This well-written novel tells the remarkable, rare and unusually insightful story of a Nazi family in Germany. It helps to explain the virtually universal admiration and collaboration by the German people for Hitler and his henchmen, while also highlighting the brutality some courageous German dissenters experienced.

—Carl H. Rosner, born in Hamburg, Germany
Survivor of Buchenwald—Prisoner #38156

Who would have imagined that the son of a high-ranking Nazi and a Jewish reporter from the Bronx would end up sharing their lives? History is filled with unexpected surprises and Stumbling Stone—a riveting story fueled by mystery and suspense—reveals how everyday life affected the children of Nazis, as well as Germans who became victims of the Holocaust. A rare, fascinating and enthralling historical tale.

—Ruth Rosen, Professor Emerita of History
University of California, Davis

Wars never end — they live on in the memories and silences of descendants and survivors — and society can only advance when we come to terms with the painful reverberations. Through an unusual accident of history, life partners Jewish journalist Julie Freestone and retired California cop and medieval scholar Rudi Raab (the emigre son of a high-ranking Nazi and the nephew of a Gestapo victim) are uniquely positioned to explore the tangled history and legacy of Nazism and the holocaust. Their personal story is framed as a "stumbling stone," the literary equivalent of a historical plaque common in Europe. Using fiction to bridge the gaps in historical documentation, this fascinating book sheds light on the holocaust in ways as unique and unlikely as its authors' relationship.

—Peter Y. Sussman, *journalist/author*

Stumbling Stone

By Rudi Raab and Julie Freestone

Alvarado Press
Richmond, California

Alvarado Press
Stumbling Stone
Rudi Raab and Julie Freestone

If you would like to do any of the above, please seek permission first by contacting us at: http:/stumbling-stone.com

Editor: Elizabeth Rosner
Cover Design: A.D. Puchalski
Interior Designer: Jim Shubin

Published in the United States of America by Alvarado Press
ISBN 978-0-9962192-0-4

PART I

CHAPTER I

April 1989

Later, I would look back and wonder what might have happened if I hadn't moved into a drug-plagued neighborhood, or if I had just done my story on the drug war and not gotten personally involved with Karl Schmidt. Of course, by the time I wondered, it was already too late.

It was a Friday evening in April and Brennan's bar and hofbrau, located near the waterfront in Berkeley, was crowded with amateur sailors anticipating the weekend, families eating early dinners and singles hopefully gearing up for a busy night.

Looking around, I spotted my friend and neighbor Beth Johnson and waved. I walked to the bar, ordered my usual draft beer and joined Beth at a table. I'd been coming to Brennan's almost since moving from New York to California two decades before, in the late sixties. I was in my early twenties then, just starting my journalism career. My hair had been mostly brown then. Well, it still was, the gray covered with dye. Sometimes, I came here to meet sources for my stories—people who were willing to talk over a drink or two. Other times, I came to escape the pressure of work, hoping not to see anyone I knew and to avoid discussing anything redeeming. In the past, I'd often come to partake of the casual camaraderie and sex Brennan's featured. It was possible to decide at nine p.m. that you wanted a partner for the evening and be in bed with a reasonable choice within an hour. Thanks to AIDS and a little more discernment on my part, those days were gone forever.

That spring night, I was in Brennan's to celebrate. I'd been following a local story for months, urged by residents in my own Berkeley neighborhood to step in and help prevent a known drug dealer from swindling an elderly couple out of title to their historic but crumbling old house. That morning, in an Oakland courthouse, I'd heard the judge nullify the sale and order the house restored to the old people. It was one of those times when I felt completely validated for putting up with lousy pay, long hours and the uncertainty of freelancing for small newspapers that were a far cry from the big time daily I'd dreamed about in journalism school.

Tonight, meeting Beth for a pre-dinner drink, I sensed that even she, a local lobbyist, had an agenda. A blonde, slightly overweight middle-aged woman, Beth was sitting with Ricardo, an off-duty, Hispanic cop we both knew. He fancied himself a poet and had gotten our attention several years before by describing his writing aspirations. Later, we'd concluded his discussions about poetry were a more creative version of "what's your sign." He didn't speak much Spanish, but had become increasingly ethnic as ethnicity had become fashionable in Berkeley. Tonight, he and Beth were discussing the drug war.

"You have to write about this," Beth said before I had even set my drink down. "This is really dynamite stuff."

I sighed. Fourteen times a day some well-meaning person suggested a story for which the world couldn't wait another second. Usually, it was something that had been done the day before, the week before, or last month by another paper, or was so obscure or boring that no editor would be interested.

But occasionally, there were ideas that I could turn into stories to be sold to one of the half-dozen editors I worked with. And often, I got genuinely excited about something pitched in my direction. I was a sucker for almost any good story and would often push it with editors because I could see an opportunity to combine my lifetime propensity for activism with my job. It probably didn't make for the best professional detachment, but it guaranteed my commitment to my stories.

Although I usually trusted Beth's instincts, I only half-listened as Ricardo described the police department's *real* attitude about the drug war. "We don't have the resources to stop the drug business," he was saying. "We're not about to stick our necks out and put our lives in danger. The courts won't send these guys away, the City won't back us up against complaints, and our weapons are outclassed. We don't want to risk our jobs or our lives." I wondered if Ricardo, a cynical veteran who seemed to be marking time, represented a prevailing attitude.

Before I could turn the thought into a question, I saw Ricardo wave to another police officer, this one in uniform. "This is a friend of mine who is patrolling the neighborhood. Mind if he joins us while he's on his coffee break?" Ricardo asked.

I did mind, but I didn't say anything. I didn't know this man personally, but I'd seen him for years. It wasn't his uniform that repelled me. I was often quick to voice my disdain for authority, including anyone in uniform. But I had admitted to myself and even a few close friends years ago that I was often strongly attracted to men in uniforms. "You know those power fantasies," I'd laugh when making my confessions.

What I had was an irrational dislike for this particular cop. So blond that his bushy eyebrows were white, he looked like the epitome of everything that I, Sarah Stern, originally a nice Jewish girl from the Bronx, had been brought up to distrust. And indeed, this cop was a German who looked like a movie Nazi and talked with an accent. If that weren't enough—and it was plenty—I had watched this cop, mostly when he was out of uniform, drinking at the bar as a civilian and concluded he was an alcoholic. I wasn't sure why I thought that, except he seemed to be at home at Brennan's. But then so many people were and in fact, so was I, something that worried me sometimes.

I'd never seen him drunk and his lithe body showed no signs of deterioration. I conceded silently as I studied him close up that he had a pretty nice build: broad shoulders, tall, a tapering waist, and a tight ass. If he hadn't looked like a Nazi, it would have been an attractive package. I'd always been drawn to blonde men who didn't look Jewish.

9

Ricardo explained to Karl Schmidt that we were discussing the real story behind the drug war. Schmidt sighed. "You don't want to disillusion these ladies, do you?" he said, lighting a cigarette. In politically correct Berkeley, even in Brennan's, that was another strike against him in my mind. I was a recent and now—though I had never thought it would happen—rabid ex-smoker.

"We're too cynical for you to worry about that," said Beth.

Schmidt confirmed Ricardo's perspective and then some. He said most cops avoid doing anything that might attract the attention of the Police Review Commission, a civilian oversight group formed in the aftermath of the sixties to keep watch over the police. He said the worst time of the night—the graveyard shift —was staffed by rookies who were running on overdoses of adrenalin but were short on experience and common sense. He thought the police chief emphasized publicly the importance of the drug war, but actually put the department resources elsewhere. My fingers started itching for a computer keyboard.

"Every city gets the kind of police protection it wants," Schmidt concluded. "Until the commitment changes, nothing else will." He leaned back in his chair and took a deep drag on his cigarette, obviously not caring where he blew his smoke.

While he talked, I watched him. He was articulate as hell, something that had always intrigued me. Over the years, I'd decided that I'd choose a good grasp of the English language and a quick mind over performance in bed. I usually arrived at those conclusions when I was sexually satisfied and intellectually impatient.

It was true that Schmidt had a distinctive German accent, something that made me think immediately of the Gestapo. But even with his accent, he had an unusually rich vocabulary and a quirky perspective I found engaging. He was cynical, but underneath the cynicism, I suspected he was an idealist. Although he was critical of the police department, he seemed passionate about the way things should be done to bring peace and tranquility to the community. He had the unabashed enthusiasm about his job that was usually characteristic of rookie officers.

In spite of all that, I distrusted Schmidt's implied condemnation of the civilian review commission. God knew someone had to keep watch over the cops or they would trample on everyone's civil liberties.

On the other hand, I had recently bought—with a female friend—a small duplex on the edge of one of the city's most drug-infested areas and would cheerfully have welcomed more police to chase away some of the unsavory elements in my neighborhood.

When Schmidt got up to go back to work, I was almost sorry to see him go. After all, I'd picked up many men in Brennan's whose politics were worse than his and who weren't nearly as intelligent. It was true they had all become one night stands—something I'd recently sworn off. But I reminded myself that if I wanted anything from Karl Schmidt, it was probably an interview.

Somewhere in the course of the conversation, Ricardo had managed to communicate the information that Schmidt had a doctorate from UC Berkeley. Ricardo was a snob about those things. He usually introduced me to people as his "reporter friend," making it clear what he believed was my value to the world. Still, I was impressed. A cop with a doctorate wasn't unknown in Berkeley, but the tidbit added to the unwilling attraction I felt.

In the days that followed, I mulled over the information the two cops had given me about the drug war, finally deciding to discuss it with the editor of the local weekly—the Berkeley Voice.

"Sure it's a story," Andy Miller confirmed. "Do you think they'll talk?"

"I think they will. But I'm not so sure they'll let me use their names and jeopardize their jobs."

He hesitated and then said, "Well, hell, go for it anyway. In this case, I'm willing to use aliases. Just take good notes so we can document who said what."

I was right. Both cops were more than ready to talk, but wouldn't say a word unless I could assure them anonymity. I assigned them code names and wrote the story.

Before it appeared, I ran into Schmidt several times. The first time, he was drinking at the bar, nursing, he told me, a broken heart. "I just split up with my wife. Again." It was the standard story, which he told matter-of-factly. A romance that should have been a short-term event but instead dragged on through an impulsive marriage in Reno and multiple separations. It was another good reason for me to stifle my interest in him, I thought as I listened.

"On the way to Reno, driving up there to the wedding in the sober light of day, I already knew it was the wrong decision," he said. His accent emphasized his Europeanness and added to his charm, despite the unpleasant associations Germans always evoked in my mind. Had I ever really had this much contact with a native-born German? Not since my early childhood.

He seemed resigned to the demise of his marriage. I asked what he had learned from the experience. "It's too soon for a post-mortem," he said. I sensed pain, and tried a few probing questions to see if I was right. He appeared reluctant to share any insights, so I dropped the subject. Why did I care what he'd learned?

When I met him a few weeks later, he said he was better. "I was prepared. It was time. It's over," he said tersely.

Our conversations got longer each time we met. At the beginning, he seemed not to remember my name. He'd eventually get to Sarah but I was pretty sure Stern wasn't in his memory. He had told me already that names weren't his thing; he remembered faces mostly. I wondered what he thought of mine. Despite my glasses, I'd always been considered passably attractive. My best features were probably my blue-gray eyes, curly, shoulder-length hair and reasonably decent body. Sometimes I wore skirts, which wasn't common in Brennan's. I was usually about two fashion periods behind, especially with my glasses, which were more functional than stylish. Karl seemed to have an off-duty wardrobe consisting solely of faded jeans and nondescript sweaters. He sometimes didn't change the outfit for weeks, but I imagined he wore his uniform most of the time anyway.

While we made small talk, he ordered his customary Irish coffee. I ordered beer. I knew we were sniffing each other out, not committed to getting into a real conversation, exchanging meaningless polite phrases. Suddenly, I looked at him and asked, "So what did your father do during the war?"

It was a subject that had been on my mind ever since I began talking to him, but my need to know was growing with my attraction to him. I wasn't sure what I expected as an answer. What had most Germans done during the war? It was murky to me, as was the distinction between the Nazi party, the German army, the SS, the Gestapo and the Luftwaffe. It seemed easier to group them all into one menacing entity.

What I wanted in his answer, I suppose, was a quick denial. Something like "He couldn't serve in the army because he was a farmer." Or maybe "He was just a soldier," which would have been bad enough but not truly horrifying. Or even better, "He was a member of the Resistance."

Karl grimaced. I knew he'd come here, much as I did, to unwind, have a drink or two and if possible, talk to someone, but probably not about the past.

"Hey," he said. "I don't want to reopen the hostilities of World War II. I usually try to avoid these kinds of conversations. People seem to look at me and automatically assume that my relatives were involved in something objectionable. It's the same kind of mentality that leads people to call World War II military helmets 'Nazi' paraphernalia."

Well, he had me there. I was one of those people. I thought Americans generally didn't make a distinction between the Nazi hierarchy and the German military. Still, I wasn't going to let this subject just go by. After all, if nothing else, I was a reporter who was used to getting answers, and finding the facts was almost instinctive for me.

"Understandable," I said. Before I had a chance to ask my question again, Karl went on, "Ever since I came to the United States twenty years ago, people have been asking me hostile questions about my past. Most of the questions have been from World War II G.I.s or their families who saw Germans as evil incarnate."

He played with his drink glass and then added, "Very few of the questions were from Jews. I actually don't know any Jews."

I wondered if Karl was aware I was Jewish. Instead of asking that, I repeated, "But what did your father do during the war?"

Karl sighed. "This was a non-topic in my family. We didn't talk about things like that."

I felt Karl was trying to avoid giving me information.

As I mulled over this in silence, Karl added, "My mother always rolled her eyes and said that it was all ancient history and then she steered the conversation to a different subject." He shook his head. "He probably did the same thing your father did, except for the other side."

His answer annoyed me. It seemed contrived and designed more to cover up than to explain. Just then, Beth, who had been listening to our conversation, tried to avert a confrontation, saying, "Hey Sarah, lay off."

Karl turned to her and said softly, "No, please, Beth. Sarah is entitled to her prejudices." He turned back to me and I knew I was frowning. What prejudices was he talking about? I decided to give it up, at least for the evening.

On our way home, Beth asked me, "Are you interested in this guy?" I could hear the faint disbelief in her voice. I groaned. In spite of his father—whatever he had done during the war—and his super Aryan looks, Karl was attractive to me. He was sexy and articulate, funny and fascinating. I could hardly comprehend feeling drawn to him but said reluctantly to Beth, "Yeah, I think I am."

Beth just shook her head in amazement, which was probably a much milder reaction than I could expect from most people, particularly my mother and my more radical Berkeley friends.

CHAPTER II

"**M**y friend wants to go out with you," Ricardo reported to me around the middle of May.

I guess this information was supposed to make me happy, but it only contributed to my continuing ambivalence. I wasn't sure I wanted to go out with him.

"Well, let him call me. I'm in the phone book," I said.

I had recently made a vow that the next man I got involved with would pursue me. I was tired of doing the initiating, the negotiating. Someone would have to find me fascinating, alluring and worth chasing, or I would be unavailable. I was tired of investing in men and relationships, only to have them go sour. To hell with it, I thought, I'll just live for my work. That made me laugh. Men, sex and relationships had always figured prominently on my list of priorities and my two marriages had not negated any of that.

"But would you go out with him if he called?" asked Ricardo.

"Well, yeah, sure—except if he's a drunk, forget it." That was another of my recent promises. No more men who drank too much or abused drugs. They were too out of control, too drained, too used up.

"He's not a drunk, he's just lonely and getting over the break-up of his marriage," Ricardo tried to explain, but I remained unconvinced. I'd heard it all before. The proof, as the old cliché went, would be in the pudding. If he behaved like a *mensch*, it would prove he wasn't just another deadbeat. Or maybe my uncertainties were an excuse to avoid him because he was German.

Karl never did phone and invite me for a formal date.

16

Instead, I ran into him in Brennan's right after the drug story hit the streets and he told me he wanted to talk about the story.

"I'd like to invite you to go for a walk on the beach with me and my dog."

It was an intriguing invitation, and a confusing one. I wasn't sure if Karl wanted to tell me more about the drug war or whether he was interested in me. So I asked him whether this was a date.

"What do you mean?" he asked, genuinely puzzled.

I remembered Ricardo saying Karl hadn't done much dating and probably none with women who asked for a definition of terms. "I mean, are we going to talk about the drug war and the story?" I asked.

"Well, not just the drug war." His answer didn't really help me figure out where he was coming from, but I decided not to pursue the matter. I wasn't sure how involved I wanted to get anyway. Maybe a little lack of clarity was just what I needed right now.

He showed up on time—8:00 am—a time I would later learn was hours too early for him. He was a night person who, given a choice, preferred to sleep until noon. I didn't realize how much he had compromised already to accommodate my early-bird schedule. I sometimes began writing at 6:00 a.m.

I also didn't realize until later that I'd never given him my address, yet somehow, there he was, sitting in his car in front of my house, expecting me to run out and join him. I didn't. I thought he ought to come to the door, although it would be the first time I demanded such chivalry. But more important, I couldn't see all that well at a distance and wasn't sure it was him. I couldn't tell one car from another, including my own. In the high-crime neighborhood I lived in, even in broad daylight it wasn't a terrific idea to go dashing out to leap into cars without exercising a little caution. If I had known at that moment, as I learned later, that he had "run me" through the DMV files to find my date of birth, my address and other confidential information, I probably would never have left my house and this story would have ended there.

When he finally got out of the car and knocked on the door, I felt an instant reaction.

He was wearing sunglasses that I suspected might have been hiding bloodshot eyes. But the rest of the package was dynamite: a turtle neck white sweater, tight jeans, hiking boots. All well within the profile of what I liked.

Climbing into his car, I encountered a very friendly, very squirmy golden retriever. "This is Rosi," Karl said with a grin, adding, "my daughter."

As we drove toward the beach, he explained that he had gotten Rosi eight years before as a puppy. "She was an adorable puppy, big feet, very affectionate, not too smart." He said this ruefully. "She's still pretty much the same." He turned slightly to the dog and said in a soft voice, "You were such a cute little puppy, Rosi. Remember the time you discovered you could bark?"

The dog wagged her tail enthusiastically and I thought I could detect a huge grin spreading across the animal's mouth. Karl looked at Rosi. "After I got divorced the first time, sleeping alone was hell. This time, with Rosi around, it's been a whole lot easier. I like to hear her breathing in the room. It lets me know I'm not alone."

I smiled along with both of them. "I've been married twice too," I said, hoping we'd find something more than two failed marriages in common. It was hard to imagine what that might be.

He explained he had named Rosi after one of the cops he worked with, a big, tough black cop with a lot of street smarts who was also a sweet sensitive guy underneath his hard exterior.

"He looks like he eats nails for breakfast, but he'd actually give you the shirt off his back," Karl said.

I wanted to reach out and pat Karl's hand or ruffle his hair. He seemed perfectly willing to show me his vulnerability and I liked that. But not everything I heard and felt that day was as appealing. Somehow on the ride to the ocean, he managed to show me the gun he had hidden in the car that was, predictably, a Volkswagen. The gun reminded me that he was a cop. I didn't need to be reminded that I hated guns and was suspicious of cops. The car reminded me once again that he was German.

Karl seemed to be having his own mixed feelings. He asked me, somewhat hesitantly, why my two marriages had broken up.

I explained that my first husband, a fellow student, had revealed himself, after we'd graduated from college, to be a conservative Republican. "We just didn't have anything in common and I hated his politics," I said. It was a tale I had told many times before, but while I was telling Karl the story, I suddenly remembered that when Joe and I were first dating, his father, an ardent Catholic with vague and distant German roots, had written Joe a letter, warning him not to get serious about me. "Jewish women grow up to be shrews" had been the gist of the message. It was the first personally anti-Semitic experience I ever had. Joe had brushed it aside, although he confessed years later that he had originally only dated me because he thought Jewish women "put out." He was engaged at the time to a Catholic who wouldn't even French kiss. "I was horny," he explained.

Karl seemed to have a harder time grasping what had happened to my second marriage. He didn't understand that I left just because I didn't want to be married anymore. "I really liked him. He was my best friend actually. We're still friends. I just had never been single and there was a whole world out there. I wanted to check it out," I said. The explanation always made sense to me but it seemed to make Karl nervous.

"You know, I'm really friendly with both of my exes," I said to reassure him. "You seem to feel a lot of bitterness toward your wives. I don't feel that way. I really liked my husbands, liked being married while I was. They were both really good experiences—and they ended before things turned sour."

He looked over at me but didn't seem much happier with my attempt to reassure him. Later, as we walked on the beach,

I asked about his marriages.

"You mean, your first wife just up and left, took all your money and you had no clue or warning?" I said in disbelief as he described his first marriage. I was also amazed that he and his first wife, an American exchange student he met in Germany, had rarely talked about their feelings.

"I have no clue about how she felt or why she left," Karl said.

I wondered how a man could make it through 10 years of marriage and have no idea about what his wife felt. That didn't augur well for his ability to perceive things. What was I doing with him? I wondered how anyone who was a cop could not make what I considered to be fundamental inquiries. But then he had apparently never asked his father what he did during the war.

Karl threw the ball for his dog to chase. While I wasn't athletic now, I'd been a good girls' basketball player once and liked playing softball. I knew a good pitch when I saw one and Karl had a great arm.

"You'd be a terrific outfielder on a softball team," I said. "Do you play in the leagues?"

"No," he said. "Growing up in Germany, you play soccer and fence and fly gliders. Once I played softball here and I didn't know what to do when I hit the ball. I perfected my throwing in the police academy, learning the techniques of lobbing tear gas grenades. When you're in the last row, you don't want to hit your fellow officers, you want to hit the bad guys," he said this last part with a mischievous grin I almost missed.

"You know, it's ironic that I'm now in the role of lobbing tear gas at the 'enemy'", he said with a laugh. "In the sixties, when I first got to California, I participated in student demonstrations against the war in Viet Nam. Tear gas grenades were then shot at me. Later, I even found out that my first application for citizenship was rejected because the F.B.I. had me classified as a 'known subversive'".

In spite of the paradox, the image of him tossing tear gas

grenades repelled me. Karl must have realized my discomfort because he said, "I was just teasing you. We don't throw grenades, we shoot them."

If this was supposed to make me feel better, it didn't.

During the walk, as I continued to ply him with questions about his past—mostly about his relationships—I noticed my conversational pattern changed subtly. "So, nu," I said, telling a story about someone I worked with. "She is a real kochleffl—a busybody."

"I know that word," Karl said, "But it has a different meaning in German—cooking spoon."

I found myself throwing Yiddish words into the conversation and I wondered why. I rarely used Yiddish except with my mother, but I was apparently unwilling or maybe unable to stop. It was ironic. As a child, I'd glanced around furtively whenever my mother or aunts spoke Yiddish in public. I hated their heavy Austrian accents and the way, even in English, they pronounced words like value, turning the v's into w's. They sometimes still thought in Yiddish and would translate so literally into English that a phrase like "turn off the light" became "make the light out."

Listening to me pepper my conversation with an un-characteristic amount of Yiddish, Karl must have known I was Jewish. I know he was needling, maybe testing me, when he talked about tear gas grenades. Apparently I was doing the same to him by using Yiddish.

"You know," he said, "My doctorate is in medieval German literature and, while earning it, I had to master medieval German, which was so close to Yiddish, I probably understand more of your ancestors' language than you do."

Well, if he hadn't known before that I was Jewish, he did now. "I've wondered about something," I asked. "Why did you get a Ph.D. and then become a cop?"

Karl stopped walking and looked at me for a moment. "Which one of these questions would you like me to answer first?" I wasn't sure what he meant.

"I think I can tell you why I got a Ph.D. I think I can also tell you why I became a police officer. But if you want an explanation for me becoming a cop, even though I have a Ph.D., then you first have to tell me why that needs an explanation in your mind." He walked on, leaving me standing there and wondering why he was so defensive.

When I caught up with him, he said, "Are you asking me why I got myself a Ph.D.?"

"Yes," I answered.

"To be honest, I don't really know. I've thought about it from time to time and depending on what mood I am in, I come up with different answers. I remember when I was a little boy, at the end of first grade, my father wanted to take the family on a trip to Italy. His vacation started before school was out and I would have had to leave first grade two weeks early. My teacher had agreed, provided that I was able to read aloud the final story in my reader before I left."

Karl looked off into the distance. "My mother coached me at home, while my father looked on. No matter how long we worked, I wasn't able to tell the difference between the letters p and b. and m and w. But my mother persisted, reading the passage to me again and again for hours."

"I tried as hard as I could but the letters looked alike and the words made no sense. My father laughed and said that I was a dummy, was probably not cut out for school and that I might be better suited to become a laborer. I was ashamed. After a while, I noticed that my mother had read the story often enough so that I knew it by heart. I faked reading it by reciting it. Everyone was relieved. We went to Italy." He smiled, but I just looked back at him, caught up in the pathos of that long ago event.

"Well, what better way to show that you can read than by getting a Ph.D. in literature?" Karl said, apparently wanting to bring the discussion to a close.

When the walk ended, I knew a lot about his two marriages

and very little about his German past. He seemed to know little about me.

"Why aren't you asking me any questions?" I said. I was now feeling a little uncomfortable about having bombarded him with a barrage of inquiries and also slightly annoyed because he didn't seem to be particularly interested in me.

"I can tell a lot about you by the questions you ask. By asking questions, you show me what you're interested in and what you value." he said. "Answers to standard questions are usually pretty canned and aren't usually honest."

I wasn't completely convinced by his response. A lot of self-centered men were perfectly happy to talk about themselves, answer questions and find out nothing about the dynamics of the women they were with. But he was right about standardized answers. I had a bunch of them at the ready.

I hoped he couldn't read my mind and see how much I was now speculating on his performance in bed. While we'd walked through the sand, I'd begun fantasizing about making love with him in the dunes.

On the ride back, we were caught in a traffic jam. Karl was getting fidgety about getting to work. "We could pull in here," he gestured to a nearby motel," and wait until the traffic clears up." He grinned to show me he was just kidding. He clearly didn't realize I would have done it without thinking twice. It would have been, for me, merely a passing expression of sexual interest, which he apparently didn't share, or so I thought.

Later I would learn Karl would never have done that. It was too soon, too rushed, not consistent with his slow approach and his ambivalence about whether he was really done with his marriage. It would have been a commitment to get emotionally involved. In Karl's values, one did not have sex without a relationship. In mine, the relationship had always grown out of the sex. And I was definitely not ready to decide whether I wanted a relationship with this German, who didn't want to talk about his family's past and claimed not to know anything about it. What would my mother think?

CHAPTER III

Our second date was a hike along a trail at Mt. Tamalpais to watch the sunset. Karl suggested it and, this time he didn't bring Rosi. When he pulled up in front of the house, I didn't wait for him to come and knock on the door. As I got into the car, I could see he was checking me out. I thought my tight jeans showed off my long legs and firm rear nicely.

I brought along a baguette, a bottle of wine, some cheese and a checkered tablecloth. It was something I often did, almost second nature, whether the outing involved a man or not, but when Karl saw the food, he acted as if he had been given a tremendous gift. He was so effusive, I was almost embarrassed, wondering if he was misinterpreting what I intended as a casual gesture. I was glad he appreciated my efforts, but I didn't want him assuming anything that wasn't happening. From my experience, I knew that when men were anxious to become a couple prematurely, it was difficult to discourage them without hurting their feelings and creating a messy situation. This was just a walk to watch the sunset as far as I was concerned. I wasn't going to get my hopes up about whether we'd end up in bed today or any other time.

On our drive, Karl seemed to sense he might have been a bit too expressive about the bread and cheese.

"You know, it isn't the bread and cheese, it's that you brought it. My wife only cooked two warm dinners during the last year of our marriage, both spaghetti. She never seemed to be able to plan anything. She ran out of everything except cigarettes and wine with irritating regularity. I like the fact that even just for a walk to look at the sunset, you organized a snack, with no fanfare or discussion."

I was struck by how little nurturing this man had, with no family nearby. I discovered only later that Karl didn't really like cheese, didn't really like American wine, and his only recreational drink was Irish coffee—he disdained American beer.

The walk was pleasant. The sunset was spectacular in its variety of colors and the ever-changing shape of the clouds.

"This is great," Karl said. "My life for the past few years seems to have shrunk to patrolling the city and visiting Brennan's. I never go anywhere. The only sunsets I've seen in the last few years were from the inside of my police car."

I enjoyed traveling, hiking and skiing, so I couldn't say the same. As the sun disappeared finally from view and the shadows took over, Karl suggested that he cook dinner for us. I liked that idea. No man had cooked for me in a while.

We got lost driving back down the mountain. As we were squinting into the dark, trying to decide where we had made a wrong turn, I asked, "Do you have any idea where we are?"

Karl answered, "Nope. But there is a yellow stripe in the center of the road which means that this is at least a mid-sized road requiring traffic control. It's going downhill off the mountain, and I see the full moon from time to time through the trees, which means we are heading in a general south-westerly direction. That's where we want to go."

There was a joke among Berkeley women about the men they met, particularly the men in Brennan's. Many of them seemed to be drifters, with no real careers, sometimes with no definite place to live, not much money and no cars. Even the ones with a better economic profile were emotional drifters, dance-away lovers who avoided commitment at all costs. To find a man with a car, a job, a brain, enough money to buy his own drinks, enough sensitivity to suggest cooking dinner and, on top of everything else, to be able to feel comfortable even when lost, all that made Karl a real find. Even getting lost began to seem like an adventure.

But still, I wasn't going to be too easily won over. Although he had volunteered to cook, by the time we regained our bearings and were headed home, Karl said he didn't feel like cooking. I had been with too many men who talked a good game and had great ideas, but were big disappointments when it came to actually putting their words into action.

Karl suggested going to his house anyway, to let the dog out. I thought I knew what that meant, which was OK with me. In fact, it was more than just OK I'd been thinking sex for days now and had even considered that if I went to bed with him, the attraction would diminish and I wouldn't have to deal with his Germanness.

But once we arrived at his house, I wondered whether I'd misread the signs. He wasn't making any moves, and Nazi past or not, I was ready.

When he let his dog out, I thought he would go about setting the stage for seduction. Instead, he prowled around his house, "dancing" away from me whenever I came close. The house had a neglected look, piles of paper on every flat surface, old frayed furniture. There were books everywhere.

We finally agreed we'd go out and get something to eat, and I concluded I had seriously misunderstood the messages I thought I had picked up. In the car, on the way to the restaurant, maybe to get a reading on what he was feeling, maybe because I had an overwhelming desire to touch him, I reached over and lightly stroked his hand, which was resting on the steering wheel.

He said softly with a nod, "Yes." It should have been a cryptic comment, but I felt a jolt of heat through me and thought I understood he was confirming his attraction to me, just delaying it for some reason.

It was much later that I learned he took his time, savoring the building of the sensual energy. And he was surprised to learn I thought he was moving slowly. He wouldn't have thought about seducing me there, in the house he had shared so recently with his wife, when he wasn't even completely through with the marriage. Besides, there was only one pillow on the bed. His wife had taken hers.

26

Once at the restaurant, Karl asked for the smoking section, ordered a drink and a hamburger and raised his eyebrows as I waved the smoke away and ordered chicken. "This is an unlikely relationship," Karl said.

"Is it a relationship?" I asked.

His face fell and he looked crushed. "I think it is. Do you have a problem with it?"

I nodded. I didn't want to hurt him; he was proving to be a gentle, sweet and sensitive man under his brusque exterior. But I thought honesty was definitely in order.

"Apart from the differences in our styles—you smoking, eating hamburgers and drinking too much—I'm still concerned with what your father did during the war. My parents, particularly my mother, never trusted Germans. When I was a child, we were never allowed to buy German products, wear Loden coats, drive Volkswagens." I paused for a breath and added, "German accents make me think of the Gestapo."

Karl sighed. "You know, I said this to you before. All my adult years, since emigrating to the United States, this issue keeps coming up. Jews who suspect me and my family of having participated in the atrocities; non-Jews who fought in the war; children of soldiers killed in the war; others with good memories of propaganda films about Krauts. All attribute Fascist traits to me, assuming my looks are the window dressing for a Nazi mind. God, people even assume I served in the Hitler Youth, even though I was born eight days after the war."

He sighed. "You want to know what my father did during the war." I nodded. Of course I wanted to know. I held my breath. Was he actually going to reveal a secret? Did I really want to know?

Karl continued, "So do I, although I've given up wondering."

Karl said he knew Der Alte—the Old Man, as his father was now called—was a Nazi during the Third Reich. It was nothing his father ever tried to hide, at least not from the family. But if Der Alte was open about his association with the party, the details of his role during the war as well as what he had known or not known were not subjects of acceptable conversation in the Schmidt house.

"We—my two sisters and I—never asked and never speculated, even once, amongst ourselves. We just knew it was a forbidden subject. There was such a shroud of silence over everything related to the war, not just in my family but among Germans in general. I can't say who was involved in what and who, if anyone, was truly innocent."

Karl remembered that every time his father had to submit a resume for a job change, Der Alte had gone through periods of anxiety. He seemed to need to hide his past, perhaps more so than the average German of his age. Beyond that, from bits and pieces of information, Karl knew his father had joined the Nazi party, even before Hitler came to power in 1933, and had participated in the street battles as a part of the Storm Troopers. Later, he had been in charge of the Ordensburg Sonthofen, a school for boys.

"That answer I gave you—that my father probably did the same thing yours did—I didn't completely fabricate it. I figured he was an educator and so he probably hadn't done anything different than what hundreds of American drill instructors did for the military, preparing soldiers to fight the Germans and Japanese. And he wasn't even teaching soldiers, but rather young boys."

Karl acknowledged that his explanation about his father's role couldn't stand up under close scrutiny, his own included.

"But you know, I'm rarely in a situation requiring more information. In Germany, I lived in a nation working to process its past but not anxious to examine individual guilt. Since I came here, I've been with people who either didn't ask a lot of questions about my past or who talked to me about the past because they thought I shared their racist attitudes."

I smiled faintly. "You sure picked the wrong person when

you started to talk to me. I've always had a strong need to get to the truth. I nibble away until I get there. That's why I became a reporter. It drives some people crazy."

"Yet I can't really tell you what my father did," he began. "When I am forced to think about it, I go back and forth. Sometimes I think the worst—that my father was involved up to his bushy eyebrows but not knowing what that really means. Other times I think it's all my imagination."

He looked at me intently and said, "Mostly, I don't really want to know and, up to now, I haven't needed to know."

I had a choice. I could tell him it didn't matter, that only the present was important, or I could persist with my questions. I had plenty of questions, which I knew I wasn't just going to ignore. I could hardly process what Karl had told me about his father. From first saying that he knew very little, Karl had just described—in some detail—what might be some fairly shocking information implicating his father. And if he had actually known all this when I initially asked him, what more was he concealing?

I didn't have to wait long for that question to be answered. Into my silence, Karl said, "Not everyone in my family was involved with the Nazis. My father had a brother. He died young. He was referred to as a 'bad apple.' I think he was a rebel. He wasn't a Nazi."

Before I could react, Karl sighed and almost glared at me. "Honestly, that's all I know about my uncle. Just vague information."

He reached over and took my hand. "Sarah, are we going to let our pasts govern our future? Or even our present?" he asked wryly, realizing I guess that I wasn't ready to talk about a common future any more than he wanted to talk about the past.

I frowned and said, "My god. I know that I annoy people— you included—with my endless probing about subjects that I think need to be explored. But you of all people ought to understand that. You're a cop. You guys are relentless in trying to pursue justice. I can't believe that all these years you've never tried to find out anything about your uncle. Think hard. What else do you know about him? What's his name?"

"His name was Gerhard. He was younger than my father. My grandfather said once that Gerhard was a good-for-nothing and a rabble rouser; my mother once implied that he was a 'homosexual'." Karl insisted there was no way to find out. "No one ever talked about him. They told me he died at an early age. As a kid, you believe what your parents tell you. I never had any reason to question that."

"Maybe he didn't die. Maybe he was a spy. Maybe he was in the resistance. Maybe he escaped and went to South America," I said.

Karl actually laughed. "I think you are getting carried away and anyway, there's no way for us to know unless my father or someone tells us."

"So wrong," I shot back. "We can start with the Red Cross. They have a tracing service. We can at least try to see if he's alive."

I can't say Karl seemed thrilled with this idea, but he finally agreed—maybe to shut me up—that we should try the Red Cross. And days later, he did mumble, as we mailed the letter to the Red Cross, "Wouldn't it be amazing if he were alive?"

I wondered a number of times after that why I had pressed Karl so quickly to try to find his uncle. Was I looking to redeem the family in my own eyes to make the idea of being in a relationship with him more palatable? Or was it my usual motivation, always looking for a good story?

CHAPTER IV

While we waited for the answer from the Red Cross tracing service, I decided to halt my interrogation about Karl's family. Instead I asked him one afternoon, "Doesn't it bother you that I'm Jewish?" It was too soon for me to know whether he shared any of his father's attitudes, but it was hard for me to believe that anyone who grew up in Germany with a father who had been an adult during the war, whatever his role had been, could be completely free of all such attitudes.

"No. I'm not sure why it should bother me."

Was I going to let the past govern the future? Would it be wrong not to even consider the past? I wasn't sure, but I did know that at least I wanted to see where my physical attraction to him was going to lead.

"I think we should go to Brennan's and have a cocktail and dinner," he said.

I hesitated.

"Don't you want to?" he asked.

"Sure I do. It isn't the cocktail that's the problem. It's Brennan's. It's a Saturday night. If we go to there on a Saturday night together, walking in at this hour, it's like putting up a billboard that we're having a relationship. Is that what you want to do?"

Karl shrugged. He didn't seem to care about these nuances. "I had no idea there were rules at Brennan's. Are you going out with someone else you're afraid you'll see there?" he asked. We had never discussed whether there were other people in our lives. I didn't really even know if his wife was completely gone from his.

I patted his hand. "That's not it. No, I'm not. I'm just wondering if you understand the implications of being seen together, there, on a Saturday night." But as I explained that Brennan's was a singles bar, I wondered if a part of me was reluctant to be seen with him, the stereotypical Nazi cop, on what was obviously a pre-arranged outing. It was something far different than just hanging out at Brennan's and having a casual conversation. As a reporter, I wasn't sure I wanted to be seen on a date with a cop. And as a Jewish woman, did I want to be seen with a German?

"Oh, hell," I said with a smile, my body telling me what to do. "Let's live dangerously. I'm up for it."

It was a short drive to Brennan's and on the way, I became aware of how frequently we seemed to be making physical contact, punctuating our conversation with short touches and pats. Once we reached Brennan's, we decided to sit at the bar and there, as we talked, our knees collided, arms brushed and the sexual tension between us became almost palpable.

"I think we should get out of here," Karl said finally. I knew we were both feeling that it was too light in Brennan's, too noisy, too public. I nodded and we walked silently out the door, waving to a number of people who called our names.

In the parking lot, walking back to his car, we looked at each other, took a step forward and found ourselves in a passionate embrace, pressing our bodies together. "Your place or mine?" he grinned, putting his tongue in my mouth and wrapping his arms more tightly around me. Despite the excitement of discovery that raced through me, kissing him felt familiar.

My place was closer. In the darkness of the living room, we shed our clothes, walking silently to the bedroom, falling into bed and rubbing against each other. He was gentle but surprisingly demanding. The sex was sweet but short, and he seemed chagrined.

"Am I the first woman you've had since you split up with your wife?" I asked.

"Yes, you are. I expected to be celibate for several years. I was between my first and second marriage." I sensed he felt guilty, not yet really severed from his marriage, still working through issues of fidelity.

"We have plenty of time," I said gently. He seemed relieved, as if he expected me, efficient and outspoken, to be sarcastic and critical about anything I perceived as not meeting my standards.

He put his hands behind his head, lay back on the pillow and said, "Tell me a story. Tell me about your childhood. Growing up in New York City. Introduce me to Sarah Stern, the nice Jewish girl from the Bronx."

By way of answering, I got up and went to my bookcase to get an album my father had made for me before he died. I settled back on the bed and started flipping through the pages, through the photos of my parents standing cradling me in front of an apartment building in the Bronx. Aunts, uncles, family gatherings. About half way through the album, Karl put his hand on a page I was about to skip.

"What's this?" he asked, looking at the yellow identification card, imprinted with the words "Allied High Commission, Occupation Forces, Hamburg, Germany 1950."

It had been a long time since I'd talked about that period of my life. I looked at the card, with a photo of me as a six year-old. "You said your father did the same thing as my father did during the war. My father was an immigration inspector during the war. He was too old to be drafted."

Sitting there, wrapped in a shared blanket, I told Karl that my father, Philip, was a mid-level bureaucrat, who had toiled away in anonymity in Newark, New Jersey until the war ended.

"He never realized his potential, giving up his law practice to work in obscurity for the government and writing long scholarly essays about the failure of the Immigration Service to keep out Nazi sympathizers. When the war ended, my father was assigned to Germany to oversee the resettlement of the displaced persons, concentration camp survivors, victims of the Nazi Holocaust. I don't really know much more than that about what he did. My mother and I went with him, first

33

to Bremen and then to Hamburg. I was only four years old when we arrived in Germany. We lived there for about three years.

My father never said much even when I was older about the people and their stories. My mother hated to talk about that period and claimed my dad hadn't talked to her much about his work."

As I told this to Karl, I knew that the family silence had made my awareness of the war and people's roles in it minimal. But I had been freelancing for a Jewish newspaper for several years. Many of my assignments involved interviewing Holocaust survivors, listening to people talk about their war experiences, reliving the Germans' treatment of the Jews. From that, a picture began emerging that haunted me when I allowed myself to think about it. I regretted that my father had died several years before I began writing for the paper, so I couldn't question him about his impressions of post-war Germany and the German people.

Karl seemed mesmerized by the yellow card, rubbing his finger over the "Allied High Commission" inscription.

"I lived in Hamburg in 1950," he said tersely. "We were the occupied."

Karl turned the rest of the pages of the album, looking at the pictures of me playing with little German girls, at the snapshots of my family in front of an enormous house where we lived in Hamburg.

"I think it belonged to a German ship builder," I said, wondering for the first time where the ship builder and his family had gone when my family moved in.

"Not exactly growing up in the Bronx," Karl said sarcastically.

I shook my head. "I don't remember a lot from those years. I know my mother distrusted everyone she met there in Germany."

I didn't add that my mother still distrusted all Germans and had taught me to feel the same way. It wasn't an attitude I'd questioned much, since every Jew I met got similar messages growing up. I also didn't think this was the right time, lying in bed with Karl, to give voice to my recurring doubt about whether I could have a relationship with a German, even now, these many years later.

Instead, I said, "I never thought about how the German people fared after the war. In my family, the focus was on the thousands of displaced persons, survivors, without homes, searching for family members taken away by the Nazis, desperate to make a new life in any country that was willing to accept them. We had little contact with the Germans themselves. My parents, after they returned to the States, never talked about what they saw and heard in Germany, not even in the years afterwards, when my father was called sometimes to testify at deportation hearings for Nazis unmasked after years in hiding."

Looking at the photograph of us in front of the shipbuilder's house, Karl said, "I remember not having enough to eat and my father hiding out after the war. Why he hid was never really explained."

Karl said he remembered fights between his parents, his father only being there on weekends, cramped quarters, clothes made of old war uniforms, the buttons of his sisters' blouses all bearing the letters BDM "Bund Deutscher Maedel"—the Nazi girls' association.

It was a gloomy discussion that didn't fit with the good feelings I had been having about the evening. Maybe to restore a sense of normalcy, Karl flipped back to the yellow ID card and said teasingly, "So, what did you do during the war? See, you were born during the war. You're older than I am."

I giggled. "Yeah. Six months." I stroked his arm and gave him a quick kiss. It was difficult assimilating all of the thoughts and feelings the evening had brought.

Karl looked nervously at the clock; it was nearly dawn. "What's the matter?" I asked. I was tired and not interested in more sex, but I was also leery of men who had other agendas and squeezed their sexual encounters in between their other priorities. Another one of my many vows was to avoid men who didn't consider time with me high on their list of important events. Karl seemed reluctant to voice his need to go. "Do you need to leave?" I finally asked.

He nodded. "If I stay, I'll want you again and I have to be at work at noon. I need to get some sleep." Then he laughed. "I also have to let my dog out."

I found it hard to be annoyed with him. He seemed to be pretty honest about where he was coming from, but then, you never knew.

CHAPTER V

When I didn't hear from him the next day, I began to wonder whether I'd picked yet another flake. I didn't know Karl had driven by several times in his police car, wanting to say hello but finding me away from the house each time.

I already knew he wasn't a man who used the phone readily. He was in the habit of face-to-face encounters. In fact, given the choice of driving to a store to see if the item he wanted was in stock or calling, he'd never think about calling. Sometimes he'd arrive at the store to find it closed, but efficiency wasn't a part of his make-up. "I'm a medievalist," he said in his defense when I pointed out how much time that approach wasted.

So, instead of a call on my answering machine, what I found outside my door a morning later was a book called *Those Strange German Ways*, which seemed to have been written for GIs stationed in Germany. It described German customs and language. Karl had written inside the cover, "Congratulations. You are the proud owner of a fine German product. Here is your owner's manual."

Although I was reassured to know Karl wasn't interested in a casual affair, I wasn't sure I wanted to be the proud owner of a fine German product, especially if it meant learning about German, Germans and heaven forbid, German ways. And of course I had been warned never to buy any German products.

I had to admit, at least to myself, that some of those German ways—or maybe they were Karl's ways —were wonderful. All my years as an adult, I had lamented men's inability to realize that by simply giving a woman flowers, they could achieve instant delight. Very few of the men I knew ever managed to integrate that simple philosophy. The men who did bring me flowers generally did it because they felt guilty about something and were trying to apologize, using the flowers as a gesture instead of words.

But Karl loved flowers himself and brought them to me frequently during the next several weeks, wanting to share with me his delight at what was happening between us. "What are these for?" I would ask each time, smiling with obvious pleasure. "Just because you're you," he responded.

It was the first flower he brought me—a red rose with black lace tied around it—that seemed most special and which I kept dried in a vase where I could always see it. It symbolized somehow the wonderful combination of sensuality and sweetness that was an innate part of Karl. Each time I looked at the rose, I could visualize him poking around the fabric store, as he told me he had, looking for just the right kind of lace.

But none of this romantic glow covered completely my uneasiness about his Germanness and his job as a cop, especially as the days passed and I became more involved in his life.

One Sunday, thinking to surprise him, I drove to the nearby waterfront park where I knew he would be patrolling and walked up to him. Except for the first time I met him officially, I had never seen him in his uniform. He looked like a stranger. Indeed, he was a stranger, someone I had known for only a few months. Here he was, a man in a uniform, carrying a menacing looking gun and a nightstick. He looked dangerous and alien.

His expression, sort of a beam or a delighted grin when he caught sight of me, looked like Karl's, but it didn't make me feel much more comfortable. A kiss might have helped, but it was against the rules for him to even touch me while he was in uniform. Instead, he suggested taking a walk out on the pier.

Looking at the equipment strapped to his belt, I said, "God, you have a lot of stuff there. It must weigh a ton."

"Oh it does all right," he said, "But you know, I always

thought I could remove one of these ammunition-do-hickies and replace it with a bottle of white-out. We sure write a lot more reports than we shoot guns."

Although I smiled, I was tense. With the instinctive dislike for cops I'd retained as a liberal coming of age in the sixties, I imagined I could sense the fear and antipathy people we passed seemed to feel. I felt disoriented and confused.

Suddenly a woman came running up, "Officer, there's someone shooting seagulls further out on the pier. Come quick," she said.

Karl looked at me and groaned.

"What does the guy look like?" Karl asked the woman rather matter-of-factly. The woman appeared genuinely scared. "He's a teen-ager, about this big," she said holding out her hand to indicate someone about my height. "What kind of gun does he have?" Karl asked. The woman said it was a handgun, but she was clearly becoming impatient. She obviously wanted help but didn't see the need to answer any more questions. He said "OK, ma'am, you and I will go to this guy and you can point him out. Can you do that?" She nodded, looking fearfully down the pier. Karl turned to me and said," Come with me but hang back. I don't know what will happen."

I knew that one of the main attractions Karl said the profession held for him involved the idea of seeing a problem and immediately being able to do something to fix it. Before I met him, I had never considered a cop's job in that light. Now I was going to see what he meant.

Following slowly to the scene of the seagull shooting, I could see that Karl and the woman had found the culprits. They were two teenagers who had thrown their pellet gun into the bay as soon as they saw the cop coming and were now claiming they had done nothing, despite a number of witnesses who were insisting they had.

Karl had apparently decided that administering a curbside chewing-out was what was called for. As I watched, my brain told me he was probably doing exactly what he should have been doing: scaring the hell out of the kids so they would never do it again. He listed a frightening assortment of laws they had violated by shooting at the birds and described in lurid detail the horrors that could befall them if they were ever to repeat the crime.

If I had stayed to hear the end of the interaction, I would have seen Karl escort the boys to a nearby public bus and warn them not to come back to the pier. Instead I left because watching Karl in his role as the police officer awakened all the concerns I had been ignoring. How could I—a liberal Democrat who had always argued vociferously for gun control, opposed the death penalty and thought of all cops as pigs—be involved with a man who drove a car with a siren and carried a gun? How could I be considering a romantic relationship with a man who bullied small children, even if they were shooting seagulls?

God knows I didn't want stupid kids shooting at sea gulls—or shooting at anything for that matter. But having Karl be the enforcer of society's rules raised an even more fundamental issue for me. Why had he, a German born to a Nazi father, chosen a profession that gave him so much authority over others? If he had grown up in Nazi Germany, which side would he have been on?

That might, in fact, have been the end of the not-quite-yet relationship, except that Karl later truly seemed to want to hear my views. In the process of explaining my thoughts and listening to his explanations, I began to see a different perspective on his role. Karl had watched dozens, maybe even hundreds of what he called "knee jerk" liberals in Berkeley react to him in his uniform. And of course, he'd been watching Americans and especially Jews react to his accent and his looks with the same mindless prejudice ever since he emigrated. He had gotten used to it. What he probably hadn't realizedor didn't want to acknowledge was that I was having similar reactions.

"It surprised you, didn't it?" he asked me the next day when we got together, he in his civilian clothes this time and me with some resolve to end the relationship. "You haven't seen me in that 'helper' role, just in my hang-out-at-Brennan's mode." I looked at him speechlessly. I had never considered that he thought his role on the pier had been a positive, almost nurturing one. I had reacted negatively and assumed he knew it. It seemed so obvious to me that police officers were essentially fascists.

But even residents in my neighborhood, as they looked to the cops to defend them against drug dealers, were beginning to realize their attitudes were stereotypes that didn't hold up in reality.

I told Karl what I was thinking, adding, "I feel the dichotomy myself. I want the neighborhood to be safe. I'll even admit that the anti-loitering law the City Council is considering might be the only way to keep dealers from hanging around on street corners waiting for their customers."

I sighed, having thought about this problem frequently in the last few years. "I find myself, for the first time in my life maybe, at odds with the ACLU. I agree, at least intellectually, that the law would discriminate against black youths. It's part of their culture in urban areas to stand around on street corners. God knows, a lot of them have no other place to be. It doesn't always involve crime."

In conversations like this, Karl often just listened, apparently afraid that anything he said might be misinterpreted. He had already learned some topics were definitely off-limits to argue about with me. But even I realized how absurd some of the standard reactions were. And even Karl appreciated that what was tagged "police mentality" in Berkeley would have been considered unacceptably liberal anywhere else. "Cops in other cities laugh at us and accuse us of having cotton bullets and nerf batons," he said, but I thought he kind of liked being part of a police department that knew civil rights were paramount to the community.

I hoped Karl was coming to appreciate that the intensity I brought to my work characterized my life. The stories I chose to write, when I had a choice, were about the underdog, people getting a raw deal, people needing a helping hand.

"When I started working for the Jewish newspaper, I learned the concept of 'tzedaka,' the Hebrew ideal of helping your fellow man. I subscribe to it ardently. It really captures my commitment to making the world a better place," I explained to him, adding, "And my parents believed in it too although they didn't talk about it a lot."

Before I finished processing the pier incident, Karl came by my house one night while he was working. He parked the police car in my driveway. The radio in the car interrupted the quiet evening, and neighbors began to open doors and pull aside curtains to see which house was involved.

One of my neighbors even came over to ask if I was OK "I'm fine," I said, feeling defensive and imagining I must be blushing furiously. "He's a friend."

I offered Karl a cup of coffee, wishing the radio he wore on his shoulder and the gun on his hip were less obvious, but the radio was hard to ignore, as a disembodied voice spit out numbers and addresses.

I hate guns. I've always hated guns and I knew I kept staring at his, until Karl finally said, "Look, I'm not allowed to leave this thing in the car, but I could take it off while I'm here." He unbuckled the gun belt and placed it on a chair, but in my mind, it might as well have been hanging from the ceiling with spotlight on it. My eyes kept swiveling back to look at the menacing object.

For all of it, I was still glad to see him. He looked tired, powerful but still sort of little-boy-like, despite the gun. When he stood up to leave, I wrapped my arms around him and lifted my lips for a kiss. He pulled me toward him and hugged me, but when I reciprocated, I felt a hard, unyielding wall against my hands, arms and chest.

"What the hell is that?" I said.

He laughed. "That's my bullet-proof vest," he said, watching my reaction.

I pulled the door open, rolled my eyes and said, "Oy vey. A radio and the gun aren't enough, huh?"

As he drove away, I stood in the doorway waving good-bye. To hell with the neighbors.

CHAPTER VI

As the weeks went by, we fell into a pattern, seeing each other nearly every night, but still my hesitation remained, heightened by the interviews I did for the Jewish newspaper. "Don't believe them when they say they didn't know," said one non-Jewish American soldier who had liberated a concentration camp. "The people who lived near those towns had to know," he said, showing pictures of the conditions around the work camp Nordhausen.

I continued to wonder often how much Karl's mother and father knew about what had taken place during those war years. What exactly was the involvement of Karl's family and what had they discussed at home, after the war? What role had the school that his father ran in Sonthofen played? What exactly did Karl know, and what was he keeping from me?

And then Karl started talking about going to Germany to visit his family, about having me come with him, showing me the sights and the culture. I wasn't so sure I cared about sightseeing, but the reporter in me was beginning to realize maybe I could get some of my questions answered.

"You're going to visit his father in Germany?" Beth said in disbelief. She clearly had her doubts about my relationship with Karl, about my continuing interest in a cop who seemed, from her point of view, to be a political conservative at best and at worst, a redneck racist.

I laughed. I knew that Beth found it hard to understand why I was attracted to Karl, and I often felt the same way. I remembered a party I hosted shortly after Karl and I started seeing each other. I was given to having large parties, inviting people from disparate parts of my life. There was always lots of food, conversation and camaraderie.

Karl said he would come and he did. He seemed quite comfortable and everyone seemed to like him. In fact most people made a point of telling me later how much they had enjoyed talking with him and how pleasant he was. Few of them seemed to care whether he was a cop and still fewer that he was a German who looked like a Nazi.

It wasn't until several weeks later that I found out how terrified Karl had been about the party. "I was sure all of your friends would hate me because I was a cop or a German," he confessed, telling me he was sure all of my friends were probably liberals and almost all were probably Jewish. And since remembering names—especially in English—had always been a problem for him, he had a hard time sorting out who he had enjoyed talking with and who he wanted to know more about. Karl's inability to remember names was frustrating to me, since I liked gossiping after a party and could discuss people and their foibles endlessly.

Rationally analyzing the relationship, I found it was difficult to define our areas of commonality, yet something powerful drew me to Karl, beyond the fun we were having in bed. There were moments, when I'd mention a family custom that was similar to his, that I felt we'd come from the same background. Sometimes, he told me stories that made me realize he felt the same sense of being connected.

Preparing me for our trip, he told me sheepishly that his family didn't call him Karl. When he was born, his great grandmother, clucking over him in his mother's arms, said, "Oh, what a cute little Bueblein," meaning little boy. Now, his father addressed him as Karl, but no one, including his nephews, called him anything but Bueblein. "When I'm an old man, a grandfather, I will be called Opa Bueblein—Grandpa little boy," he laughed. I could see the name pleased him, almost as if it were a tangible reminder of the times in his life when he was cuddled and protected, sheltered from the cruelties of post-war Germany and from his stern father.

I particularly liked the nickname because it sounded like *bubeleh*, the Yiddish word, dear child. In fact, Karl laughed quite gleefully when I read him a story I happened on one day in *The Joys of Yiddish* that seemed to be written for him.

"A Jewish mother sent her son off to his first day in school with customary pride and precautionary advice: So, *bubeleh*, you'll be a good boy and obey the teacher? And you won't make noise, *bubeleh* and you'll be very polite and play nice with the other children. And when it's time to come home, you'll button up warm, so you won't catch cold, *bubeleh*—etc, etc.

Off went the little boy. When he returned that afternoon, his mother hugged him and kissed him and exclaimed, 'So did you like school, *bubeleh*? You made new friends? You learned something? ''Yeah,' said the boy. 'I learned that my name is Irving'."

Little things drew us closer, like discovering we had both saved our teddy bears from childhood, carrying them around with us across continents and countries. And even more bonding was the fact that both bears had been bought in post-war Germany, maybe in Hamburg. When I saw Karl's teddy bear I thought of him walking down the pier during the seagull episode, the equipment on his gun belt clanking with every step. I remembered how the people looked at him with what I thought was fear and apprehension, and thought none of those people would have imagined this cop had a treasured teddy bear at home.

Then there were the puppets. The miniature stage I remembered playing with in post-war Germany as a child was lost over the years, but I still had the wooden puppets: the policeman, the queen, the witch. Karl had the same toys in a larger size, saved from his childhood. Both sets of them, although clearly carved to a different scale, showed the same distinctive style of the woodcutter who had made them. Even the fabric of the dresses was apparently cut from the same piece of cloth.

"I remember when I got these," he told me one day, holding the witch.

His family had lost all their possessions and had no income. His father was a disappointed man whose world had just collapsed. Karl could remember vividly that cold and rainy November when they were in the Alsterhaus in Hamburg where the puppets were bought. He had no idea what his parents had used for money to buy them.

"We must have been in the same store at the toy counter as children pretty much at the same time, with our parents buying them for us," Karl said. "I can picture your little girl's face and rain-soaked hair."

Karl remembered far more from his childhood than I did. I realized I knew very little about my parents' roots. They had preferred to dwell on the here-and-now and not the past. They never talked about what they and their parents had left behind in the old country. I wasn't even sure precisely where the old country was, other than somewhere in Eastern Europe. They had never talked about the early years or about the war.

"My parents never talked much about the past," I told Karl and he said, "neither did mine." He looked at me and added, "when we did ask questions, my mother made it clear that this was a subject that was not to be discussed. Not now and not in the future."

I frowned. My parents certainly hadn't encouraged my questions, if I ever had any, about their past either.

When he was trying to find things we shared, Karl sometimes laughingly said, "Well, you call them latkes and I call them potato pancakes, but they're the same food. Latkes are just potato pancakes with a Yiddish accent."

Actually, as a lover of history and lore, Karl was able to trace the origin of the traditional treats, describing the arrival of the potato into Europe by way of its discovery in the New World and its adoption by both Germans and Jews.

It was a nice feeling to be a part of all that history, I thought in my more optimistic moments. It was true Karl didn't cook his potato pancakes the same way, and ate applesauce on them instead of sour cream, but the flavor was similar enough to feel familiar. Still, in my darker moments, I knew it took more than just a common food to make for a feeling of kinship. Grated potatoes didn't wipe out the blood of six million people.

Furthermore, I had a hard time feeling sorry for his parents' loss of all their possessions when I thought about how many millions of people had lost their lives and families at the hands of the Nazis.

I was lying in bed with him one sunny morning, basking in the afterglow of our love making. He was a gentle but demanding lover who made no secret of his ardor. His sense of urgency inflamed me. Stroking his body, I touched his penis, examining it more closely than I had before. I was fascinated by what he jokingly called his "turtleneck."

"I've never been with an uncircumcised man before," I said, leaning over to take him into my mouth. After I felt him harden, I slid his penis out of my mouth so I could watch as his erection arose out of the skin. But then, Karl broke the mood, saying he thought circumcisions were barbaric. "Don't ever try getting me to do that," he said with a laugh.

The comment irritated me because of its absurdity and the faint, worrisome possibility that it, like many other seemingly innocuous and slightly thoughtless comments Karl made, was actually anti-Semitic. There were remarks and observations of his, like assuming all of my friends were Jewish, when clearly, many were not, that seemed to smack of something more than just a misunderstanding.

Finding myself on guard for his possible anti-Semitic remarks was ironic. All my life, I had dismissed my mother's contentions that unthinking comments by insensitive people were, in reality, purposeful anti-Semitic aspersions. "I suppose there's a Nazi under every bed," I used to say sarcastically whenever my mother recounted an episode of what she believed to be anti-Semitism. Now, with this man who clearly cared about me, I was scrutinizing his every word and nuance.

When I told Beth I was thinking about going with Karl to visit his parents, I said it would make a great story. That was one of my favorite lines, an explanation for many of the oddball things I did—that and my theory that since you only live once, you should seize the moment. "When else could I travel around Germany with a German and meet his Nazi family?" I laughed.

"Well, you'd better figure out where the American embassy is before you settle in for the night at his father's house," said Beth.

CHAPTER VII

As the weeks passed, the tickets were purchased and I tried to sell some of my story ideas, I began to think even more seriously about the trip. Why was I doing this? Would I feel comfortable in Germany at all, never mind at Karl's family's house?

"I want you to tell them I'm a Jew before we leave," I said to him one night.

"Why can't you just let it be?" he asked. "What difference does it make? You don't look that Jewish."

I was offended by that comment and by the thought of going there without his family knowing I was Jewish. "I'm not going to go to Germany under false pretenses. I'm not going to try to "pass" as a Gentile. I want them to know now," I said with some heat.

So Karl dutifully wrote what we began referring to as his "guess who's coming to dinner" letter, receiving a prompt reply from both his mother and father, separately.

"You and your friend will be welcome," wrote his father. "I will reserve two rooms in the house for you. You will let me know when to expect you." Karl suggested facetiously that Der Alte wanted the two-bedroom arrangement to avoid violating the Nuremberg laws prohibiting sexual interaction with Jews. Actually, there were no other double beds in the house and perhaps it was his way of diplomatically communicating that information.

Ingrid Schmidt wrote simply that she was excited about seeing her Bueblein. "I'm especially looking forward to meeting the woman who is taking care of you now," she wrote. Knowing we would be going to some of the places I had lived in Germany after the war, I showed Karl some more of my old pictures. "That's me in Hamburg with my mother."

I had finally called my mother, who lived in New York and was a spry 85, to tell her that I was dating Karl. "Well, times change," was her response. She had weathered my two marriages to non-Jewish men. She had borne both divorces in stoic silence and had, in the main, refrained from interfering with my life.

"What do you think about my trip to visit his family?" I asked point blank.

My mother laughed. "Well, it looks serious, huh?" It was an old joke between us. I rarely told my mother much anymore about my love life. In the past when I had, her inevitable response had always been to question whether the man's intentions were honorable and whether marriage would result. She never asked anymore if I were planning to get married again, but once in a while, she permitted herself to express a little curiosity about the future.

"I suppose it might be serious," I replied, surprising both of us. "But I mean, don't you think it's a little weird, me visiting his mother and father?"

My mother reached back into her past for the answer, giving me information I had never heard before. "When we lived in Hamburg after the war, we had a German neighbor, a woman. She was always inviting me over for tea. I always tried to get around it. I didn't want to socialize with those people; it had only been a few years since the war. I couldn't be around them without wondering what they had been doing during the war, why they hadn't stopped it."

On one particular day, when she was feeling low, homesick and abandoned by her busy husband, she had finally succumbed to the neighbor's offer. "The mother had three children and they spoke only German, but they entertained you," my mother said. "And you know, with the language barrier and all, it was ironic, but this woman was much warmer and more cooperative and responsive and friendly than any of the

American women—the wives of your father's colleagues, the military people, even the women from the agencies that were helping the DPs. For the most part, the Americans were anti-Semitic, petty, crude and nasty."

When I shared my mother's story with Karl, maybe to show him how much anti-Semitism there was everywhere, he described another issue I had never considered.

Although Karl adjusted to having people mimic his accent once he moved to America, and even greet him by saying, "Sieg Heil," he wasn't prepared for having people assume he shared their sometimes anti-Semitic feelings. He was taken aback when first confronted with the assumption from a new acquaintance, who slapped him on the back in a buddy-buddy manner one day, apropos of nothing and said, "We'll get them all yet. Just because Hitler failed doesn't mean it can't be done." That Karl thought the comment was despicable was clear, but when I asked him what he said in response, he told me he had said nothing.

Shortly after the discussion, I clipped a poem from a newspaper and hung it on my refrigerator. Written by Protestant German church leader Martin Niemoeller, the now-famous words were, "In Germany, the Nazis first came for the Communists and I didn't speak up because I wasn't a Communist. Then they came for the Jews and I didn't speak up because I wasn't a Jew. Then they came for the trade unionists. I didn't speak up because I wasn't a trade unionist. Then they came for the Catholics and I didn't speak up because I wasn't a Catholic. Then they came for me and by that time there was no one left to speak for me."

It was just a silent reproach, which I didn't follow up with any discussion. I didn't tell Karl that part of the reason I had put up the poem was as a reminder to *myself* not to stand by idly when there was a clear need to act. With even more self-scrutiny than usual, I worried about what I would have done if I had been a German, faced with the same dilemma. As a reporter, covering stories about guilt and inaction during the war, I had often been struck by the question. I remembered hearing from a Dane who had participated in rescuing hundreds of Jews, explaining why so many of his countrymen had been willing to risk their lives.

"The king got a letter from the Germans saying they would take care of the Jewish problem. The king telegraphed back 'we don't have a Jewish problem. We are all Danes.' We had people go to Germany and tell the Nazis we weren't going to allow them to treat our Danish Jews the way the Jews in other countries were being treated."

Another of my assignments involved a man whose parents had been rescuers in a small town forced to witness the Nazis' torture. "It's hard for people to understand why virtually no one did anything, why people said they didn't know." He said he was lucky to be in a family where a sense of right was never lost. "My father worked in the underground. But make no mistake, I lived in a tiny village, way up north, but we knew. We all knew. Even the children knew."

I had come to realize it wasn't just individuals who pretended they didn't know, leaving the rescue to the few compassionate, brave souls who were called somehow to perform heroic acts. And it wasn't just individuals acting alone who refused to speak out.

Other experts I wrote about spoke of the way whole nations had turned their back on the Reich's victims. One immigration specialist had said, "Choices were clearly available to those in leadership positions. The reason a helping hand wasn't extended was because of anti-Semitism, reaching historic intensity." He pointed the finger at nearly every country and every leader, even U.S. President Franklin Delano Roosevelt, who had been regarded in my family as a god.

Although Roosevelt did convene two conferences to discuss the problem, no action was taken. "Europe looked to Roosevelt for leadership. He did nothing," the expert said. "After 1941, the borders were closed and the State Department blocked the Reich refugees from entering. Roosevelt did nothing to change that."

Where, I wondered, did that leave people like my parents, who had supported Roosevelt and the Democrats and wanted to hear nothing bad about their hero?

"Jews were powerless to do anything to influence more positive immigration policies," said a commentator at a panel discussion I was covering. "The Jews were entirely marginal, peripheral. They were powerless and fearful, operating on eggshells. Some were afraid to call attention to what was happening in Europe for fear of triggering similar actions here. Only within the Democratic Party were the Jews enfranchised and FDR knew the Jews had no place to go, no matter what was done about Germany. They were captives of the New Deal."

I didn't tell Karl about my confusion and doubts, about my fear that I wouldn't have had the moral courage to fight the tide or about my concern about what my own father had or hadn't done as an employee of the Immigration and Naturalization Service to influence the government's policy to accept fleeing Jews.

I believed that my being Jewish didn't consciously matter to Karl. But I couldn't imagine what his perceptions about Jews could have been based on. In Germany, there were no Jews in Karl's life. He had never been confronted with the issue of anti-Semitism or what he thought of Jews because there weren't any. When he emigrated, he was surrounded by a blue-collar world that came complete with a whole set of preconceived ideas about groups of people. Karl bore their assumptions about himself in silence, but at least silently had condoned all their prejudices about other groups.

Because Karl was becoming a major presence in my life, I began putting him on the phone with my mother for a brief hello now and then. Maybe I was trying to adjust her to hearing his German accent, which wasn't so different from hers. Maybe I was testing him. Maybe it just seemed like the normal thing to do at that stage of our relationship. Both Karl and my mother were clearly uncomfortable at first, but gradually, as they began to share information about me, I sensed they were beginning to relax with each other. I could almost hear my mother saying to her friends, "Well, he's a German, but he seems like a decent fellow. He does nice things for Sarrie."

In fact, I was conscious of "feeding" my mother information about those nice things, making a special point of telling her whenever Karl brought flowers, or worked on my car, or when we went to a place for dinner my mother would have liked.

Now I became obsessed with hearing more about my mother's memories of those long-ago times in Hamburg and Bremen. I would call her, once, twice, three times a week and ply her with questions. She had clearly been paranoid about the Germans, assuming all of them had been implicated in the atrocities. Going to post-war Germany in 1948 to be exposed to thousands of concentration camp survivors was the last thing she wanted to do, but her husband had gotten a promotion. Her place was clearly with him.

My father's career, before the war ended, had been boring and at a standstill. The opportunity to work in post-war Germany represented the chance of a lifetime. Living there, with all the privileges of the victors, my parents were overwhelmed. Our small, two-bedroom apartment in what was virtually a Jewish ghetto in the Bronx was a stark contrast to the opulence of our lifestyle in Germany, despite the food shortages and hostility of the *goyim* there.

That my father worked 18 hours a day, taking the plight of the DPs home with him, leaving my mother to navigate on her own the difficulties of food rationing, language problems, fears of the Germans and the growing political threat of the Russians seemed a small price to pay for the contribution he was making to resettling these people whose lives had been destroyed by the Nazis.

"About the German housekeeper we had—Clara—such speed you never saw," my mother said in one conversation. "She would bring you to school, bring you back, dress and undress you, iron beautifully, cook like the best hotel chef. Mostly, she seemed to be honest—for a German," she added.

I had heard a few stories over the years about Clara, seen pictures of the young German woman. Once when I was in high school, years after leaving Germany, I wrote to her and received a warm letter in response. Clara explained that she and her husband were trying to find an apartment in Darmstadt, where he had just gotten a job, but were having difficulty finding anything they could afford. Consumed with my high school activities, I had never written back.

Thinking about Karl and my upcoming trip, my mother suggested I try to find Clara, long married and the mother of several children. "She tried to keep in touch with me after we came back, but I just didn't feel like writing to her—I never really trusted her completely," my mother admitted.

When I told Karl about my mother's suggestion, he thought it would be a good idea to try to connect with Clara. "Maybe she can tell us more about what it was like, working for the Allies, especially for a Jewish family," he said.

He told me Germans moved rarely and that we would probably find Clara in Darmstadt. He called information, found a listing for her and placed the call.

"This is Karl Schmidt," he said when he reached Clara with remarkably little difficulty. "I have here Sarah Stern. Do you remember her?" Clara, after little hesitation, responded with amazement, "Yes, Yes, little Sarrie. How is she?"

Karl explained to Clara that we were planning a trip to Germany and would be at his parents' house, not far from Darmstadt. "Would it be possible for us to see you when we are there?" he asked.

"Indeed, not only possible," she said, "but absolutely necessary. You must call us when you arrive and we will arrange a time."

I wondered if I would be able to talk to Clara about my mother's fears. Would Clara have been aware that my mother hadn't trusted her or any Germans?

Sometimes during my calls with my mother, I would hear previously untold memories of horrific sights and experiences. Some I had heard from Jews I interviewed, but I had never heard them from my mother. Now they sounded even more wrenching than the stories I had written for the newspaper.

"We had just come back from the Bremen airport where we saw a plane off—hardship cases, orphans, infants, pregnant women and old people," she recalled. "It was certainly pathetic when people that age had to start out for a new life in a new country. One of the "orphans," a boy of 17, was very handsome and charming. An American family who was stationed there had become interested in him and offered to adopt him. His parents agreed and signed away their son. They had come to the airport to see him off. They said he was the youngest and they had nothing to offer him. They couldn't read or write and you couldn't immigrate if you were illiterate."

Responding to my interest, my mother sent parts of a diary my father had kept during those years, one I had known nothing about. I shared it with Karl. "Today I got into a conversation with an English businessman about the Germans," my father had written. "He was in Germany under Hitler. He did business with the Germans. He agreed that they indulge in self pity and have no feeling of horror or pity over the atrocities, which they all deny all knowledge of. They all deny they were Nazis. But the businessman says that he witnessed them all enthusiastically marching under Hitler and enjoying it."

My father apparently saw a lot of the countryside and what he saw dismayed him. "The scenery still depresses me," he wrote. "Nothing but ruins, partly or completely demolished buildings. Curious sights: a fairly well dressed youngish woman, wearing a hat and coat on the street, shoveling manure, just to take home. I saw a man on the autobahn doing the same. Apparently fertilizer is hard to get."

Karl laughed when I finished reading that, realizing he had his own memory about fertilizer. "Fertilizer was actually impossible for us to get. It contained nitrates and with nitrates, Germans could make explosives, so it was banned by the occupation forces." What Karl remembered was that because gasoline was unavailable, some Germans used horses for transportation, sometimes using them to pull cars. Following close behind the horse was at least one person, frantically shoveling manure for their gardens, which meant food in the long run.

Seeing a soldier in those years in Germany meant, for Karl, seeing a foreigner. All the soldiers, and there were a lot of them, were occupation forces.

After my conversation with Karl, I asked my mother what she remembered about the living conditions in the occupied zones, particularly in Hamburg, where the British were rationing food. She and I had never talked about this before.

"When we were in Bremen—where I suppose we had enough to eat, although it wasn't what we were used to—we heard that in Hamburg the occupation forces had hardly anything to eat," she said. "Even the families who could buy in the Commissary had very little to buy and they told me they were half-starved. I remember one fellow from the occupation forces saying that the matzoth the Red Cross handed out for a Jewish holiday were all he had to eat for a week once."

The Red Cross handing out matzoth in Germany when there were virtually no Jews left there to eat them struck me as a supreme irony.

I remembered an episode from those years, maybe in the school in English-occupied Hamburg, when I was forced to eat grapefruit sections mixed with condensed-type milk, the milk curdling from the acid in the fruit. A fussy eater as a child, I had at first refused to consider putting the vile-looking offering in my mouth.

58

"We have rationing," I recalled being told by a teacher with a clipped British accent. "You must eat this." I had, with clenched teeth.

But my mother said that in Bremen, things were much better. Almost everything could be bought—somewhere. "Fresh vegetables were a little scarce, but I always found cabbage and carrots and green peas. After a while, they brought in lettuce and radishes," she said.

Describing the menu for a meal with guests—men from the British zone who worked with the DPs—my mother said, "Can you imagine anyone wanting second helpings of soup? They all said they were fed up with the canned soup at the hotel. After the soup, we had leg of lamb, small browned parsley potatoes, fresh garden beets Clara swiped from a neighbor's garden, Italian grapes, hot biscuits, a heart-shaped cake."

That sounded like a feast, but I could understand why my mother might not have considered that an adequate meal for guests. I remembered the plates and plates of food my mother and aunts cooked for family get-togethers when I was a child.

Commenting on that "sad" description of life for the occupation forces, Karl said, "I remember being hungry until sometime around 1953," he said. "We received rations—for my sisters, but not for me because I was considered too young. My most favorite and most frequent meal was hard bread softened in hot barley coffee with a little sugar." Karl fell silent. He said he remembered when, as a little boy, he had made his way down to the ground floor in the apartment house where they lived in the attic. On the right side in the entrance way were dark brown double doors that led to the pub. Karl's eyes were about the height of the keyhole.

"I looked through it and saw all the older children in the neighborhood sitting at long tables and eating from steaming plates. I had no idea why they were there and I wasn't."

Later he was told they had gotten the food from "Boernebespiesning," the program of the Danish government to feed starving German children. Karl had not only looked but also breathed in the scent that came through the keyhole. It was a combination of stale beer and old cigarette smoke mixed with the aroma of hot food. It had smelled strange and delicious.

"Sometimes now, when I walk into Brennan's while they are serving food, especially on rainy winter evenings, I remember that smell of those terrible years: stale beer, old cigarette smoke and hot food."

Karl said he had once taken himself out for a special treat in a nice restaurant sometime after his first divorce. He picked one that featured rabbit, remembering from his early childhood what a delicacy it had been. But eating it that night in Berkeley didn't remind him of those long-ago meals.

"I complained about it later to my mother in a phone conversation," Karl said. "There was a long silence after I told her that the restaurant fare had suffered by comparison to her cooking. I thought I was paying her a compliment. But she said, 'That wasn't really rabbit, Bueblein. It was cat. That was all we could find'."

He described his family's two-room apartment in Kiel, a place his father built of scavenged boards in an attic, unheated for the four years they lived there.

After I told my mother about Karl's life in Kiel, she recounted to both of us in a phone call about her own scavenging during those years in Germany to find clothing for the family to wear. "I wrote often to my sister, requesting that items be sent from the States. I told her if she should hear of hand-me-downs, please arrange to get them. I had to explain to her that clothing in Germany was expensive and inferior. I knew I could always give what I didn't need to the maid."

"The girls who worked at your father's office looked awful," my mother went on. "They wore dresses above their knees and long socks they knit themselves. None of them, even mature women, wore stockings. It was worse in Hamburg. There they wore rags."

60

Karl, who lived in Hamburg during that time, said he was too young to have noticed that.

Later, as my mother and I talked about those years, she remembered something else I had never heard. "You know, when your aunts and other people did send things for me to pass out, your father wouldn't let me do it. He said there was a rule for all occupation personnel prohibiting fraternizing with the enemy. He was a stickler for obeying the rules, but even so, sometimes I snuck things to Clara anyway."

Karl pointed out that everyone who wasn't serving in the Army during the war had belonged to either the Hitler Youth or Nazi girls' organization—the BDM—so those uniform shirts were the only thing in ample supply and were used for making clothes after the war.

"My mother was in the BDM," Karl said matter-of-factly. I remembered laughing as a teenager about how my mother thought every German she encountered during those post-war years was a Nazi. Maybe my mother hadn't been so far off.

"My shirts were actually made out of my sisters' old dresses, cut in half," Karl recalled.

I showed Karl pictures of our "family" car, provided by the occupation forces, complete with a chauffeur, to drive my father around. "It was a pale green 1949 Chevrolet," I said. "We never had a car in the States, couldn't afford it and no one in the family knew how to drive."

"My father knew how to drive," said Karl, "but before 1950, we didn't get around. There was no money and no place to go."

"I wonder if there wasn't another reason for our low profile in those years immediately after the war," Karl commented. "Could we have been in hiding?" Once the Schmidt family moved to Hamburg, public transportation was available. It was 1954 before the family had a car. "Maybe we'll get some answers during our visit," he said.

After each of these conversations, I felt torn. It was painful to think of Karl, who was, in some strange way, even now, very vulnerable and childlike, having to go without food or adequate clothing. But I thought about the conditions in the concentration camps, the starvation, torture and degradation, and wondered how many people would feel sorry for the way the Germans had to live after the war, even the children. All my life I had been told that all Germany should pay for the crimes of the war. But did one wrong justify another?

And what exactly had Karl's father been doing during that period? Was he hiding out and if so, why? Where did Karl's uncle fit into the puzzle?

CHAPTER VIII

Even while I was struggling with those unresolved questions, Karl started trying to teach me German. Learning the days of the week and colors, I found an essay I had composed as a child in Germany, dictated to my mother, "Clara took me to the Osterwiese—park—for Easter. She bought me a bird's nest with Easter eggs. I speak German. Aschenbecher means ashtray. Affweider Schoen means goodbye. Bitte Ein blume haben means can I have a flower."

Karl laughed heartily at the spelling of the words in my mother's handwriting. "Your mother had no idea how to spell German," he said. "Everything is spelled totally wrong."

Speaking the language, hearing it now in my own voice, made me feel uncomfortable. Even though Karl heard the similarity, to my ears it wasn't enough like Yiddish to remind me of my childhood, when my mother and aunts would speak Yiddish almost exclusively. Visions of stormtroopers still came to mind whenever I heard German. I struggled with numbers, remembering that I had learned to count to ten in German as a child.

There were times when the child and the adult blurred for us. Riding in the car, sitting at the table, walking in the supermarket, I would point out objects and ask Karl to say them in German. I learned the word "Tuete" for bag and decided it could be used for virtually everything from a sock to a glass case. Although Karl recognized the liberties I was taking with the language, he would merely grin whenever I used the word generically.

In the spirit of "if you can't beat them, join them," he even began referring to my bras as Tueten.

Lying in bed one night, I playfully pointed to his penis and said, "Und, was is das?" Karl grinned. He had a dry sense of humor, overlaid with the blue-collar mentality of ethnic jokes that I deplored. I wasn't given to telling or even understanding most jokes, but I did find humor in everyday events.

"Das is mein Maennlein," he said, stroking himself.

I pointed to my furry mound, which Karl began to finger. "Und hier ist mein Fraeulein," I said. Karl grinned. He had clearly never heard the word Fraeulein used quite that way, but if his third-grade use of Maennlein made sense, certainly my application was equally as logical. He was pleased that I was feeling at least a bit more comfortable with the German language.

Showering together one day, while he was soaping his penis and lathering his pubic hair, Karl began to sing "Ein Maennlein steht im Walde auf einem Bein, sag, wer mag..." Karl grinned as he sang, but I missed the smile. The German singing made me think of Nazis marching. I frowned and said sarcastically, "Great, so being in the shower with me makes you think of military music?" Karl looked puzzled, then broke into laughter, singing the song in English. The song described a mushroom standing in the forest as a "little man with a hat standing on one leg," a silly song he had learned in second grade, where the slang word for penis was "little man."

He and his classmates had tried to suppress their embarrassed giggles when Fraeulein Fischer had unknowingly made them sing about their penises. "A little man stands in the forest, on a single leg, say, who could be that little man..." It was the first song Karl learned in primary school.

Such moments made me feel distinctly better about our impending trip and decidedly guilty about my own stereotyping.

Planning where we would visit, we decided we would definitely go to Hamburg, to see the houses we had each lived in in 1950. I thought about Bremen, where my family had belonged to a military country club. Even though I couldn't recall it and hadn't thought about it in years, my mother remembered it well.

"The country club at Camp Grohn was wonderful. Golf, tennis—not that we played—ping pong, badminton, dancing, a snack bar, lounge chairs, a swimming pool. All for free." It was a country club where, in the states, no Jews would have been welcome. In any case, my family could never have afforded the membership fees.

"That makes me feel sort of ashamed," I said, "Like somehow my family benefited from the war, got something we wouldn't have had if there had been no war, no displaced persons, no camps." Karl liked it when I was confronted with confusion and was forced to realize nothing was really black and white.

"One of my main playgrounds was the rubble of buildings," Karl remembered. "The great sport was to search for grenades or to pry open scorched bomb shelters, looking for skeletons."

"That's pretty disgusting!" I interjected, "What were you thinking, looking for skeletons?"

Karl shrugged. "I don't remember what we thought about, but put yourself into our place. That's all we knew. As far as we could tell, that was what the world was like and all kids were looking for dead people."

Karl described the castles he wanted to take me to, the trip down the Rhine, the cathedral in Cologne. My mother remembered, from going down the Rhine in the spring of 1948, that everything would be in full bloom. "Words can't describe the beauty of the flowers and trees," she said. She sent me a fold-out map of the castles on the Rhine, saved by my father.

"Maybe," I suggested to Karl, "We could go to Sonthofen and try to solve the mystery of what your father really did."

Always, in the back of my mind as we planned our trip were the unanswered questions. What did Der Alte know about the Nazi machinery? How much was he involved with them?

"I have to admit, I keep wondering how much of what I've been told about my father's role is true," Karl said. Without actually saying so, it was understood among his friends and schoolmates that if your parents hadn't been tried at Nuremberg, they must have been blameless. But how many people were actually tried for their war crimes and how many more went free? It was another thing no one discussed.

Karl too had pictures, most from several years after the war, after rationing was over. "There was no film available right after the war," he told me, but I wondered if there was another reason why the Schmidt family took no pictures during those years. Were they trying to be invisible?

Karl took me to his house one day to search for the pictures and old school books that he thought we might have in common from the occupation period.

"Look at these old pictures. I'd forgotten I had them. I remember taking them out of my grandfather's house in East Germany." Karl handed me a cardboard-mounted print of a young man standing, holding a sword and wearing a helmet with a plume of feathers on the top. "That's my grandfather wearing his class-A police uniform in Leipzig."

Putting the pictures away, Karl said, "I bet there's all kinds of stuff still there. My father still owns the place. He once, a few years ago, offered to deed it over to me." Karl laughed. "That's about all he's ever offered me and a piece of worthless farm property in a godforsaken place I can't even visit. The Communists have incorporated it into a commune owned by the State."

He described the years when his father had ordered him to stand straight, think straight, do better in school. In fact, Karl had been a marginal student, in trouble much of the time, indifferent all of the time. Karl's relationship with his father, never good as a child, had worsened when he emigrated, until Karl's contact with him now was limited to a one week visit on his very infrequent trips to Europe. And Karl knew, were it not for his mother, he would never visit at all.

But when he observed to me that he had fled Germany to get away from his father, I said, "Well, it's not that easy. I think you took some of it along with you. You chose a very structured situation for yourself, working for the police, where there are rules and orders for everything. Isn't that going along with the program?" I asked.

"Maybe so, but for me, the Nazi regime didn't end until I left Germany and my father's house," Karl said. Neither of us gave voice to the question of what Karl's attraction to rules and order would have meant fifty years or more before.

CHAPTER IX

One night while we were having an after-dinner cocktail at Brennan's, the television suddenly flashed to a shot of the Berlin Wall.

"My God," said Karl, pointing to the screen. We could see swarms of people standing on the top of the Wall, attacking it with sledge hammers, tearing holes in it. The camera angle shifted and we saw men with steel cables pulling whole sections of concrete to the ground. Not one East German soldier could be seen. Men, women and children were dancing on the Wall and in the streets.

"They're tearing the wall down," Karl said in disbelief. I looked at him as he watched the action. While he looked elated—smiling and pumping his fist—he also seemed almost dazed at times.

At one point, he looked down at the table and said in a sad voice, "As a young child I would always hear my grandparents talk about the reunification. 'It will happen someday,' they would say, adding, 'But not in our lifetime.'"

He would always tell them, not really understanding what he was saying, that they would live to see the country be one again. They hadn't. Later, as a teenager and young adult, Karl said he never repeated those reassurances. Instead, he agreed that a united Germany would be dangerous, and that keeping the country separated was the best plan.

"When I moved to the United States, I realized that if I said that, it reassured people, made them understand I wasn't a power crazy warmonger, or a Nazi."

But watching the Germans dancing for joy on the crumbling Wall, Karl said, "I really believed what I told my grandparents.

Germany did belong as a single united country. You can't keep 17 million East Germans imprisoned, deny them the vote and the right to travel."

In the days that followed, we watched many such scenes, people climbing onto and over the wall, chipping away pieces of the wall. And in the weeks that followed, it seemed that the two Germanys almost catapulted toward reunification, exhilaration on both sides.

"By the time we get there," said Karl. "There will be only one Germany. My God, my father's house will actually be worth something. I think we should visit it. There will be bargains to be had as the East Germans try to sell things off to get American and West German money. I like that really old stuff."

Suddenly Karl was talking about his East German cousins, whom he had seen rarely in the past decades, and the two trips he'd made to East Germany to visit his grandparents. Letters from his family these days included news of the East German branch of the family and how quickly they were seizing the opportunity to cross the border freely.

"Greta brought us schnitzel from their farm," wrote Karl's mother, describing the trips relatives were now free to make to the West. Commenting on the food shortages and poor conditions in the East, Ingrid said, "We realize we'll have to give them money," adding, "I guess since we started World War II, it's only right that we should pay."

But if Karl was obviously happy about the fall of the Wall, I knew that most of the Jewish community was not. People feared that a reunified Germany would become once again a nationalistic Germany. Cartoons began appearing showing reunification as the path to the revival of the Reich.

As the trip drew nearer, my editor Bruce Kaplan at the Jewish newspaper became more interested in my visit to Karl's family. "I want you to interview the old man," he said. "People are really interested in how the Germans feel about their future. They'll be really interested in what an ex-Nazi thinks. It'll make a great story."

"I'm not sure he's an ex-Nazi," I said. Nothing Karl had said made me think his father had renounced Fascism.

"Well, if he isn't, that might be a story too," he responded, but he warned me about what kind of story he wanted. "He has to be contrite about what happened or the readers won't stand for it," said Bruce. "If he still believes that Hitler was God, forget it. He has to show contrition, remorse, atonement. And Sarah, don't mention your relationship with Karl in any of your stories."

"Huh?" I was genuinely puzzled, but a knot was forming in the pit of my stomach about what I thought he might mean. "Who is the old man supposed to be then and exactly what don't you want me to say?" I thought I kept my tone even, but Bruce clearly noticed my reaction.

"Calm down," he said. "I just don't want you to say you're having a romantic relationship with the son of an ex-Nazi. Say he's your traveling companion, or part of a group of people you're with."

"Why?" I could feel myself getting angry. In the world of freelance writing, antagonizing editors wasn't recommended, but I suspected a principle might be at stake here.

"Why? Because our readers don't want that kind of confusion. They hate Germany. They want to condemn the Germans. We don't want to destroy your credibility as a reporter by letting them think you're dating a German."

I thought about the things I could point out to him, high-minded principles about manipulating the news, letting the readers decide for themselves, but I said stiffly, "I am dating a German. I don't think I can write an article and pretend my relationship with Karl doesn't exist."

My editor chuckled. "Oh, I have faith in your good sense, Sarah. I'm sure you'll see the light. Start thinking about some story ideas and get back to me."

I wasn't sure why I didn't want to tell Karl about my conversation with Bruce Kaplan. Maybe I didn't want Karl to see the Jewish community in a bad light. When you are trying to be aggrieved for past sins committed against "your people," you can't be displaying your own bigotry. It was a *shande*, that is, a scandal you didn't divulge outside the family.

And then there was another, even more unpleasant possibility. I didn't like to think about why I hadn't argued more vehemently with my editor, who was responsible for assignments that paid my mortgage and bought my food. How different was my silence from the failure of the average German to speak up about the Nazi atrocities? Was I being overly dramatic about a trivial issue?

I wondered if Karl would be able to distinguish between Kaplan's instructions not to reveal my relationship with him to my Jewish readers and my own reluctance to be seen in public with him in Berkeley, where I wrote articles that criticized the city administration and the police department.

"It's better for both of us if we aren't seen together," I had explained the first time he suggested I go with him to a police department-sponsored party.

It was hard for Karl to dispute the logic of that, but I wondered how long that rule could last. If I continued to see him, I would eventually have to take him places where people would recognize both of us. And I would have to attend some kind of function where the room would be full of police personnel, many of them probably carrying guns.

I wasn't sure how much of my reluctance came from not wanting to create a situation where people would question my professional integrity and how much stemmed from my continuing distrust and dislike for the police. I didn't want to even consider that I could still be reluctant to be seen with someone who looked like a stormtrooper.

I eventually told Karl about the confrontation with Kaplan. Maybe it was because keeping secrets wasn't my strong suit. I also thought it was dishonest to withhold the information. "I think it's outrageous that he wants to manage the news, that he wants me to pretend I have nothing to do with you. How does he know his readers would be upset? Maybe his readers are a lot more broad-minded than he thinks."

Karl was always taken aback when I launched one of these tirades, sometimes not realizing that I wasn't really as angry as I seemed. He shrugged, but he was clearly irritated by Kaplan's attitude too.

"In Germany, which I'm not sorry I left because it was such a structured society with so many rules and so much silence, at least I was treated as a person, judged just for who or what I was," he said. "I was never condemned just simply for being a German. I was never confronted with how I felt about Jews, or what they thought of me. There weren't any."

He was silent for a minute and when I asked him what he was thinking, he said he'd suddenly remembered a trip his school had taken to Amsterdam when he was a teenager. On their sightseeing tour through the famous flea market, Karl had seen an old Delft tile which he wanted to bring as a souvenir for his mother.

"I approached the proprietor of the stand and asked if he spoke German. The old man immediately began to shout in Dutch, apparently very upset. I could make out fragments of sentences now and then. Everyone around me stopped and stared as the old man yelled at me."

"He was blaming me for killing the Jews in Holland and for the murderous bombing of Rotterdam. Then the old man began to spit at me. I didn't know how to react. I had learned in school what the Nazis had done to Holland and that all Germans shared a collective guilt. Despite that, I did not feel any personal guilt, so I was confused about why the merchant had singled me out and spit at me. At the same time, I understood the rage."

"So what did you do?" I asked. I could see the scene as if I had been there.

"I slowly melted away in the crowd, followed by reproachful eyes of the onlookers." He paused. "That certainly was one time I was judged just for being a German. And the fact is, I assume that any Jews I meet are suspicious of me or dislike me. I've never gotten to know any before you. I assumed they all thought I was anti-Semitic and they wouldn't have anything to do with me. I thought the minute they heard my accent, they would wonder about my father's involvement in the war. So I never started a conversation with them about anything substantive, fearing their disapproval."

I wondered if I should acknowledge that I too had judged him exactly as he feared. He added, "Each time I looked at someone I thought was Jewish, I wondered whether their families had died during the Holocaust."

As I gave him a hug, I understood that he had been troubled about this for a long while, and meeting me had brought all these issues to the surface.

To slightly change the subject, I told Karl about Bruce Kaplan's interest in an interview with Der Alte. At first, Karl agreed enthusiastically, almost gleefully, that it would be a good idea. He was so positive about the idea that I wondered if he didn't think I might uncover information he too wanted to hear. Was I also in some odd way a tool of revenge against Der Alte?

But when the time came to write to Der Alte and describe what I wanted to ask in an interview, Karl had second thoughts. "Why don't we just play it by ear? Let's wait until we get there and see how it goes. You can interview him and he won't even have to know you're doing it."

I objected. That sort of underhanded approach didn't conform to my professional ethics and I disliked not having all of the loose ends tied up, but the scenarios Karl described—Der Alte refusing to talk, canceling our visit or forming an opinion about me before he'd even met me—these outcomes were not at all attractive. Finally, I agreed I would wait and see what happened.

CHAPTER X

When Karl began bringing me books and maps, describing places we'd see, suddenly the trip became more of a reality.

"What am I doing this for?" I groaned to Beth one night over a beer. "Why am I going to Germany when I could be going to Tahiti or Hawaii? Do I really want to expose myself to anti-Semitism? Do I want to get into a hassle with my editor about censorship? It's supposed to be a vacation."

Beth smiled. "Is it? I don't know how you do it, Sarrie girl— I think I remember that all you really wanted from writing an article was to be able to write off the trip as a tax deduction. Now you've lined up a bunch of stories you're going to write; you've decided you're going to conduct an exhaustive interview with an old Nazi to find out what he really did during the war. You're going to watch Karl like a hawk to see if he transmogrifies into a stormtrooper when Lufthansa lands in Frankfurt. If that isn't enough, you're also going to investigate what became of this mysterious uncle. Does that sound like a vacation?"

I shook my head. "Nope. And that's only about half of it. There is the Germany I remember dimly from my childhood. How will I feel about the new Germany, the reunified Germany and its people heading toward some unknown future? If everyone, including Karl's relatives, is going to be delighted about the fall of the Wall, how am I going to feel? Is a reunited Germany something good?

"Will I really enjoy castles and other sights my mother raved about?" I asked Beth, adding with a laugh, "An ordinary tourist visiting Germany would go up the Rhine watching castles and quaint towns. What kind of a trip will we have debating not whether to visit the Alps but whether to see the concentration camp in Bergen-Belsen?"

Not to mention the impact my doubts had on Karl's feeling about the trip. Together we had read a book—*Born Guilty*—about the children of Nazi families—and I was moved by his reaction. "These people feel the same way I do," he commented as we read case histories of family after family, describing the impact of their parents' profound involvement in the Nazi atrocities. "I thought I was the only one who felt this way. My sisters and I, my friends and I, we never talked about this."

Now I groaned to Beth yet again. "Instead of carrying a German guide book we will be schlepping *Born Guilty*."

She shrugged, clearly bemused with my soul searching.

At my house I showed Karl a story I'd written about a young German woman talking about her childhood and what she knew of her parents' involvement. "I feel I contributed to my parents' silence," the woman had said. "I sensed when to stop asking, but I knew somehow, something was not right. There was an incredibly loaded silence in our families—especially if our fathers were not heroes of the Resistance. And most were not."

The woman had said she later decided the silence was maintained by the children to keep their parents as strong role models and by the parents to rehabilitate themselves after the war. "For me, there was intuition that something else had happened in their lives. We became suspicious, began to distrust our fathers. The father image was destroyed. Much later I was told a few family members were active Nazis." The question of what they knew and how they could have kept silent was always in her mind. "There's a suspiciousness, a doubt, a disbelief that stays with me today," she said.

Karl shook his head. "We had no suspicions that Der Alte had been involved in atrocities, but my mother always removed us children from the room when my father started into politics with his old friends. She would say 'the old Nazis and their horrible stories,' as she ushered us out. We were given to understand the Nazi time was a different era that one should not discuss. We were always cut off when we began to ask questions. For me the message was clear. This was a topic that was taboo."

And Karl said it was bizarre to watch movies in school in the morning that showed starving concentration camp prisoners and then go home and sit down at the table for a meal with a father who must have been implicated in some way.

When I tried to explain to Karl about some of my concerns for the trip, he nodded and sighed. "I know what you mean. I have my own fears. This isn't going to be a trip like the others I've taken to Germany to visit the family. I have so many more doubts about my family than I ever had before." He started pacing. "There is my father—who was in charge of the school in Sonthofen; my mother—who did that which she felt was expected of her: she joined the BDM, gave birth to three children and gave them good Germanic names."

"Then there are my two sisters, one a conservative housewife married to a conservative surgeon, and the other a very left-leaning member of the SPD, the Socialist party. And now we've added a new wrinkle. My mysterious Uncle Gerhard."

He shook his head. "I'm confused myself. Maybe we'll get answers but I wonder—do I really even want those answers?"

I assumed it was a rhetorical question for him, but not for me. "I know I want answers."

Karl winced. "I hope this trip will not just be a quest for information. Sometimes, I wonder if you are interested in going with me, meeting my family and seeing the sights, or do you just want to get a good story or two."

"Why does this have to be either or?" I asked, adding, "we can do both and I'm sure you're interested in seeing how your family reacts to me."

When I told my mother about this conversation, she seemed to side with Karl. "Why can't you just see the sights, meet his family, eat German food and enjoy being with him?" she wondered.

When I told her there seemed to be so much that Karl didn't know about his family and those war years and what happened to his uncle, my mother said, "Why do you think you and Karl have a right to get answers? So many families tried to find out after the war what happened to their relatives, only to learn there are no answers."

"Mom," I said. "I'm a reporter. I ask questions. I get answers. And Karl is a cop. He investigates. It's part of who we are."

I had reason to remember this conversation a few weeks later when Karl received a message from the Red Cross. "The British Red Cross advises that they have been unable to contact the sought person—your uncle. We presume this also means they were unable to get any information concerning him. It states that all available avenues of inquiry were explored."

While this was an answer, it also deepened the puzzle. The letter didn't explain why our inquiry to the American Red Cross had been investigated by the British Red Cross. Although they said they had been unable to contact Gerhard, they didn't say definitively that he was dead or that he hadn't survived the war. When I told my mother we still had no concrete facts and that I wasn't convinced that Gerhard was really dead, she suggested I concentrate instead on building my relationship with Karl and exploring how he was with his family. "Maybe they will tell you they all regret the Nazis and want to apologize to you." We both laughed after she said that and so did Karl when I told him.

Karl wasn't sure much had changed in his father's mind about the Jews since the war. He remembered on a trip to Italy in the sixties, at a campground near Ravenna, when Der Alte and Karl's older sister had been discussing her history class. Der Alte was telling her that the depression of the thirties was engineered by a conspiracy of Jewish bankers and the Communists. He also explained to her that international Communism was led philosophically by Jews. "Yes, even Karl

Marx himself was nothing but a German Jew," Der Alte had said.

And yet, Karl allowed for the possibility that maybe Der Alte had considered altering his attitude about Jews. Traveling without Ingrid, he had gone so far as to visit Israel in the seventies. He reported, with a certain awe, about the country that had been built out of a desert.

Gesturing to the books about Germany spread across his table, Karl said, "You seem to be avoiding looking at these, but this is supposed to be a holiday. We want to go down the Rhine on a boat, visit the Cathedral of Cologne and walk through the Hanseatic town of Luebeck. I want to take you to Goslar in the Harz Mountains, to Emperor Friedrich the Second's palace and tell you the story about how the people felt about him. I want to show you where I hiked when I was fifteen." He paused for breath.

Intrigued by his passion, I asked, "Who was Emperor Friedrich?"

Karl described an emperor who lived into his seventies, which was almost the span of three generations in the Middle Ages; when he died, the legend that he would return was born. "His nickname was Barbarossa—Red Beard—and they say he lives in the mountains, waiting to come back at a time when Germany needs him."

"Where was he during the Holocaust?" I asked, framing the question without thinking.

Karl shot me an exasperated look. "Well, your question is the point I'm trying to make. I would like to show you a part of my heritage. You can't put it in any context but the Holocaust. Even as a German, born eight days after the surrender, I find I have acquired a heritage that is overwhelming to me. There is nothing that I have done to feel guilty, but the feeling of guilt is in me nevertheless. Sometimes I wish I could feel proud of my heritage, especially when I walk among the Renaissance buildings in Luebeck. After all, there's more to German history than just the twelve years of the Nazi era. But when I travel in Germany, I always notice—with a certain bewilderment—that the trains still run on time. Germans still have a need to organize everything on a vast scale and be absolutely efficient about it."

"Well, that's how the concentration camps happened, I suppose," I said.

"Is this specifically German? Is this what made the Holocaust possible, and if this is German, is that then also part of my heritage?" he asked, more to himself than me.

When I said nothing, Karl told me he was reminded of an acquaintance he had made when he first emigrated. Sigfried Holmann had been about his age and, like him, a student. He had confided to Karl that his own father, some 15 years older than Der Alte, had been a military judge during the Nazi years. Sigfried had often made anti-Semitic comments to Karl, telling Jewish jokes and assuming Karl had sympathized with his sentiments.

Then suddenly, without any explanation, but perhaps because of a woman, Sigfried had announced he was actually Jewish. "My family made their name sound more German during the war years," he had said, thereafter including in nearly every conversation a smattering of Yiddish.

"Well, maybe he really is Jewish," I said. "Maybe he never felt safe about announcing it before."

Karl shook his head. There was no way Sigfried could have been Jewish. His father had been a member of the Stahlhelm, a virulently anti-Semitic group more right wing than the Nazis.

"Well, then why did he do it, pretend he was Jewish?" I asked.

Karl had theories, but no real answers. He figured other Germans his age had the same problems he did trying to reconcile their parents' roles. Some observed the utter silence that seemed to surround the entire country when the war years came up in conversation. Perhaps Sigfried was only doing what others had tried, revising history to better cope with their revulsion and their confusion about their parents' histories.

"Were you ever tempted to make up a different version of

your father's story?" I asked, the reporter in me somewhat intrigued by an option to change the past.

Karl thought about my question for a minute. "I don't really know what my history is because I don't really know what my father did. Maybe when I find out—and if it's worse than what I think—maybe I would be inclined to tweak the truth."

"Well, what would be 'worse' in your mind? That your father helped design the camps? Or worked in one of them? Or was responsible for executing Jews in conquered countries?" My voice rose as I considered these options. They all could be true. "Would you be tempted to lie to cover up that history?"

"I don't think so. That's the cop in me. You raise your right hand, you swear to tell the whole truth and nothing but the truth. No matter how distasteful it is."

PART II

CHAPTER XI

After landing at the Frankfurt airport and taking the train to the downtown area, we checked our luggage at the station. Although we never discussed the reason, we seemed to have silently agreed to delay our arrival at the Schmidt house. Now that we were actually on German soil, surrounded by German signs and people speaking the language, I was wondering again why I ever agreed to the trip.

We strolled around Frankfurt's downtown, slightly dazed from the ten-hour flight, but even our fatigue didn't dampen Karl's enthusiasm for pointing out the historic old buildings, mixed in with the newer ones. "This was bombed during the war," he said, uttering a sentence that would become a theme. "But you can see that some of the buildings were preserved and then new ones were built around them."

After an Eiskaffee at an outdoor restaurant, we retrieved our bags. Waiting in the station for the train to Heidelberg, listening to the announcements about arrivals, departures and track numbers, I was reminded of movies I'd seen of the war, with Gestapo agents lurking in public places and citizens hurrying from place to place, avoiding eye contact. It was frightening, hearing the German voices amplified on the distorted public address system throughout the huge building. *My life would have been in danger*, I thought. Suddenly I cringed against Karl and closed my eyes.

"What's the matter?" he asked, sounding annoyed. I suppose he thought I was imagining Gestapo agents in raincoats, not far from the truth.

"It's the pigeons. They're flapping. I keep thinking they're going to dive-bomb me," I said. He knew I hated birds, especially when they fluttered.

Karl laughed. "This vacation is already so intense, nothing that happens seems attributable to something as mundane as bird phobia." He gave me a reassuring hug.

As we arrived at the Schmidts, I began to feel even more apprehensive, but only Karl's mother was home. Der Alte was out somewhere. Ingrid shook her head. "He is always out somewhere, doing something." She said it not fondly but bitterly. I knew that Karl felt his parents' relationship was a model for everything bad in a marriage.

Karl had warned me they fought constantly. Der Alte was always yelling abuse at his wife and she always ended up being reduced to tears, usually after he slapped her around a few times. She was constantly threatening to leave him, and she did many times. Their fights were about money—first not having it, then how Ingrid spent it, then whether the children should have any, then what Der Alte was spending it on. And when Ingrid chose to start the arguments, they were about the hours Der Alte spent with his war buddies and the women Ingrid suspected he had on the side. Her suspicions, she had told Karl, were not completely fabricated. Twice during the war, arriving from out-of-town for surprise visits, she had found him in "compromising positions." Ingrid had never forgiven him for that, or for the many other transgressions she suspected or knew him to be guilty of.

If they had ever shared anything, those common interests were long gone, along with the glory of the Reich. The dashing Nazi star she had married was just an ordinary man. In her mind, anyway, he had never regained the power and influence that the Nazi party provided. In some respects, Der Alte had adjusted better to the fall of the NS and the end of the dreams than Ingrid had. And he had spent too many weeks away on business, working late at the office, taking refuge with his friends at local taverns. She had been too long a victim, never finding any interests of her own, never finding any contentment in her daily life. All of this Karl had explained to me before the trip even began.

They had long since given up sharing a room, it being a symbolic statement of the life they no longer lived together. In his room were large collections of books, most about the war, some about the places he traveled, always without Ingrid. She was terrified of flying and now, at 75, said she was too old to leave home.

"I think she looks forward to his trips as vacations," said Karl. In fact, she did take one vacation each year, by train to the Baltic Sea where she always stayed at the same place and visited with old friends nearby.

Since Der Alte wasn't around, Ingrid set the table for the three of us, the coffee pot steaming in readiness. As Ingrid stood next to Karl, lovingly putting her arm around him, looking at him with pride and the smile only a mother could have, I was surprised. The pictures I'd seen, and maybe my own stereotypes about German women, had prepared me for a tall, albeit aging, Germanic goddess, slender, with chiseled features. Instead, I saw a small rotund woman, maybe a head shorter than Karl, the epitome of a mother figure, except for her blonde hair. Her pearl-gray dress with white piping and the carefully coordinated jewelry she wore made it clear she thought this was a special occasion.

As I was stowing my clothes away in my bedroom, Karl came in, walked across the room, silently motioned me over to the dresser and pointed to a framed picture on display.

"This is a picture of my father with his brother Gerhard." He spoke in a whisper as he held up the picture, turning it over, looking at it intently. "This is when they were young—maybe pre-teens. I've never seen this picture out on display—or any picture of Gerhard at all—except at grandfather's in East Germany."

I stared at the faded sepia-toned picture. "Why do you think it's out now?"

"I don't have any idea but I'm going to take a picture of it," said Karl, laying the photo back on the dresser and adding, "Maybe this means they are ready to finally talk about Gerhard and the past."

As we ate cake and drank coffee, Ingrid seemed to want to talk—with Karl translating—about the war, an old woman's remembrances about the hardships of giving birth and making do with Der Alte gone all of the time.

"Did the women who were left behind talk and speculate about what was happening?" I asked.

Ingrid wore a displeased expression. Even with the translation delay, she understood. "What was happening? What do you mean?" I didn't want to be too combative, sitting there in the living room of Karl's boyhood home with his aging mother, so I rephrased the question.

"Well, did they talk about the evils of the regime?"

After Karl translated—perhaps not quite literally, Ingrid shook her head. "There was nothing to talk about. We didn't know. Even Der Alte, who was high up, didn't know. Only about twenty people must have known and they didn't tell anyone."

Karl and I exchanged a look of amusement, amazement, confusion. But I had decided, in planning for the trip, that I would merely ask questions, remember the answers, ask follow-up questions and avoid confrontations. Beyond that, I had no expectations. And the truth was, I had not expected, after less than an hour with Ingrid Schmidt, to already be involved in a significant conversation, one in which Ingrid had casually mentioned that the old man was "high up."

Like many unhappy women, Ingrid was more interested in complaining about her husband than in talking about life issues. Karl had told me many times that his mother sheltered him from his father's wrath and abuse during his childhood, taking his part, hiding his failures, protecting him. Ingrid turned to Karl now and, changing the subject, said, "You know what he's like, always criticizing, always sarcastic."

"Maybe Karl's relationship with his father is aggravated by the fact that Der Alte was a Nazi. Maybe all the children of Karl's age carry around that extra burden that alienates them from their fathers," I suggested.

To my surprise, Ingrid agreed. "No one will ever forgive the Germans or forget. My generation will have to be dead and gone for that to happen," she said. But she disagreed that Karl's problem with his father was related to that ancient history. "Der Alte is and always was a cold man. He was not a real father, he was never there. His own father was like that too." It was obviously a familiar theme for Ingrid, almost a refrain for the rest of her dialogue.

"We had it hard during the war, we women. When Dresden was bombed, we knew we had to leave. The Russians were coming. I walked for ten days, almost in a circle, to avoid the Russians."

The first part of Ingrid's walk, from Dresden to Pirna, was for naught. By the time she arrived there, Ingrid found the Russians had preceded her. So, still lugging her two little girls, she trudged on to Nonnewitz, where her parents lived. She was nearly nine months pregnant with Karl, and Karl's two sisters were still in diapers.

"One day I was walking by the side of the road. I don't know how many days into my trek that was. I was pushing one of the girls in her baby buggy. You know, she had had polio and couldn't walk. The other girl I carried on my arm, she had dysentery. And Bueblein here, he was a few days away from being born," Ingrid spoke softly, remembering those difficult days.

Suddenly, a Russian soldier had stepped out of the woods onto the road. "He looked at me and then he slowly raised his rifle until it pointed at my head. I thought it was all over, that he would kill me and the children. Just then my younger daughter started to cry, I don't know why."

The soldier may have heard the baby cry. Whatever the reason, he lowered his rifle and then vanished back into the woods. Ingrid stopped talking and looked into the distance. Then she turned back to me and said, "Yes, those times were hard, especially for us women."

"And how were those times for Gerhard? Der Alte's brother," I asked, leaning forward and looking intently at Ingrid. Was it possible I could get information about Karl's uncle this easily and this soon?

The old woman was silent for what seemed to be a long time. "You know, I never met Gerhard. By the time Der Alte and I were married, Gerhard was gone."

Karl stopped talking and seemed stunned. Into the silence, I said, "Where did he go?"

"He died. I think you should ask Der Alte for more information. He knows the whole story."

And before Karl or I could ask anything else, Ingrid continued to talk about her flight from Dresden, describing the panic she felt, fleeing on foot, carrying her possessions on her back, dragging her children after her, artillery shells flying overhead. She talked about the terror she and the other women experienced when they considered what the Russians might do if they caught up with them.

"Eight days after the war officially ended, I arrived in Nonnewitz, my parents' village and asked someone to get help. I was already in labor. My father arrived with a hay wagon. A few minutes later, when we reached their house and I climbed into the bed my mother had just made for me, I said to my father, 'We can thank the Fuehrer for this,'" Ingrid recalled, sighing heavily. "Bueblein was born four hours later. It wasn't easy."

The supreme irony of Ingrid's flight was that shortly after she gave birth, in what she assumed was the American zone, the Yankees pulled out and the Russians moved in. Fearing she would be detained—or worse, raped or murdered—she left

Karl with his grandmother and fled again with the two little girls, determined to be in a safe place when her husband came looking for her. "He wouldn't come to the Russian sector. The Russians would have sent him to Siberia," Ingrid said.

I asked why.

"Well, he was a Nazi. But they felt that way about every Nazi, even the "little" ones. My own father would have been shot, but he knew a Communist and that saved him from the prison camps," Ingrid said, without explaining whether her father fit into the category of a 'little' Nazi. She didn't describe how she eventually found her husband or elaborate on whether he was, indeed, a "little" Nazi. Karl didn't know the story about how the family came to be reunited. There were time gaps and information gaps that neither parent had ever spoken about.

Did my mother know stories about women like Ingrid, women with whom she might have empathized no matter what Hitler was doing to the Jews? Had Ingrid known what Hitler was doing? Had she known what her own husband was doing?

"Well, he was a soldier," was all Ingrid said of her husband's actions when I asked. "It was like that for all women. He was fighting the war."

I wondered if Der Alte really had been just a soldier. Surely Ingrid didn't think that Der Alte's directorship of the school in Sonthofen would just be forgotten. But what had the school been for, really? Did Ingrid really remember nothing and did she truly know nothing?

I had written a story, just before leaving on the trip, about a panel discussion in which three concentration camp liberators recalled the camps and the towns around them.

"There were close to 4,000 bodies," one of the speakers had said. "I don't think there were more than a few survivors. The beds were six high. We had doctors with us, but it was too late. Everyone was dying."

Describing what happened in the days following, he had

said, "I still remember the commanding officer standing there with tears streaming down his face." He read from the graveside ceremony conducted by an American Army chaplain, "The victims were allowed to starve to death within sight of your homes. The world has been horrified by these crimes. This is murder. Though you claim no knowledge, you are individually and collectively responsible. It should be the firm resolve of the German people that never again should such degradation be allowed."

That theme had been repeated by the other speakers. A first lieutenant explained why he, as a non-Jew, had gotten involved in describing the Holocaust and his experiences as a liberator at Camp Dora near Nordhausen. "I saw this. I keep reminding you. A lot of people say the Jewish people are exaggerating. I'm a non-Jew. I saw it. They weren't."

Speaking to a hushed audience, he had apologized in advance for his graphic description of what he had seen. "I'm not holding back. I hope people here have strong stomachs." He had gone on to describe a freight train that was leaking fluids. "We opened the locked door. Bodies slithered out. It was a horrible indescribable stench. The people of the area denied any knowledge."

While I reflected on the revolting memory of this story and after we had finished our coffee and cake, Ingrid began to think about dinner. "Does your friend eat pork?" she asked Karl. I explained that I had no dietary restrictions. It reminded me of my ex-in-laws, ever uneasy about my Jewishness. They never stopped, in the five years I was married to their son, apologizing for serving bacon or shrimp or a dozen other things they thought I wouldn't eat, even after I'd explained carefully that I didn't observe dietary laws and even served some of those foods to them in my own house.

"I had three Jewish friends," Ingrid said suddenly. "From school, three sisters, two of them twins. They were Orthodox, but when they were away from their parents, they ate everything." We laughed, but while we were still smiling, I thought of Mengele, the Nazi who specialized in experiments with twins.

"I wonder what happened to those friends," I said to Karl, who translated the question to Ingrid.

"In 1934, they went away, as usual, on a summer vacation. Only that year, they never came back. They had a lot of money, they owned a chain of shoe stores. I used to buy my shoes there. They just disappeared. The stores just abruptly closed."

I listened to her, telling the story in a flat tone of voice, no emotion visible. "What did you think happened to them?"

Ingrid said stiffly, "I assume they went to safety. Thank goodness." She shook her head again. "It was all so very, very regrettable."

She seemed to have no explanation for why they might have had to flee, suddenly, leaving everything behind. And I wondered whether Ingrid really felt the word "regrettable" adequately described the extermination of six million people.

She might have wondered that as well, because she said, "During those same years, I would sometimes pass by a place where there were women behind a fence. They looked hungry and we—my friends and I—we would push bread through the barbed wire to them."

Apparently Karl had not heard this story before, because before I had a chance to respond, he asked Ingrid, "Who were those women?" Ingrid said she didn't know.

It seemed clear, with still no sign of Der Alte, that she was tired of the discussion and wanted to change the subject. She began to show me pictures, of Karl as a child, of herself and her twin brothers growing up. Karl had told me the boys had been only fifteen at the end of the war and had been aides in the Luftwaffe. One of them had been taken prisoner by the Russians. He had been buried in the ruins in Berlin for days and later was beaten repeatedly as a POW. "Still not right in the head," the family always said about him.

"Ah, here, this is my wedding picture," Ingrid said.

Smiling, I took the photograph, and saw a much younger, much thinner Ingrid, braids around her head, a crown of flowers in her hair. She was wearing a long white gown, looking lovely. My smile faded when I realized the groom was wearing the official Nazi uniform, looking every inch the dedicated party faithful, one arm stuck in his jacket, an iron cross dangling in front.

And lining their path as the bride and groom moved toward the camera, on either side of the walkway, were the Hitler Youth, their uniforms crisp, their arms raised in a Sieg Heil salute. I felt the blood draining from my face. I must have looked ashen as a feeling of revulsion coursed through my body. For all of my doubts about this trip, I had not expected to be faced so quickly with the obvious manifestations of Karl's heritage.

Karl tried to change the subject right away. He was clearly uncomfortable with this dramatic confrontation with the past and seemed to have a pretty good idea about how I was reacting to Ingrid's recollections. I wasn't sure whether he was protecting himself, Ingrid or me when he said, "Let's talk about something lighter."

But Ingrid apparently didn't want to be protected. She said, "He doesn't like to talk about this." I wasn't clear whether "this" was the past or his father. Was that true? Was it Karl who had hidden the past behind a wall of silence?

Ingrid acted quite comfortable reminiscing, even about things that weren't all pleasant. What's to discuss, I wondered, when you didn't know anything—if only twenty people knew?

Maybe sensing my impatience with the answers—or non-answers—Ingrid suggested we all take a walk along the Neckar River. During our stroll I thought about what kind of peace Ingrid could make with herself over the guilt for deeds too staggering to comprehend.

Later, I asked Karl, "How could your mother say only

twenty people knew? There must have been more than twenty guards at one concentration camp, on one train, in one city's Gestapo group."

He shrugged. "She's not too bright. You can't expect much from her. She told me she's really glad to have someone to talk to about all this."

But I was sure that "all this" didn't mean the war, the Holocaust, Der Alte's role in the war machine, but rather his transgressions as a husband and father. Ingrid was obviously glad to have her ally back in Karl.

CHAPTER XII

It was almost nightfall when Der Alte returned, and I wondered if he hadn't stayed away deliberately, as reluctant to see Karl as Karl seemed to be about meeting his father. But if Der Alte had any negative thoughts, they were well hidden. He greeted Karl warmly, giving him a hearty handshake and a thump on the shoulder, and then he pumped my hand enthusiastically. Though he had a wiry build, at 82, he was beginning to show definite signs of aging. While his steel-blue eyes were alive with the fire of a sharp intellect, his hair was now white and wispy. I thought that the deep lines history had carved into his face actually improved the youthful good looks I had seen in earlier photos. All the same, his sharp nose and square jaw made it easy for me to recall pictures of the younger man in his military uniform.

"I have a plan arranged for you," he said in German with an almost mischievous grin. "A little bit of dinner at the local pub with some local wine and some conversation, then tomorrow maybe a look at the downtown and we go to see the castle. Maybe the next day, we will go up into the mountains to see the cloister ruins."

The old man was so much more effusive than Karl had described him, and I could tell from the tenseness of his body and voice that Karl was on guard and distrustful. He was probably worried that I wouldn't believe all of his stories about how distant and tyrannical Der Alte had always been.

Since his father's plan involved the very things that Karl had suggested we see, Karl couldn't very well object. The truth was that they shared an interest in old buildings and an appreciation for all things artistic. He had told me that through most of his life, as he aligned himself with everything that was warm and loving about his mother, he had worried about anything that he had in common with his father. Indeed, Karl's interest in architecture had grown only as he distanced himself from his father and from Germany. He was reluctant to admit the interest had its roots in his childhood, fueled by his father's enthusiasm.

"Where is the old lady?" Der Alte asked, without much interest. I wondered how the two had survived nearly fifty years of marriage. Ingrid was a simple woman, content it seemed with pictures of her children and grandchildren, kaffeeklatsches with her friends and complaints about her spouse. I suspected that as a young woman, she had probably been similarly inclined, concerned with clothes, decorating the house and the small details of life.

In contrast, Der Alte seemed greatly interested in the loftier things of life. At the pub during dinner, he talked with delight about the symphony, which he attended without his wife, and about trips he took—also without Ingrid. If he bore his son any ill feelings for emigrating and having only sporadic contact, it wasn't apparent.

"So Karl," he said, "What do you think of the Wiedervereinigung?"

Although all of his conversation was in German, as was Ingrid's, and Karl was translating continuously, I caught that word before it was explained. We had been here in Germany less than a day and reunification was mentioned so constantly that it was impossible to ignore.

Before Der Alte had returned, Ingrid talked about Wiedervereinigung and the related news on television. She seemed mostly concerned with the plight of relatives still living in East Germany—cousins on farms, one niece who was an official in the Communist party and was having difficulty adjusting to the changes.

But Der Alte was especially worried about his property in

Leipzig. He didn't mention the proposal he had once made to deed the property to Karl, but he discussed at length his concern that the state might take his house, as they had others, and auction it off. "I've been in contact all through these years and have a manager on the premises. I even have furniture and things stored there. I was just there for a visit. I want to be as visible as possible so they can't say I abandoned it," he said.

Beyond his concern for the land, he was obviously relishing the new era that was dawning in Germany: unified elections, a common money standard, and one government.

Back at the house after dinner, he began reminiscing about the years after the war, when he would travel to East Germany—the Deutsche Demokratische Republik, or DDR—for annual trade missions. On some occasions, he was able to make contact with old friends, colleagues from the school or the army who were caught in Russian territory when the war ended.

Those recollections seemed a good opportunity for me to ask about his other memories. What did he remember about the war and the school, I wanted to know.

"Everything." he grinned. He seemed relaxed about talking, almost eager. Long after Ingrid retired for the night—mumbling about "old men and old Nazis"—he seemed eager to go on. He handed us a book describing the school, which he urged us to read.

"I joined the party in 1929, when I was a student," he said. "We wanted to undo what the Versailles Treaty had caused. To allow Germany to stand back on her feet proudly with the other nations. It was for patriotic feelings and for economic reasons." He looked into the distance and said," You know, Sarah, I was young then. I saw the economic misery and poverty that the Weimar Republic had given us. I saw myself as a social revolutionary."

He paused, and smiled while he leaned towards me. "I joined the NSDAP because it was the National Socialist

German Worker's Party, that is what the initials stood for. I was opposed to the old, losing ways of the Weimar Republic. I also was opposed to world Communism, same as I am today, so I joined the Nazis, which offered the only viable alternative for our country."

As it grew dark outside, the old man opened three more bottles of beer. "At first, when Hitler needed to make a coalition with business, we thought he had become their puppet. But then unemployment did begin to go down."

Sitting there, listening to Karl's father with his posture slightly stooped and his passionate recollection of those days, I felt disoriented. I was sitting here, being "entertained" by this Nazi who in many ways seemed like a harmless, almost charming, not-yet-so-old man.

I'd had similar conversations with my own father, who had talked with equal passion about running for Congress on the Socialist Party ticket, an effort doomed to fail but filled with the energy of idealism.

"When did that change, when did you sense something was wrong?" I asked Der Alte, expecting him to deny that he ever believed anything was wrong, ever doubted that the Reich would be anything but victorious. But he surprised me. He described a series of events, including lying on the beach in France and watching the Spitfires shoot down German planes. "I think that is when absolute certainty changed to only hope. That was about 1940. I realized the war was unwinnable." And almost as an afterthought, he said, "I told them when we were discussing the invasion of England that we couldn't win with the ships we had."

Karl and I looked at each other. We had speculated about some of this before, although we hadn't had as much specific information. What was his real role in the Reich? How could he have been in a position to provide input about a planned invasion? Was he telling the truth or just exaggerating his importance? What would the book he wanted us to read tell us about the purpose of the school?

99

If he were lying, why would he be so brutally frank about his realization—rather early in the war—that the Germans were not going to triumph? All my curiosity now seemed to revolve around how much of what he said was a lie and how much really happened.

"But wasn't that discouraging? That bright dream disappearing?" I asked, through Karl. He was doing a masterful job of translating, inserting almost no commentary into the conversation, asking no questions of his own, and he seemed to want to keep it that way. Although I knew it was exhausting to translate almost without interruption for hours on end, Karl was fully present and engaged. I was asking questions that Karl had formed silently himself, but had never voiced. He could probably feel the taboos of his family—developed over years of evasions and prolonged silences—crumbling as I pressed on.

Amazingly, the old man did not refuse to respond to even a single question. Der Alte's concentration remained unbroken as he gave me answer after answer. The only interruption of the give-and-take between Der Alte and me happened when Karl suddenly was silent during a long and complicated explanation his father gave.

"Why have you stopped translating?" I asked, slightly irritated. I suspected that Karl had begun censoring the old man's comments. I looked first at Karl and then at the old man, both silent now. I felt fear rising in me, especially as I noticed suddenly how much Karl looked like his father. I also became aware, sitting in that semi-dark room, that I was in Germany, that I was a Jew who was interviewing a Nazi about his past, and that I was depending completely on the son of that Nazi.

"I am waiting for the damn verb," Karl said with a half-smile. My impatience was apparently at odds with the way in which German had to be translated. "His sentence has three sub-clauses, all of which are waiting in my head. I can't say *what* happened until I know *how* it happened. In a German sentence the verb comes at the end. When the thought is complicated and the sentence has many sub-clauses, then the verb comes at the very, very end. The old man is intelligent and when he gets complicated, you just have to wait."

Relieved, feeling a little guilty, I realized I had not thought of the mechanics involved in simultaneous translating. Nodding at Karl, I reminded myself, not for the first time, that there were often other explanations for things besides the ones that came most quickly to my mind.

"OK, so when you saw the dogfights above you with the Spitfires, didn't you find that discouraging?" I seemed unable to stop asking questions. I was skilled at asking what journalists like to call "follow-up" questions. People came to trust me during interviews, forgot that they were doing anything but chatting, and often revealed information they never intended to share. Yet I doubted that Der Alte was going to fall into that trap, perhaps because of my inability to talk directly to him.

"Discouraging? Well, to have the school collapse because all of the students had to go to war, that was discouraging," said the old man, staring at me intently.

I sat forward in my chair, sipping my beer. "The school. Tell me about that. Who was it for? What were the underlying principles of the place?"

The old man also leaned forward, clearly relishing this discussion. "It was to provide a new generation of leaders. The Adolf Hilter Schule: it was modeled along the lines of Eton."

The name alone repelled me. I asked him how it was modeled after Eton and he explained in some detail how the students were selected. Each year, 300 students were chosen to attend, recommended by the Hitler Youth and German schools. They would choose the best, the bravest, the brightest of students, natural-born leaders, and offer them the toughest and most selective education possible. And it was provided for free, regardless of their social background or their parents' ability to pay. All they had to do was fulfill specific requirements about their character.

"So they were the creme-de-la-creme," I said, thinking that those "selected" were drawn from a universe that depended on weeding out anyone deemed undesirable by the Nazis.

"Well, they were not the elite, the leaders, not yet," he laughed and added, "Not until after six years at the school." He got up and walked to the bookcase, taking a pile of photos. "Look here, some of these were taken at the school."

I picked out one photo which seemed to be of him and an older man in uniform, standing on a field. "What is this?" I asked, wondering if this was Der Alte's superior officer.

He smirked. "Well, this was just before the unification of Germany with Austria. The school was being visited by an Austrian army colonel. When he arrived—with 800 of our students in the stands around the field—I yelled at him, commanded him to stand at attention and dressed him down for his sloppy uniform."

"Did you outrank him?" I asked, trying to sort out how this German school director could reprimand an officer in another country's army.

"I did. Someone had to show them who was going to be in charge. And it was fun," he added. "Also, it was a foregone conclusion that in just a matter of hours Austria would again become part of the German Reich."

Finally, he was ready to quit. He stood and stretched, looking, in the dim light, suddenly quite frail. "Well Karl, I will say good-night. We will meet again in the morning. The old lady will prepare breakfast and then we will set off."

We crept into the bedroom where Karl had slept as a child. "How much of what he told us do you think was true?" I asked.

"Shh. I don't know. I don't think much of anything he's been saying could be true. How could he have been in on the plans for the invasion of England? Where does the school fit into it all?"

"God, six years of brainwashing," I responded. "Could you tell where the school fit into the hierarchy of the Reich? Were all of the teachers party members? Was your father considered an important Nazi official? What happened to them all? The teachers, the students when the war ended?" My questions flowed out of me.

"I have no idea." Although he was whispering again, Karl was clearly upset.

"Why are you so angry, Bueblein?" I asked.

"Damn him!" Karl whispered. "When I was a kid, I remember once crying when I fell and skinned my knee. My father grabbed me and began hitting me. He was furious with me for crying. He yelled that as a man, I should damn well learn to take pain. Crying was an emotion of a wimp. He forbade me to be a wimp."

"How horrible." I pulled Karl's head to my breast and rocked him, wanting somehow to give him the comfort he had missed those years before. "My poor little Bueblein. How could he have been so cruel? You were only a little boy. You had fallen and hurt yourself. He should have kissed you."

But Karl was shaking his head. "He was not cruel. Don't you see? At least not in his own mind. He was just following the maxims of steeling me as a man, the same way they did it at that damn Adolf Hitler Schule. When the Third Reich collapsed, the old man lost his school but then he used his techniques on me."

Karl yawned. "I have to go to sleep. You should too."

I knew I was too keyed up to sleep. As Karl kissed me and silently left to go to the bedroom next door, I continued to think about what the old man had said. Being alone after all I had heard that day, alone in a country I had been taught to distrust, I felt vulnerable and uneasy.

Suddenly I remembered Beth's suggestion that I find out where the American embassy was. I hadn't. I had no German money, relying on Karl to change our American dollars and conduct our financial transactions. Without trying to reason through the logic of my fear, I rose quietly from bed and searched quickly for my passport and penknife, the only thing I could find even close to a weapon. Putting the papers under my pillow and clutching the knife in my hand, I fell asleep, vowing to be vigilant.

CHAPTER XIII

When I woke up in the morning, I was still clutching the knife. With the sun streaming in the windows and the smell of coffee in the air, I felt slightly foolish about the thoughts I'd had, but my uneasiness hadn't completely dissipated. I dressed quickly after taking a shower, not yet used to the hand-held shower head that required kneeling in the bathtub to wash.

Karl came to my room while I was still getting dressed, giving me a perfunctory kiss. I felt more like talking about our conversation with the old man than I wanted to kiss and whisper sweet nothings, but before we could even begin our conversation, Ingrid knocked at the doorway and announced it was time for breakfast. When we were seated and drinking coffee, Ingrid gazed fondly at Karl, shaking her head about how much time had elapsed since his last visit. "We're getting older," she said. It reminded me of discussions I had whenever I saw my mother. In fact, Ingrid's next action really reminded me of my mother.

Licking several of her fingers, Ingrid approached Karl and used them to smooth down some hair that was sticking out of his head after his restless night of sleep. Karl cringed, as he probably had when he was a little boy, squirming away from his mother. "Na, Bueblein," Ingrid said, unmoved by his objections.

I laughed. It was so reminiscent of times my mother had buttoned my sweaters when I wasn't cold, given me kisses when I didn't want them, clucked over me when I was trying to be independent. I would have liked to share the story about Irving, the boy called buebelah, with Ingrid. I thought it would have entertained her, but again I was frustrated with not knowing the language. Though I could have asked Karl to translate, I was trying to save his interpreting for essential conversation. He was doing a wonderful job, but it didn't always make for the most natural exchange.

If I was amused by Ingrid's interaction with Karl, the old man clearly wasn't. Karl had told me his father had always felt Ingrid coddled Karl too much, making a pet of him when she should have been enforcing the old man's harsher discipline. She had conspired with Karl to hide bad school grades from his father, undermined punishment meted out by the old man, and fought valiantly but mostly unsuccessfully against edicts the old man issued that made Karl's life miserable.

Today, Der Alte was anxious to describe his plan for our outing. "So, we will let you go to the Tourist Racetrack for some souvenir hunting this morning. Then, you will come back and we will take the car to the Heidelberg Castle, O.K.?"

I said I didn't like racing.

Karl grinned, translated my comment, and the two men began to laugh. "The Tourist Racetrack is a section of downtown Heidelberg. It has a lot of shops and places where people can buy trinkets. You'll like it. It will satisfy your need to find souvenirs—*tsatskes*," He added the Yiddish word with what looked to me like a smirk.

Karl decided that he would invite his mother to meet us for lunch, since the old man was monopolizing us and we would have no time to talk privately with her. Ingrid seemed delighted at the invitation.

"Whew, that was an intense first day," I laughed as we walked toward the train for downtown Heidelberg.

"Wait a second," Karl said, pulling me into his arms. "I haven't said good morning to you, kissed you, touched you or anything." He ran his hands over my curves slowly, feeling the contours of my body, absorbing my heat, burying his face in my hair. "Umm, nice." We pressed together. "Not bad for a crack reporter in her forties," he said with a smile.

106

"More later?" I said, thinking of the night before and how incompatible the penknife would have been with any lovemaking activities.

For the next few hours, we were tourists, strolling along Heidelberg's main street, looking at the old buildings, listening to the hubbub of voices and accents.

"Hey, look at this T-shirt," I said. It showed the Berlin wall coming down. "I like T-shirts with historic significance." Paying the vendor, I slipped the shirt over my blouse. Karl gently laughed at my choice. He'd often commented that I wore my political opinions across my chest. I had shirts that promoted use of condoms, shirts that proposed more money for schools and less for defense, Nelson Mandela shirts, no smoking shirts, more walking shirts, anti-war, pro-seniors, no drinking shirts. Once he said he was going to have a shirt made for himself that said, "Liberalism is the most intolerant religion," just to offer a somewhat balanced view when we were walking together.

Soon, it was time to meet Ingrid for lunch. Walking to Bismarck Platz, I said to Karl, "About your Uncle Gerhard. Are you sure your mother used to tell you about him? Didn't your father ever say anything?"

Karl shook his head. "She did tell me about Gerhard. I was shocked when she said she had never met him and no, my father never said anything to us children about his brother." We walked the rest of the way to the restaurant in silence, each of us lost in thought. Ingrid had chosen an outdoor cafe with typical German food. She was already seated when we arrived. Karl ordered for me while I kept busy staring at the passers-by and the sights.

"So what do you think of Der Alte now?" asked Ingrid. "Did you have a good talk with him?"

I sensed that Ingrid felt excluded and wanted to score some points of her own. "I enjoyed the conversation," I told her. "I learned a lot about the war years."

Ingrid tightened her lips. "Yes, those were his glory years all right. Nothing has ever been as wonderful since. He joined the party to have a family. Then, when he was nearing 30, they pressured him to get married so people wouldn't think he was a homosexual. Actually, I think he probably was or would have liked to have been. In any event, there was a big celebration, I think it was the anniversary of the Machtergreifung, the day Hitler came to power. The Nazi Party fixed up a group of us BDM girls with these handsome officers. It was wonderful. That's where I was introduced to Der Alte. Of course he was young and good looking then."

I had not heard Karl describe his mother's thoughts about Der Alte and homosexuality. I wondered if she had ever mentioned this before, but I decided not to ask Ingrid.

For a moment, Ingrid's voice trailed off. There was a wistful expression on her face; it appeared as if she was looking into the past and finding, after all, some pleasant memories. She turned again to talk to me, saying that the old man had been her only lover, but there had been other suitors. "I met them all after I started a relationship with him. He was away by then, with the army, but I was writing to him. I felt disloyal when I was with the others. He wrote wonderful letters and he was charming and intelligent. People said he was a good catch."

Listening to Ingrid reminisce, I began to wonder if both she and the old man had decided to ignore my Jewishness. "What does he think, do you suppose, about Karl bringing me, a Jewish woman, home?"

Karl winced, but he translated the question.

Ingrid struggled with her answer, then said, "Well, maybe the old Nazi has learned something new."

I wasn't sure I knew what she meant and I remembered that Bruce Kaplan wanted contrition in my stories about Der Alte. "So do you think he lost his anti-Semitism? That he's contrite about what happened during the Nazi years?" I asked.

Karl asked her what she meant and she was silent for a

minute, then said, "Oh, I don't think he was ever anti-Semitic himself. It was all Himmler's idea."

That comment was so silly I decided to let it pass—at least for now.

After lunch, we took the streetcar home, where the old man was waiting, seemingly eager to renew our discussion. "Ach, very interesting," he said, looking at my Berlin wall shirt. "You know, the Wall fell on November 9. That was also the date of the 1923 Beer Hall Putsch," he said, adding, almost in a mumble, "and the date of Kristallnacht."

"Oh my god," I thought, reaching down immediately to peel off the shirt. "The Wall fell on the same date as Kristallnacht, the Night of Broken Glass?"

"Yes. Do you know what caused Kristallnacht?" Der Alte asked. I shook my head. I had heard about Kristallnacht every year since I had been writing for the Jewish newspaper but I was too dumbfounded to respond. Of course, I would never wear that T-shirt commemorating the date that the Nazis had rounded up Jews throughout Germany in 1938, vandalized and burned their stores and homes.

Der Alte ignored my reaction and continued with his story. "Well, a German diplomat had been killed in Paris and three people were involved in the shooting. One of the people was someone called Rosenberg."

"So what?" I said, looking at Karl. "What's he trying to say, that Kristallnacht was an uprising by the German people in response to that shooting?" Karl asked his father the question, but the old man quickly shook his head.

"Oh no, it was the Storm Troopers' idea. They did it and Hitler went along with it. He was like that. He often wanted peace but didn't always know how to get out of what other people got him into."

Before I could ask another question, the old man went on. "There was so much property destruction, the insurance companies complained, so Goering had to apologize. Then they had a trial and decided that the Jews with their business practices were ultimately responsible and that they should pay for the damages."

I was stunned. This was revisionist history at its worst. Although I had vowed to maintain a neutral position, to gather information and not debate his perspective, this was so patently untrue that I couldn't just leave it unchallenged. I decided to try a personal approach.

"What did *you* think about that?" I asked.

"I? I was a soldier in Dresden. I didn't even know about it," the old man said firmly.

Remembering some of what I had heard about Kristallnacht, I said to him, "But how could you not notice? Buildings were destroyed all over Germany that night."

"Well, yes, that's true," he conceded, "But the Storm Troopers cleaned it all up within twelve hours."

He said it all so matter-of-factly, but I remembered the plaques I had seen in Frankfurt and downtown Heidelberg, commemorating the Jews who had been taken away on Kristallnacht and the homes and businesses that had been destroyed that night. I wondered if the old man really believed what he was saying now, fifty years later. But further questioning seemed futile.

"I heard about it afterwards," he added, seeming to encourage my questions. Was he toying with me? Was he trying to see how much he could get away with, growing bolder each time I failed to challenge him?

I told myself he was an old man, he was the parent of my lover, and I wasn't there to conduct a belated version of the Nuremberg trials. I was trying to collect information, determine the depth of his involvement, learn more about Uncle Gerhard. It was a fine line between simply asking questions to get those answers and directly accusing him of lying. Maybe he was merely being evasive?

As I had done the evening before, I used my concealed

voice-activated tape recorder, feeling as though I were betraying the Schmidts' hospitality, but not wanting to forget a single sentence.

Although I had told Karl ahead of time about the recorder and he agreed we should use it, I wondered if part of my motivation for recording what the old man was saying was because I didn't fully trust Karl to translate every word, especially anything incriminating.

"Well, if you didn't know about Kristallnacht, what *did* you know about? Did you know about the camps?" I challenged him.

"There were no death camps on German soil. Only in other countries. And yes, I knew about them."

Frantically trying to remember my geography and history, I said, "What about Bergen-Belsen? What about Nordhausen? They were in Germany."

But the old man repeated, "There were no death camps in Germany."

I realized he was making a technical distinction between camps whose purpose was extermination, and labor camps, where thousands were worked and basically starved to death. Feeling defeated, I said, "Who built those death camps in the other countries?"

"Oh, the Germans, of course," he said and then went on. "I knew about a few camps in 1934 and I must say that I was in full support of the idea. They were supposed to be for seven specific groups, like child molesters, habitual criminals, and for homosexuals." He didn't explain the other groups, only repeated that the camps were for child molesters.

"My friends and I have tried to decide when we first knew about Auschwitz," the old man said. "We watched a television show recently where they tried to get the person who was an ex-Nazi to identify when he first knew. We all agreed that it was only after the war that we heard the word—Auschwitz."

But I wouldn't let this go by, for he seemed to be implying that the death camps didn't exist, while admitting he knew

111

about them. "What are you saying? Where did these people go? Are you implying that they didn't die in the camps?"

In answer to my question, he retrieved a piece of paper. "These are my notes from a television show I watched the other day about the Jews of Eastern Europe. After it was over, I called my old comrades so we could discuss the numbers they used on the show."

"What numbers?" I said, feeling the knot in my stomach growing by the minute. These were the sort of conversations that I had read about and never believed, people pretending that the atrocities didn't really happen.

"Well, look at this. On the show, they said there were 500,000 German Jews before the war. Then about 350,000 left with visas. So that left 150,000. I'm trying to make sense of these numbers."

"What do you mean, 350,000 left with visas? Where did they go?" I remembered the story of the St. Louis, one of the last boatloads of fleeing Jews to leave Germany, headed for one of the few countries that would accept them. But when the boat, loaded with women and children, arrived in Cuba, the government there decided it would not accept any more immigrants. The ship was turned back, refused entry by President Roosevelt, and eventually returned to Europe. The nearly 1000 would-be settlers were divided among France, Belgium, Holland and England. Only those who emigrated to England survived. Nearly all of the others perished in Nazi concentration camps. There were other, similar stories, many even more horrifying.

But none of those numbers were written on the old man's piece of paper. He said again, "I don't know, I'm trying to make sense of the numbers."

Was he truly trying to determine what happened to six million people or was he simply working on a way to revise what he knew? In desperation, I said, "OK, suppose you couldn't prove that six million people died. Suppose only a million died. Would that make any difference?"

Immediately, the old man said, "No. It was the worst mass murder ever. The worst." Later, I realized that acknowledging the scope of the murder wasn't the same thing as expressing dismay, regret, agony or any emotion. He hadn't.

I remembered an argument I'd had with Karl several weeks before when we were talking about the number of Jews who died. He pointed out the Germans didn't have a monopoly on genocide. He listed nearly a dozen other examples, from the American Indians to the killing fields in Cambodia.

"It wasn't just the Germans," Karl said.

Those kinds of comments created a dilemma for me. Brought up as a liberal, I agreed the treatment of the American Indian, for example, was genocide. But I was also conditioned by years of messages from my family and the Jewish community that the Holocaust—the Shoah—was a special case, an effort to annihilate a whole group of people using the most brutally efficient methods. In fact, the Holocaust was a special word, reserved to describe how the Nazis murdered six million people in gas chambers.

And the point made by Karl, which sounded like an effort to exonerate the Nazis, was especially bothersome to me because it made me worry anew whether he was really anti-Semitic. Could someone raised by a good Nazi, indeed an ardent Nazi, turn out to be anything other than a Jew-hater deep down?

While I never doubted his dislike for his father, I began to wonder how much of it had anything at all to do with the old man's role in the Third Reich and how much was related to the normal friction between an overbearing, violent father and a rebellious son. In the old man's case, could the two be separated? The horror I felt about the old man's involvement in the Nazi machinery, the possibility that he might have been fully aware of the atrocities, those issues Karl seemed relatively unconcerned about.

Karl had told me stories about his parents' arguments when he was a child, his father's abuse of his mother and his own defense of her. I knew Karl felt his father was critical of everything he did and said, but I thought now that maybe Ingrid had manipulated Karl into being her ally, preventing him from ever forming a relationship with his father, who was certainly on a higher intellectual plane than Ingrid.

I was torn between wanting Karl to have a healthy relationship with his parents and a sick feeling for what his failure to hate his father's complicity might mean about Karl himself.

CHAPTER XIV

Our trip to the Heidelberg Castle was not without incident. The old man was a frightening driver—Karl said he had always been like that. He tended to get involved in his conversations, gesticulating to emphasize points, removing his hands from the wheel to point out important spots. Ingrid sat stoically through it, gripping her purse and occasionally mumbling things like, "You can see why I never go any place with him." The old man ignored her, along with Karl's occasional suggestions that he move over or slow down.

"I can see what you're going to be like when you get older," I joked. Karl stuck his tongue out at me. His driving, when he wasn't behind the wheel of a police car, sometimes suffered from significant lapses of concentration. "I'm giving myself the day off," he would explain.

Arriving at the castle, the old man led us through the gates. "You know, of course, Karl, the history of this place?" he said.

I knew that questions like that irritated Karl. He had explained most of the history of the castle to me before we left California, using a book about Heidelberg to illustrate his points. He had been to the castle with the old man at least a dozen times, and listened to the same description about the war with the French that toppled one tower. He could recite from memory the story about the prince who built—in one night—a towering gate for his wife.

Under the best of circumstances I barely tolerate museums, but I tried my best to look interested in the stories, translated painstakingly by Karl as his father droned on. Once, leaving the old couple behind, we walked down into the bowels of the castle to see the largest wine barrel ever created. In spite of myself, as we strolled around the park-like grounds, I began to be drawn into a picture of what life must have been like.

"Here's the hunting lodge. They would build huge fires here and roast whatever they killed, spending hours drinking and carousing," Karl said.

"I can see them all sitting around after a boar hunt, or whatever, and drinking themselves into oblivion," I laughed. I was enjoying myself and beginning to feel like any tourist in a foreign country.

My interest was apparent to Karl's parents, and even Ingrid, who trudged along grudgingly, seemed sparked by it. "She has a good imagination, your friend," Ingrid said after Karl translated a few of my comments about what life must have been like.

"Yes. I'm looking forward to having her see some of the really old sights so she can think about life in Celtic times," Karl said.

When I asked Karl what else he had in mind, he rattled off an ambitious list of places he wanted to see, conceding that we'd be exhausted if we hit everything on his list.

"My mother always says to leave some ink in the inkwell for the next time," I said. "What are your priorities?"

Confessing that he had a yen to go back in time himself, Karl described a side trip to Goslar, in the Harz Mountains, where he had hiked as a boy.

"I'd like to see what it's like now, since it was so gorgeous then and I'd like to show you Barbarossa's castle."

The old man, hearing Barbarossa's name, wanted to know what we were saying. Karl described his plan to drive from Heidelberg to Goslar. "Sarah can see the old palace and realize that this is an ancient country. In the United States, old is 1650. Some of the buildings she'll see were built before then."

"Why Barbarossa?" asked the old man.

Karl explained that I was fascinated with the legend of the old ruler, said to be hiding in the caves. He refrained from telling his father that I'd asked where Barbarossa was during the war. But the old man brought up the war himself. "You know, we NS liked Barbarossa ourselves. He represented what we wanted in restoring Germany—a proud heritage, with strong, revered leadership. We even called our campaign to take Russia 'Operation Barbarossa.'"

Continuing to walk, the old man reminded us that it had been exactly 800 years since Barbarossa's death. "We are all still waiting for his return," he chuckled.

"If he was supposed to come back to help Germany in her hour of need," I asked, "where was he during the war?" Karl grimaced. At least I had used the neutral term war rather than the emotionally laden Holocaust. In fact, there wasn't a German word for Holocaust. The German word Judenvernichtung, Jew annihilation, had always been used instead.

The old man said provocatively, "Maybe it wasn't dire enough for his appearance. There's still plenty of time for Barbarossa. Maybe now that the Wall is down he's out and about." Although he was showing signs of fatigue, the old man suggested we ride into the mountains around Heidelberg and look at the old cloister. Karl had told me about the spot, where there had been a Celtic settlement, then Roman altars, and finally a monastery. There were still traces of all of them there, tucked away above Heidelberg in the hills where few tourists ventured.

"That's a good idea, but let's go by the Tingstaette instead," said Karl. His father looked at him, but said nothing. Ingrid asked to be dropped off at the house so she could begin preparing the afternoon coffee.

I knew that Karl wanted to show me the cloister but he had never mentioned the Tingstaette; he must have thought it was pretty important if he was choosing it instead. When I asked what it was, Karl explained it had been built by the Nazis as one of their sites to stage rallies. It had only been used once or twice, but had never been removed.

Winding through the hills, the road narrowing, we exchanged exasperated glances. Karl had offered to drive and been turned down, but the old man was driving slowly, maybe in no hurry to confront one of the remnants of the Nazis' thirst for building massive meeting places.

Indeed the Tingstaette was a truly unnerving place. Built of huge stone blocks in a half circle for a huge audience, it had a stage for the orators. Towering over the city, with a breathtaking view of the Neckar Valley, it should have been a picture postcard scene, but the feel of evil was everywhere. Even though it was deserted and overgrown with weeds, I had no trouble as we walked around envisioning thousands of jackboot-wearing Nazis shouting "Sieg Heil" as they stood listening to frenzied speeches. The only reassuring part of the place was the graffiti that had been painted on the walls. "Nazis Raus" and, in German, "Never Again, Germany."

The old man silently studied the writing and the weeds.

I turned to him finally and said, "So, when you look back at all this now, from the perspective of fifty years and longer, what would you say about those years from 1929 to 1945?"

The old man paced around, staring down at the huge outdoor meeting arena, maybe remembering the few gatherings that he had attended. "What would I say?" He paused before speaking. "Of course it was war. The war was bad. But I will tell you that for my mother, bringing up her children with not enough to eat, the most she could ever hope for was to see Austria. For me, I was able to give my three children so much more: food, clothes, a nice place to live and a good education. I was able to see the world. What do I think? I now think it was worth it."

Karl made no comments as he translated his father's words. They seemed to ring out in the silence of the Tingstaette as a horrible memorial to the dead. I wondered how the old man could tell me about his improving his lot in life and never mention the six million Jews who died. My mother would be appalled at the old man's ability to pick up the pieces of his life after the war, build a new career and create a comfortable middle class existence on the graves of the dead Jews.

But I got an insight into how he might have been able to do that on the way back to the house. Karl insisted upon taking me to a synagogue he had visited as a student at about age 14. He remembered his class going there and being greeted there by an older man.

"I am Gustaf Gruber," the man had told the class. "I am a native of Heidelberg. I survived the Nazi concentration camps. This is where my synagogue stood before the Nazis came. See? We have rebuilt it. I want you to know about my people and my religion."

The students had gazed at the simple, stark building. The man explained some of the Jewish rituals, including the reading of the Torah. Karl remembered being impressed with what a clear picture the man had of his history.

"How could you have come back here?" one of Karl's classmates had asked in a hushed tone, reflecting what most of the group had been thinking. The man, not sounding bitter, had said simply, "This is my home. I was born here. I am a German." As we walked around the rebuilt synagogue with Der Alte, we noticed there was a display of art depicting Auschwitz. Karl led us to the room where the paintings were hanging, a mute memorial to the horrors. Images of emaciated, tortured souls stood at barbed-wire fences, staring, hopeless.

The old man motioned us over to one of the canvases. "Look here, this picture was painted in 1947. That one was painted in 1946. The war was over." I realized the old man was implying the paintings did not reflect something the artists had seen, but maybe something they imagined or only heard. So this was how he was able to resume his life with no guilt; he could explain away atrocities as possibly rumor or folklore.

"This one here," Karl said, pointing at a canvas with bodies piled up. "Look here at this one. It was painted in 1941". The old man said nothing more, looking silently at the paintings, reading the commentary about how much slave labor had been used in German factories. He had already told us about how the Krupp family had rebuilt their empire after the war and how the Krupp son had served his father's prison sentence for war crimes because the older man had been too ill to go to jail.

The ride back to the house was a quiet one. At dinner, we talked about mundane issues. Although I saw Karl's parents as two old people in the last chapter of their lives, at the same time, Der Alte was clearly an unrepentant Nazi. He was not, as Bruce Kaplan had hoped, contrite or apologetic. I found that more disturbing than ever.

CHAPTER XV

Although I was frustrated about not being able to speak directly to Der Alte and Ingrid, I wondered if I would ever be able to bring myself to learn conversational German. I knew there were times in our day-to-day life, especially when he was tired or frustrated, when Karl would have liked to speak German with me. In fact, he and his first wife had used it exclusively, even though she was an American.

It was, for him, the language of his childhood memories. His grandmother had sung to him in German. He had told his first girlfriend he loved her in German. But for me, when I heard the language, especially in places like the train station where announcements were being made, I thought only of the Gestapo and the Nazis.

"I can say Ich liebe dich to you," Karl once said, "And you hear me saying Achtung."[1] In some way, though, German sounded enough like Yiddish to set off memories. And Karl sometimes told me my recall of the German I had learned as a little girl was more than I realized.

Now I hoped some of it would come back to me as we set out to visit Clara, my family's maid from Bremen. We took the train to Darmstadt, where Clara and her husband Hans, a retired government worker, met us at the train station. We drove to a nearby restaurant and over lunch, in response to my questions, they described their children and their life. At the beginning, the encounter had the feel of a meeting with an elderly couple rather than a confrontation with history.

---

[1] Based on a poem by Hans Stahlschmidt

Soon after we ordered, Clara looked at me and said sadly to Karl, "I don't remember her at all. I don't see any trace of the little Sarrie I remember." It had been forty years since Clara, a young woman being courted by Hans, had seen me. Those had been desperate times, with not enough to eat and tattered clothing. Clara said she had been grateful to have a job, delighted when my mother gave her cast-off clothes or a little extra food to share with her parents. She hadn't cared about whether we were Jews and had come to feel protective and fond of me.

But now, as a sick woman with grown children and grand-children, she was sitting across the table from an adult American who could recollect very little of those years.

After Clara inquired about my parents and expressed her sympathy over my father's death, there seemed little to talk about. I didn't really remember her either.

"You know," I said. "My mother believed in those days that every German was a Nazi. She was terrified of living in Germany. I don't know what kind of a relationship you two had, but she was frightened. Did you ever connect as two women?"

Clara shook her head. "No, I don't think so. I don't remember," she said sadly. "My memory isn't so good."

I wanted to be certain, for some reason, that Clara understood that we were, after all, just middle class people and that those years in Germany, with a car and household help, were aberrations in our life. Clara looked amazed when I explained that. "I never knew that. And I never knew your mother didn't trust me."

Hans leaned forward, his meal forgotten. "I knew your parents. I used to talk with them when I came to see Clara. I know your mother was suspicious of us all. She never understood how the German people couldn't have known about what was happening."

I didn't want to disrupt the pleasant mood by asking discomforting questions, but I thought it was quite likely we might never see these people again and my need to know, as usual, was overpowering any politeness.

"Wasn't it strange," I asked Clara, "working for people who had been the enemy?" I didn't mention that we, after all, had also been Jews.

Clara didn't answer, but Hans said, "Well, the Third Reich had fallen. We knew we had lost the war." It was a pragmatic answer, but I could understand suddenly why my mother hadn't trusted too many people she met in those years in Germany. What had Hans, for example, really been doing just prior to their arrival?

A teenager at the time of the war, Hans had been in the Luftwaffe. "Actually, I was an aide—Luftwaffen Helfer. Half of the Luftwaffe was against the effort. So many Germans were terrified of the Gestapo."

"My mother was BDM," Karl said, apparently not wanting the couple to feel he was passing judgment on them. It seemed to me an odd way to establish commonality.

Clara nodded. "Naturally. So was I. We all were."

I understood the conversation without needing it translated. What would my mother have done in 1948 if she had known the young woman who lived with us had been a member of the Nazi youth organization? Would she have entrusted her only child to her and sung her praises? Maybe my mother had known and simply hadn't wanted to cope with the truth, enjoying the extraordinary experiences of having "help," a car and a mansion.

Karl told them his mother had said only a few dozen people knew about the camps and the atrocities. I found it astonishing that Clara also thought this was true.

"My mother said until this generation of Germans is dead, the world will not forgive us," Karl said.

Hans agreed. "Collective guilt. We will pay forever."

We talked about the memorial in their city that was built to remember the Jews and the rebuilt synagogue. "There is forgiveness here," said Clara.

On our train ride back to Heidelberg, Karl said, "I'm worried about whether you are getting any good feelings about this trip, about Germany, about the people. Is it all black goop you're digging up?"

I leaned over and gave him a lingering kiss. I knew he felt the trip was his responsibility. It was his country and, despite his own conflicts, he wanted me to like it. "There are tons of things I really like. I love the lace curtains everyone has in their windows, the beer that each town makes, the food, the fact that I'm starting to understand the language. And also that I don't have to share you with the Police Department."

We laughed about Hans and Clara bringing their dog to the restaurant and being amazed when we told them such a thing would be unheard of in the States.

That night back in Heidelberg, we packed, getting ready to begin what Ingrid called "the real tourist" part of our trip. As the first part of our visit with Ingrid and the old man came to an end, even that seemed to be less a historical confrontation than a ritualistic meeting every couple has with each other's family.

The old man seemed eager to suggest tourist sites in other parts of the country to see, and said he was looking forward to hearing our report when we came back.

When the old man asked where we were headed, Karl told him we were going to the area formerly known as eastern Germany. "We just want to see the changes," Karl said. "Maybe we'll find some bargains as people throw out their old things to make way for the new. Maybe we'll go to Leipzig to see the grandparents' old house."

The old man seemed to like that idea and offered us the key to the house so we could look around properly. We took it, and Karl was excited about seeing the house again after so many years. We also told the old man we might go to Zeitz to see the Three Swans Inn where Karl said he remembered going once with his grandfather.

124

That distracted the old man, sending him off on a description of what he remembered about the small city and the luxurious hotel where they had never been able to afford to eat a meal. The story lasted until, breathing heavily, he walked us out to the street where our rental car was parked.

Karl and his father stood on the sidewalk, facing each other, shaking hands as we said our good-byes. There were never warm hugs in their greetings or farewells. Outside in the sunlight, Der Alte looked old and small. He had to look up into Karl's eyes. The deep creases in his face seemed to give witness to the turmoil of the many years he had lived through and maybe the horrors he had witnessed.

It was sad that the stiff handshake with almost military correctness was all they had of a relationship. Then Der Alte turned his attention to me. He came forward, took me in his arms, hugged me and we smiled at each other. I said one of the few German phrases I had picked up and could remember when the occasion arose, "Ja, dann auf Wiedersehen!"

I felt uncomfortable speaking German, worrying about whether my accent sounded strange or the words were right. Hugging him reminded me of how old he was and how tenuous was his hold on life. It reminded me of the last months of my father's life when it was clear he was dying.

The symbolism of us hugging good-bye, a former high-ranking Nazi hugging a Jew, saying good-bye like friends who had been visiting for the day, was also in my mind. I could see Karl watching me intently and probably thinking the same thing.

When the old man seemed to feel the tension he abruptly released me, but of the three of us, he seemed the most relaxed. Karl got into the rented Renault, small and underpowered, and started the engine. It gave him something to do. The old man waved one more time as I closed my door and then he turned back to the house where Ingrid stood in the doorway waving her lace handkerchief and mopping her eyes.

CHAPTER XVI

"Well, let's go," I said. "I've got the map, you concentrate on driving. Do you know the way out of Heidelberg to the Autobahn or do you want me to get out the city map?" I didn't have any real confidence that I could guide him out of the city, but I was suddenly anxious to leave the Schmidts behind.

Karl found the main artery leaving Heidelberg and shortly afterward was on the Autobahn. "OK, Sarrie," he said, "close your eyes for a while and only look if you must. This is going to be hairy. On this highway system pure Darwinism applies. There is only one speed limit. It is what your car can do. No one goes faster or slower. You screw up and you are allowed to remove yourself from the gene pool." With that, Karl accelerated until the engine whined.

"What are you doing?" I said, as I looked at the speedometer and saw 140. "Are you going 140? Are you crazy?" I yelled.

Karl said calmly, "I thought I told you to close your eyes. What this speedometer tells you is kilometers, not miles. We are going a lot slower than you think. A little over 80." Just at that time our car jerked to the right into the slow lane and a sportscar went by us.

More than the high-speed traffic was bothering me. "I don't get it. You've been telling me since I met you that all through your childhood, there was silence about the Nazis and your father's role in the Third Reich. But here he is, apparently willing to talk freely to us. Was it maybe that you and your sisters and your mother never really wanted to know?"

"I'm not really sure," Karl said. "As a child, I clearly remember him at our house, sitting with his old Nazi buddies. They spent hours talking about the school and probably lamenting the loss of the war. But my mother didn't want us to hear any of it."

"So do you think that if you had just asked a few simple questions, you might know a lot more now?" I wondered again whether the answers had been given, but had fallen upon deaf ears.

"Think about it, with your reporter hat on. How many of your questions did Der Alte really answer? Didn't he really tell you what he wanted you to hear? Do you really know anything more about his role and how he was privy to high level conversations?"

I had to admit the old man had been very talkative, but maybe not all that forthright.

As Karl continued driving, I mostly pretended to squint at the map, trying to distinguish one German town from another, I wondered why the old man was so interested in knowing exactly where we were going and what we were going to do. I suppressed my paranoia—sort of.

Gradually, as we drove through the countryside, Karl pointing out familiar towns, the interaction with the old man faded, although we both knew we would discuss it later. It was finally time for us to be vacationing tourists and I knew Karl was looking forward to driving up the Rhine.

To the right, I could see an occasional castle. The rocks of the cliffs looked reddish in the sunlight. To the left and right of the smooth concrete ribbon of the autobahn were small villages surrounded by fields. From time to time we passed through sections of forest. I wanted to enjoy the ride, but Karl's driving was truly disturbing. He rode up onto the tailgate of slower trucks too fast and too close. Then he would suddenly pull into the fast lane, make the engine scream and pull right back into the slow lane, almost cutting off the truck. I noticed my right leg becoming tired as I continued to press on the imaginary brake pedal as we again approached a truck.

"Karl, please, do you have to drive like this? Why are you going so fast? You don't do that at home."

"It's a different ball game on the Autobahn," Karl answered, giving me a complicated explanation of why Germans build small cars and how they have to compete with more powerful vehicles on the road. I didn't say anything when he concluded, "I guess you might say that when you swim in a shark tank you just don't act like food."

I think he believed what he had just said, however, for me this was something entirely different; in that moment I saw him conforming to the German driving style in a heartbeat. *Shark tank… food… I thought. Is that how the Germans conformed to the Nazi regime? Fitting in and acting safely?*

"How about setting some sensible speed limits?"

"Sarah, that is just not possible. I guess it would make sense, both the fast and the slow lanes have about the same speed and passing would become safer. Think of it this way. Would it not be safer if all firearms were outlawed and people would not have them to commit crimes? I think it would. Try to outlaw firearms and disarm the American public. I think that is politically impossible. The Nazis, by the way, did that. They are, however, totally committed to their right to drive as fast as their car can on the autobahn. Think of it as their Second Amendment right."

"Just typical for you. Not only do you compare apples with oranges, but as usual your analogies are off," I patted his knee to take the edge off my words.

Karl seemed to think about this in silence and then said, "You win. But I guess analogies are always a bit off. If things were identical one could not compare them. It's just that some countries hold things dear that make absolutely no sense to an outsider."

Karl interrupted himself to ask me to look at the map and see what route we needed to take to Mainz. I was feeling stressed, not being familiar with the towns and names. After telling me to hurry because the decision had to be made soon, Karl laughed.

"Let's just take one of the choices. If we are wrong, we double back and all it takes is more time. We are on vacation. This is not do-or-die."

All of a sudden the pressure was off. We took the middle of three choices and that proved to be the right one. We did not know that it was right until after a few kilometers when we saw that we were indeed headed towards Mainz and then Bingen. That was where we would leave the Autobahn. I was relieved that soon we'd be driving on a smaller roadway.

As we neared Mainz, I saw a number of old castles, towers and fortifications on the hills looming above us. To me it looked like a fairyland: beauty and history packed between little towns with charming houses and cobbled side streets, church steeples and vineyards in between.

Karl decided to stop in Bacharach, a beautiful little town with half-timbered houses with shutters on the main street and carefully tended boxes of flowers under the window sills, which I came to love more and more. I promised myself that one day I would have those in our house.

We parked in a small satellite lot near the center of town. In the middle of the parking lot was a stump of an old tower flanked by a crumbling wall and some arches that reached down into a fenced-off ditch. "What is that in the middle of this lot?" I asked. "Wouldn't it be better to either repair the building or tear it down? They would be able to get many more cars into this lot."

"Well, let's see," Karl said as he approached the sign in front of the tower. "These were the original Roman baths about 1800 years ago. I don't think they will either repair this building or tear it down. They mean to preserve it."

I looked at the walls and arches. "You mean that this has been standing here for almost two thousand years?" What had seemed at first to be an obstruction in a public parking lot now looked entirely different to me.

We left the car and sought out a restaurant. Just as we were rounding the corner to a little market square, not much larger than a tennis court paved with cobblestones, I saw the street sign "Judenstrasse".

"What does that signify, Judenstrasse?" I knew it literally translated as Jew Street, but that meant nothing to me.

"In the Middle Ages the Jews were required to live in their own streets, a form of early ghetto. Either by subtle pressure, a matter of choice, or custom, most likely a mixture of all to varying degree, this continued until the Nazis came," Karl explained.

"And then, as your father said, they all moved to different countries, right?" Anger started to well up in me.

Karl chose to take my sarcastic remark literally. "No, all of them lost their property, most probably died in concentration camps, and all of the streets got new names. Look at it. This sign "Judenstrasse" is quite new. I think that returning the street name is one way to commemorate."

Maybe Karl was right. But returning the name of the street did not return the people who died and the houses were still owned by someone else.

"How did the people who own them now get title to them?" I asked.

I could see in Karl's face that he was uncomfortable with the direction our conversation was going. He shrugged and I decided to drop the subject.

We walked in silence to the restaurant, which totally fit what I imagined *gemuetlich* must mean. There were wooden booths, checkered tablecloths, a low-beamed ceiling and a friendly waitress who brought the menus.

Karl opened his and began to read. "Oh, look they have venison. I think I'll have the elk stew, boiled parsley potatoes and red cabbage. Yum! What are you having?" he asked.

I was confused. "What am I having?" The menu was in German. I couldn't read it.

"Sorry, I forgot," Karl appeared to be embarrassed. "I'll try to translate. The menu is divided in sections of fish from the Rhine-area, beef and pork and venison. What category are you interested in?"

"Why do you have to make it so efficient and systematic?" I asked. I knew I should not be so confrontational with him, but shortly after the "Judenstrasse," I found Karl's systematic way of thinking was especially irritating.

"Well, I don't want to have to translate the whole menu if I don't have to. This is not easy to translate. The words are clear, but what they conjure up in the description of the dishes is like trying to translate the back label of a wine bottle. You read it, it sounds great, but you couldn't summarize the prose or accurately translate it."

Maybe he had a point. "What do they have in beef?"

Karl looked at the choices and began to summarize rather than translate. After a while he just said, "I don't think you want any of this. This is just run-of-the-mill German roast beef in various forms. With various sauces with the choice of potatoes or spaetzle." When he got to "succulent junior swine" I began to laugh. "Junior swine?"

"Well, yes. 'Jungschwein' may be translated too literally. It means a very young and tender pork, somewhat older than suckling pig but still small and tender." I laughed again and the waitress started moving in our direction, thinking that we had finished reading the menu and were ready to order.

"Ja bitte, was darf's denn sein?" Karl told her that we needed more time since he was still translating the menu for me.

She said "Ach so, eine englische Speisekarte! Kommt gleich!" She returned with an English translation of the menu. Karl looked sheepish but relieved as I started to study the choices. After all that, I ordered elk and Karl chose wild boar. We were in an adventurous mood.

We were amply rewarded. The food was excellent, with

flavorful sauces, unusual seasoning and generous portions. After our meal we continued up the Rhine valley. More vineyards and names I vaguely remembered from wine labels: Andernach, Remagen.

"Remagen. That's a town that is hard to forget," Karl said. "Did you ever see the movie 'A Bridge Too Far'? It's about the World War II battle at the Rhine bridge of Remagen. A horrible waste of life when the war was essentially over." And on Karl went with his explanations and memories. It was a bit after dark when we finally arrived in downtown Cologne.

I was exhausted. I had seen so many quaint villages, castles, old towns and relics from the past. Sometimes had even enjoyed myself. I almost felt like a tourist. After a short search we settled on an inexpensive bed and breakfast in the downtown area where Karl wanted to be. We had to climb two narrow stairs with our suitcases until we got to our room. It was small with a high ceiling and furniture from the 1940s, making me feel caught in a time warp. Karl put down the luggage and we sat on the bed. "The mattress is the same age as the rest of the furniture," he said.

"It feels hard. I think it's actually three mattresses."

"You are probably right," Karl groaned. "I used to have a mattress like this when I was a kid. Springs, horsehair and three parts. Hard. But, you know, they last forever. Just like this one has."

At that point, I did not have the energy to care. After a short while we turned out the lights. Thinking of castles and the Judenstrasse without Jews, I drifted off.

CHAPTER XVII

The next morning, I didn't need an alarm clock. The much earlier dawn in northern Europe and the clanking of the trucks in the street making deliveries early to avoid traffic congestion woke me up. I was ready to begin the new day, though Karl was still asleep and softly snoring. Under the quilted blanket, he had rolled himself into a little ball.

"Wach auf, Bueblein," I said. Karl sat up bleary-eyed and said a string of sentences in German. I just looked at him. He looked back, obviously expecting some sort of response.

He appeared baffled and then he said, "Sorry, let me flip my language switch. What I said was, 'I hate those mattresses.' I hated them when I was a kid and didn't know that there was something better. But now I know, and that certainly does not help. So. Good morning. How did you sleep?"

"Thanks," I said wryly. "The same. I didn't like the mattress either."

Untangling himself from the blanket, Karl said, "Let's get going. We have a lot of plans for the day." He stumbled over to the shower booth, which seemed to have been recently added to the room. He opened the plastic door and looked inside. It was essentially a telephone-booth-size contraption with a drain at the bottom and wide open at the top. If one took a shower, the steam would fill the whole room. We stood side by side studying the thing, then looked at each other, neither of us saying a word. Karl closed the door of the stall and we both began brushing our teeth. I pulled some new clothes from the bags and we dressed.

Once out in the street Karl found a bakery, which sold fresh and warm pastries and strong fragrant coffee. They had tables in a corner and we ate breakfast in silence, watching the city come to life. I felt surprisingly good.

A little while later we headed toward the Cologne Cathedral. As we rounded the corner and came to the square at the banks of the Rhine, I saw the enormous twin towers and the roof of the nave with flying buttresses and alcoves containing statues. It was monumental, extraordinary. I had seen something like it on postcards from France. But to walk up to a building like this was something totally spectacular.

Karl began. "What you see here is the biggest-ever façade of a Gothic cathedral. That style of architecture was developed in France and spread into Italy, Germany and England. Each region developed its individual distinctive style, but this one was the largest ever. See the arches over the portals? They all have a peak at the top. During the previous era, the Romanesque period, the arches were all round. The Gothic period of architecture lasted from roughly 1200 to 1450."

I was silent as we walked closer.

"Look at the portals. The arches are columns, which in turn are dissolved and divided into narrower columns. Some of them are saints and patriarchs standing on pedestals which in turn serve as a roof for the next figure. Look at the clothes they wear. That's what church people wore at the time this was built. Just imagine: All this is chiseled out of sandstone, just rock."

Karl was increasingly enthusiastic and animated as he described what we were seeing. As we entered the church, I saw the immense stained glass windows. Each was at least 40 feet high and narrow and replaced what would have been a wall between the columns. They were beautifully red, blue and yellow, in all colors of the rainbow, featuring figures and scenes. The rising sun was shining through, forming shafts of multiple colors diagonally through the hazy air in the building.

"This is the main nave." He explained that the word derives from "Navis," Latin for ship. "Typically a Gothic church has three naves lengthwise and one to three crosswise, called

'Transept.' That's symbolic for the Father, the Son, and the Holy Ghost. See up there in the ceiling? That's where all the columns meet in a latticework. Just look at the huge space that is created. Every single stone rests on another and the weight is directed to the sides and downward." He explained the different little chapels in the multiple alcoves around the perimeter and the golden Sacrament next to the altar. It was a miniature Gothic spire about 30 feet high.

I noticed that we were being followed by people who were listening in on Karl's explanations. Did they think he was an official tourist guide? He either did not notice or he didn't mind. He knew his stuff and it was obvious that he deeply loved medieval architecture.

Later Karl showed me the "Bauhuette" on the outside. His "audience" hadn't followed us. I could see stonemasons making statues and column sections by hand with mallets and chisels.

"You know, this is the place where they carved the original stones and where they still continue to do that. They never stopped since the very beginning of construction. Now it is no longer to build the cathedral. Now it is just repair and replacement."

"So when did they begin working here?" I asked.

"Well, it all began in 1248. The first architect was Gerhard von Rile. He designed the whole thing and they stuck to the original plans. Just imagine. That man had all this in his head before he made drawings and began work. At the time they started, the city of Cologne had about 35,000 inhabitants. There was absolutely no way that the local economy could support the creation of a building of this scale. When Gerhard von Rile made his plans he knew that he would never, in his lifetime, see the completion of the cathedral or even a significant part. He knew that this would take centuries. But he believed that the city would grow and attract more people and commerce because of this building and one day, it would be completed. He could see everything in his mind. In 1880, they completed the last parts of the towers. That's how long it took. Sure there were setbacks and pauses during wars and epidemics. But they continued to build."

"By the way, have you ever looked at the label of a bottle of original cologne? I mean the brand that has the 4711 on it? That was created here in this city right around the corner. The number 4711 is the address in the Glockengasse, the bell alley next to the cathedral. On the label of this brand you can see the picture of the cathedral the way it looked in the 1700s. The cathedral did not have spires then. On one of the towers there is the construction crane depicted. This is the way it looked until they took the crane down and began the push for completion in 1842. Look at one of those bottles of original cologne in the drug store when we get home."

I was amazed by both Karl's knowledge about this building and his enthusiasm.

I amused myself with the thought of my perception of him as a "Nazi cop" at Brennan's. What I had here was a medievalist with a Ph.D. from UC Berkeley, showing me around. The contrast was a bit mind-blowing.

Eventually, we were hungry and tired of walking so we went to a little pub across the street. As we sat down and ordered, Karl looked through the smoke-stained window toward the cathedral. He was quiet and subdued.

"What is it, Bueblein?" I asked him.

After a long silence, he looked at me. "You know, all these years when I was asked in America—by you for instance—'What did your father do during World War II?', I evaded that question by giving my standard answer: 'Same as your father, except for the other side.' That usually brought an acceptance, a chuckle and that was the end. And when I was questioned about my feelings about German superiority or the Nazis, I evaded further inquiry by telling them that I was not born until eight days after the Nazi defeat and that I was, if anything, one of the first German Democrats. And that usually ended the discussion." Karl again became quiet.

"But why are you bringing this up now?" I asked.

"I just explained the history of that magnificent cathedral across the street. I felt a lot of pride in my history when I did that. Hell, the cathedral was started in 1248. I think of that period as part of my history. But the 12 years from 1933 to 1945, which is like almost yesterday, I always thought I could say that it was before my time."

He grimaced. "But that, too, is my history. If I take pride in the cathedral, then I have to also own up to the Nazi years as being part of my history. All of it. The whole shebang."

We both fell silent and took small sips of now-stale beer. It was time to get back into the car and head toward Leipzig.

CHAPTER XVIII

"You know," Karl said as we were approaching Leipzig, "The last time I was here, I was just eleven years old. When Der Alte suggested we stay in the old house of my grandparents, the idea seemed kind of absurd to me, but now it's spooky. Why not stay in a bed and breakfast or a hotel instead? At least we know what to expect there. I have no idea what we will find in my grandfather's house."

I sensed that Karl was worried about whether I would be pleased with the place. "We don't have to stay there if you don't want to," I said, "But at the very least we should take a look around and see if everything is OK. If we decide that we should stay somewhere else, we can still do that."

Karl always had to have a plan and then felt as if he had some sort of duty to adhere to it once it was made. Flexibility was not his strong suit.

I was totally intrigued with the idea of visiting the house. Karl had told me that his grandfather bought it as a young man. After losing his first wife to throat cancer, he soon brought his second wife to the house. That was in the 1920s. He had raised both his boys in that house, which made them city kids, except for occasional visits to their Tante Liska on the farm.

"I remember arriving here after a long train trip." Karl said. "My grandparents had visited us in Hamburg. Both were over 65 then. I know that because you could not get an exit visa from East Germany unless you were a senior citizen. The Communists did not allow anybody to leave their country except for people who were living on a pension. I guess they actually hoped that the seniors would not return after visiting family in the West. If they did not come back, the West German government picked up their pension and the East Germans were off the hook. I remember how envious young people were of pensioners who were allowed to travel."

I could almost see Karl as an eleven-year-old boy getting off the train.

"When we arrived in the old house I noticed some strong and musty smell right when we came through the porch into the kitchen," he said. "I saw dishes in the sink and a wicker chair with a sleeping cat on it. When I approached to pet it I saw that it was a loaf of bread covered with mold. Think about it: My grandparents had been visiting with us in Hamburg for almost three weeks. That was some old bread, needless to say. My grandmother was a really bad housekeeper and a lousy cook. I had to stay there for two weeks and I did not look forward to eating my grandmother's food."

"So what do you expect when you get to your grandfather's house now?" I asked Karl. "Probably not stale bread," I laughed and hoped he was right.

"Well I really don't know. I do have some other memories which are not all bad. For instance, as we left for an outing, just outside the house my grandfather pointed to his new rain gutters and down spouts. They were brown and you could see the sun shine through them. He told me that they were made of Bakelite. He pointed out that they would never rust. Then he added that they did not have enough steel in what he called "Our Republic" and were therefore replacing things with this new material. For some reason, I remember the strange way they smelled. I also remember my grandfather taking me to the Voelkerschlachtsdenkmal."

"What in the world is that?" I asked. "Is that another one of those things like Wiedervereinigung?"

"Right," Karl answered me with a laugh. "Another of those beautiful compound nouns. It's the Memorial of the Battle of the Nations. In just one word. You know here in Leipzig is where Napoleon's armies suffered their final decisive defeat. A coalition of several European nations annihilated the French on their retreat from Russia. A great tower was erected in 1913 on the 100th anniversary of that epic battle. Remember the picture in my father's house over his old desk? That is a hand-colored print of the victory parade in front of Leipzig City Hall. I think it was printed and painted in 1815."

As Karl carefully navigated the traffic in downtown Leipzig, I gazed at the sights. I saw some old apartment buildings with ornate facades and balconies with carefully preserved wrought iron railings. Sculptures of people were standing on pedestals, holding up the stone balconies on their backs.

Karl explained that West Germany also used to have many of those old buildings that survived World War II. Sometime in the late 50s, their magnificent facades had been chiseled off and people had "modernized" them by covering them with plain stucco or even asbestos shingles. "Fortunately, they did not have the money here to do that. Maybe in the long run they can repair and preserve these buildings," he said.

It seemed to me that Karl was driving aimlessly. After a while, he gave up, pulled over and asked a pedestrian, an old man, directions to Gohlis, the sector of town where his grandfather's house was located. The old man answered Karl's questions in a slow dialect punctuated by pointing, changing positions, and pointing some more. All I understood was Karl finally thanking the man and driving on.

"Why are you grinning, Karl? Is there something funny about getting directions?"

"Not really, but this is the first time I have heard pure Saxon spoken since I was a kid. When I grew up, my parents tried their hardest to lose their dialect. It was a big handicap for them because it immediately revealed that they came originally from the East. In the years after the war, that particular idiom identified you as a bombed-out-poor-refugee country bumpkin."

There were other things Karl associated with the Saxon accent. Ulbricht, the first East German head of government, spoke with a very high soprano voice and a thick Saxon dialect. He did so in all his speeches demanding respect and equality. "It just sounded terrible and whiney," Karl recalled.

"And there are books translating all the wonderful poetry of Goethe and Schiller into that dialect, all terribly funny. There is no way to explain this. Try and imagine Shakespeare's Prospero speaking in a very slow Texan drawl. Wouldn't it be odd? Well, this dialect has been laughed about for so long, I wonder how this will work out in a reunited Germany. Somehow I cannot see a Porsche salesman in Stuttgart closing a deal in Saxon."

When I suggested that his attitude was demeaning, Karl agreed, but said, "I know this is shallow, but picture the English queen speaking with anything other than her aristocratic diction. That would not work. Dialect is a powerful messenger."

He had a point but I was quite unwilling to concede it.

"There it is," Karl pointed to a gray stucco two-story row house, as he parked the car. "Eduart von Hartmann Strasse 12. Still the same after forty years. Badly needs paint, and on the corner up there, the stucco has fallen off. What a mess."

Looking at the house I suddenly felt a lot of trepidation. "Do you want to unload the suitcases or should we take a look first? I mean, we don't have to stay here if we don't like it. I'm just suggesting..." I began.

Karl interrupted me. "I think you are right." He didn't look happy.

While we were hesitating, an old man came out of the neighboring house and approached us.

"Karl Schmidt?" he said. "Mein Name ist Kiesling..." That much I understood. What followed was a rapid conversation in German. Karl did not translate, but eventually he introduced me. Mr. Kiesling shook my hand, said something that sounded friendly, and then retreated to his front door. I waved and he waved back as he re-entered his house.

"What was that all about?" I asked Karl.

"After my grandfather's death, Mr. Kiesling took care of the house. He paid all the bills and caused necessary repairs to be made. His wife cleaned and dusted from time to time. You see, my father did not want to sell the house because the East German government would have had the right to buy it at their price. Somehow my father hoped to keep the house, thinking that East Germany could not survive in the long run. Anyway, I had never met Mr. Kiesling and he just introduced himself to me. I guess he wanted to find out if I was the real Karl Schmidt and entitled to go inside. Der Alte must have told him we were coming. He was just doing his job in a friendly way."

Karl opened the front door and entered the house for the first time in almost 40 years. "Well, this time it does not smell like moldy bread."

He stopped in the entryway and looked around. "Wow, look at this. This is a museum. Everything looks like I remember it. The rugs are gone but the furniture is just like it was then. And look. Even the pictures on the wall are the ones from the fifties. Those frames are from the 1920s."

I looked at Karl as he slowly explored the hallway and the living room. I followed him into the kitchen and was amazed by what I saw. Even the stove was an antique. It was coal-fired, had an iron plate as a stovetop and individual rings that you could remove to expose the pots directly to the fire. The countertops were made with little octagonal tiles no larger than a quarter. The grouting was cracked and missing in many places. There were ceramic canisters on a shelf along the wall for sugar, salt, flour, rice and so on.

"I like this place," I said to Karl, giving him a hug. "Maybe we should stay at least for a night and look around. But if you think I am going to attempt to cook on this stove, you are dreaming. Here is what I suggest. Let's open some windows to let some fresh air into the house. After that I would like to find a restaurant or buy a pizza and come back with a couple of bottles of beer and some red wine. What do you think?"

I knew that even though his preferred drink in the U.S. was Irish coffee, in Germany he enjoyed sampling the local beer. He had expounded on that theme often when I ordered my beer in Brennan's. He wouldn't drink it. In spite of my early concerns about whether he was an alcoholic, I soon learned that he was almost finicky about what he would drink and I'd never seen him drink to excess.

Karl agreed with my idea for dinner. We quickly opened a few windows in the upstairs and the back of the house. After that Karl brought the bags from the car and we locked up. The walk to the downtown area was just what I wanted after sitting in the car all day. Unless I get at least one good walk a day I become grumpy.

As we left the residential area and approached broader streets, I asked Karl where he was headed. "Oh, I don't know. I just follow my nose and see if we can find streetcar tracks. I just follow them until I see a streetcar stop—there you usually find a little map and that tells you where you are."

"Don't you want to ask directions?" I asked, baffled. Karl shook his head.

"Naah. Let's just walk, look, explore. We'll find something," That wasn't my style but it did contribute to the feeling that we were lighthearted tourists just looking around.

Sure enough, after just a few blocks we came upon streetcar tracks, and shortly after that we found a stop with a map. I was getting my exercise and felt that I was becoming less antsy and more relaxed. I saw many businesses that were closed, apartments for rent and houses offered for sale.

"Seems like everyone who could leave has gone to West Germany," Karl said.

As I looked at the empty windows and closed stores, I was thinking of Jewish businesses and apartments after Kristallnacht during the Nazi years. It must have looked similar. Except that the Germans claimed not to have noticed.

"I think we are there," Karl said. We had arrived at what looked like a major square with businesses and people shopping. "Now we have to make a decision," Karl said. "Do we want to eat at a restaurant or do we buy something and go back and have it at my grandfather's house? How about if we look at the butcher shop over there and see what they have," he suggested.

A short while later we were on our way back with fresh rolls, some cold cuts, smoked meats, Russian red wine and some beer. Karl retraced our route, and soon we were back at the house.

Karl was carrying the paper bags and looked around, unsure of himself. There was no dining room, but the kitchen had a cleanly scrubbed wooden table. "Here, let me handle this," I said, taking the bags and setting them on the table. Karl looked relieved. I started searching through the cabinets and managed to find a cutting board, some knives and a few plates. I began to set the table. Karl went into the living room and found two old cut-crystal wine glasses which looked like they were a hundred years old. One of them was slightly chipped around the rim. He even found a corkscrew. I laid out the goodies we bought while Karl opened one of the bottles. We sat and began our dinner.

"So," I asked. "Does it feel less spooky now?" Karl shrugged while I cut a piece of bread, spread butter on it and took a few slices of sausage.

"This tastes great," I mumbled as I chewed.

Karl said, "Why can't we make sausages and breads like this in America? After all, we are in the former East Germany, an unworkable outcome of World War II, where nothing really functioned and that finally collapsed under its own weight. In American supermarkets you buy bread that has no substance, no taste, and you put bologna on it. Consider this, Sarah. In the U.S., we conduct a survey to find out what people like and don't like. Then we have the computers evaluate it. Then we produce a beer that no one objects to and an unobjectionable bread that can be mass produced. That's what we do with everything we make. Then we have beer, bread, and meat that can be marketed to 250 million. We have no tradition. No local specialties because they can't compete in a national market. Everything is cheap. And average."

"You want some more wine?" I asked. A rant about American commercialism seemed at odds with our very German dinner in this old house crammed with memories and ghosts.

Karl shook his head. "Later. Let's look around a bit. I want to see what is left here of my grandparents."

CHAPTER XIX

When Karl got up from the table, I followed him into the living room. "See that? That is a picture of my father's stepmother when she was young. I remember when I was eleven, I asked my grandfather who that pretty-looking woman in the photo was. He looked at the picture then for a long time and remarked, 'That is your grandmother—when she was young. She had a very strong back.' That struck me as odd. I never forgot his description. I don't remember her being pretty or young. She did not look anything like that picture."

Karl reached out to touch the old piano and picked up a little brown canoe that was lying on it. "I made that when I was eight or nine. It's carved from the soft bark of a pine tree. I always liked the rich brown color and the light layers in between. Almost looks like it is made of planks." He put it back carefully.

Seeing this very tangible object that Karl had actually made by hand brought into focus the sharp reality of where we were. In his grandfather's house. In Germany.

Karl started up the steep stairs to the second floor. The wooden steps creaked. "When I first got here when I was a kid, I noticed that the railing was sticky. I always hated sticky stuff. Funny, I still don't want to touch it."

I ran my hand over it, and—maybe it was my imagination—it still felt sticky to me.

Karl opened the door at the top of the stairs. "This was the bedroom of both my father and his brother Gerhard. I stayed in it when I was a kid. At the time there was only one bed. Just like now. There were little antlers of roe deer on the wall. My grandfather explained that he had not hunted them himself. They were a gift from an old friend."

I looked around at the wainscoting along the walls, the old hardware around the door locks. In America, these would be antiques. Here they were just old and outmoded stuff.

"This was my grandparents' bedroom," Karl said, standing in another doorway. "I was given to understand that it was off limits for me when I was a kid, so I never came inside." Following him into the room, I saw a heavy-framed double bed, two narrow bed stands, a dark wooden dresser with a marble top and an oil painting of a mountain landscape with a lone deer on a meadow.

"Who did that?" I asked.

"My uncle Gerhard. It's hung there as far back as I can remember. Good, isn't it?"

I didn't know much about art but I nodded. It seemed almost professional. "So Gerhard was a painter?"

Shrugging his shoulders, Karl said, "I don't know. He died young. I never asked."

Karl pointed to a set of stairs. "That's the way up to the attic. I never was up there. Let's see what they stored away."

Thinking of discarded toys, old furniture and dust, I was reluctant but intrigued. Karl led the way up the narrow steps. At the top he opened the door to the dark attic. He twisted the knob-style light switch next to the doorframe, and it responded with a loud clack. As a dim light shined through the opening, Karl stooped to pass through into the room beyond.

"What a mess!" he exclaimed.

I looked into the attic and saw women's clothing hanging on an old wire clothesline. I held up a dress. "Look at the style— it must be from the 20s."

An old washstand complete with a washbowl and water pitcher stood in the corner. Next to it was a stack of newspapers.

"Oh, I love old papers," Karl said. "When you go through old papers you can find out what people thought was significant enough to save. It tells you a lot about them." He squatted down next to the stack and began reading.

"*Neues Deutschland.* From 1948 until the fall of the Wall, this was the official publication of the SED—the German Unity Party—that was actually the ruling Communist party. See here, next to the banner at the top of the paper, the overlapping profiles? These are Marx, Engels, Lenin. The founders of Communism. Does that look familiar to you?" Karl smiled.

"Yep," I said, "I can't place it. Where do I know this from?"

"The official emblem of the City of Berkeley," Karl laughed, pointing out that on every public works truck and every city business card is a similar logo showing different ethnic faces— instead of the founding fathers of the Communist Party.

"The Communists tried to show a united front through uniformity, while Berkeley tries to show a united front through diversity. While there is much difference there is also much similarity," he chuckled. I thought that was silly of him. But so typical too.

"This is the grand announcement of what turned out to be the last Five-Year-Plan. Look here, they asserted that it would be possible to surpass the West German economy in the foreseeable future. Interesting." He then unfolded a paper that looked like a certificate. "Wow, look at this. It's a certificate from April 11, 1911." He read it with an amazed expression.

"Jesus," he said. "This is a certificate giving my grandfather Royal Saxon citizenship. Before his name, his title is listed as Schutzmann—'police officer.' I had no idea my grandfather was a cop."

"I guess being a cop is in your blood. Wonder what that means," I teased. I stood by as Karl moved the stack of papers, including a wrinkled drawing of a sunflower. "I wonder if that is also Gerhard's?"

"I'm sure it is. My grandfather didn't know how to draw. Neither did my father."

Picking up another newspaper, Karl said, "Here is one from

1948. I think it is from the Berlin Blockade. They called it an American provocation. Well, I guess everyone has their view points."

Karl kept digging and eventually uncovered an old shoebox full of yellowing cards of some sort. He pulled one out and began to read it, not translating for once. His face became ashen.

"What is it?" I asked, moving across the room to put my hand on his shoulder. Karl did not answer. He took another card. I could see that it had red printing and handwriting on it.

"Holy shit. Let me translate this for you. First of all, this is a postcard. The red printing says, 'Concentration Camp Buchenwald. Write clearly. Illegible mail will be discarded by the censor.'

The little red box says:

"It is too early to state a day of release.
Visits to the camp are prohibited. Inquiries
are pointless.

Excerpt of the camp rules:

Every inmate may receive two letters or two
postcards per month and may also mail two
letters and two postcards. The lines of the
letters have to be neat and legible.

Mailings which do not comply with this order
will not be forwarded. Packages, regardless of
content, will not be received. Money may
only be mailed via postal money order, a
receipt of which must be attached to the
letter. Mailing cash is prohibited. Writing
notes on the back of the postal money order
is prohibited and the receipt will be refused.
Everything can be bought in the camp.
National Socialist newspapers are permitted.
However, they have to be ordered by the

inmate himself through the concentration camp postal services. Letters that are difficult to read cannot be censored and will be destroyed. Mailing of pictures and photographs is prohibited.

The Camp Commander

As I listened to Karl and glanced down at the postcard, I struggled to comprehend what he was reading. In spite of all my interviews with camp survivors, no one had ever mentioned that prisoners were allowed to send and receive mail. And beyond that, what were these cards doing in Karl's grandfather's attic? When I asked him, he pointed to the handwritten part of the postcard and began translating.

"Dear Father and Mother. Thank you very much for the package which arrived on time for Christmas and my birthday. I like the brown sweater very much. We don't have many clothes and in the winter the warmth of the sweater is very good under my prison uniform. My fellow prisoners liked the sausage very much. They have not had a treat like that in a very long time. I had to give the sausage away since I don't have teeth anymore and was not able to eat it. I enjoyed the cookies very much. I was able to dissolve them in my mouth and so had a nice treat from home.

P.S. Father, could you perhaps check if my prescription for my glasses is still in my bed stand? I need a new pair. My present pair is all smashed up. I am sure that the prescription has not changed much. Thank you again. Your son Gerhard."

None of this was making sense but I seized on a small inconsistency. "I thought the rules of the camp were that no packages were permitted? How could Gerhard have received sausages?"

Karl was clearly stunned, as was I. We looked at each other in the dim light. Karl whispered, "These cards are actually from my Uncle Gerhard, sent from Buchenwald."

I knew we were both thinking: how could this be?

"Do you realize what he was trying to do?" Karl said. "He was trying to tell his father that he was beaten. His teeth were knocked out and his glasses were smashed. Look at the date—January 6, 1939. A 21-year-old does not lose his teeth naturally!"

"But how could he be in the concentration camp while his brother—your father—was a Nazi big-wig on his way up?"

Karl shook his head. "I don't know the answers to that, but now I'm sure of one thing: he was imprisoned in Buchenwald."

I was dumbfounded. I looked at the postcards as if somehow further explanations would spring from them. Karl slumped as he pulled several more postcards from the box and read them silently. I sat down next to him on the floor and hugged him. I felt sorry for Karl. I wanted not to be in the attic.

"What now, Karl?" I asked.

"I don't know. I can't read any more now."

He carefully put everything back into the box the way he found it. He collected the newspapers and stacked them the way they were on top of the box. He took my hand and led me from the small room with the dim light. The room seemed oppressive now. We closed the door, turned off the light and made our way back downstairs to the kitchen. Karl fell heavily onto the old kitchen chair. We both poured another glass of the Russian red wine and opened a beer.

"I had no idea," Karl looked at me. "I remember that night at Brennan's when you asked me what my father did during World War II. I thought I knew and I did not want to talk about it. I gave you some bullshit answer that I had practiced. At my parents' house, when I translated for you when you were talking to Der Alte, I had a clearer idea. Now I don't know what to think."

We discussed possible scenarios for how Gerhard might have been sent to Buchenwald. None of them made sense. As it grew dark outside, I asked Karl what the plan was.

"I hate to say it, but I think we need to go to Buchenwald

and see what is left of that concentration camp. We can stay somewhere nearby tonight. I don't want to spend the night here."

I agreed before he was even finished with the sentence.

We quickly cleaned the kitchen, took the bags back out to the car and drove away.

CHAPTER XX

Buchenwald was located on top of an isolated hilltop ten miles from Weimar. Karl and I walked quietly toward the barbed-wire enclosure, past the rows of barracks the SS guards had occupied. It was colder here than just a few miles away in Weimar, where we had stayed overnight. I felt more and more reluctant about being here at the camp. The feeling of evil was palpable.

Karl read me the inscription on the metal gate. "Jedem Das Seine—everyone gets what he deserves."

"Oh my God," he whispered. "Once, when my grandfather talked to me about Gerhard's life, he made it sound as if Gerhard had been at odds with everyone, contributing nothing to anyone. Then my grandfather said, 'well, jedem das seine,' sighing heavily and shaking his head. The way my grandfather used that phrase made me think then it was just a maxim, a way for my grandfather to express his disapproval of Gerhard's life."

"I didn't know that the Nazis had incorporated those words into the entrance gate of the camp, surely knowing most of those who entered there were doomed. And of course I didn't know that Gerhard had been there. Now I wonder if my grandfather knew those words were on Buchenwald's gate and if he did, what terrible cynicism, or perhaps complicity even, his comment reflected."

Confronted now with the physical reality of the camp, we discussed if we really wanted to continue our visit here. But Karl was determined to try to find out what he could about Gerhard. With some difficulty, we located the Buchenwald archivist, tucked away in a nondescript building.

Frau Schwarz was a middle-aged woman and—like many other East Germans—wore drab unstylish clothing.

When we explained why we were there, she told us all the records at the camp were kept by number, not by name. "We don't have a cross reference from name to number. You'd have to go to the city archives and get his number," she said. But Karl remembered the number he had seen on the postcard in the attic, and after a long search, she handed him a sheet of paper.

At the top, was the number 632, followed by a list of three names. In the middle was Gerhard's. "That's him," said Karl. His date of birth and place of birth was printed, along with the notation "Pol" and 13/12/40.

One of the other names said "BV." The third name also said "Pol."

"Who were these other two people with the same number?" Karl asked.

Frau Schwarz stumbled through the explanation. They were prisoners who had preceded and followed Gerhard. The prisoner number had been recycled.

"What does Pol mean?" Karl asked Frau Schwarz, who explained that Gerhard had been classified as a political prisoner and that he was "transported away" on December 13, 1940. BV was the designation for professional criminals.

"Does that mean that Gerhard was released, allowed to leave?" I asked.

Frau Schwarz shook her head. "No. It says Ueberfuehrt. Transported while still in custody. I don't know where to."

We both had hoped the whole thing was a mistake and that we wouldn't find any trace of him here. When we said as much to Frau Schwarz, she said many people came with that hope. She had worked there at Buchenwald, in the upstairs dingy room of the massive building, for eight years, trying to find answers to questions that could hardly be formed. She described one family she had been able to find information for. "They came from Israel, wanting to know what happened. I found out for them that the brother had been part of a work detail. He had died outside the camp. I was even able to tell them where he was buried."

But she wasn't able to tell us any more about Gerhard.

Leaving the archives, we noticed a newer building. Inside was an exhibit that explained what had happened to the Jews of Weimar. All had been swept up by the Nazis. None had ever returned. On the walls, there was also artwork done by the Buchenwald prisoners. Karl and I passed silently, looking at the pictures and the dates. There was one, a pastel in chalk of sunflowers. Karl stood in front of it for a long time. The artist was listed as "Unknown."

"Uncle Gerhard drew in this style," Karl said. "Doesn't it remind you of that wrinkled drawing of the sunflower we found in the attic? Look at the light coming from the left, reflecting on the petals. It's almost identical, even in the pastel colors." As he spoke, his voice rose and his eyes teared up. "Unknown," he repeated, barely audible.

I began to lag behind as we walked back down the hill toward the entry gate, past a clump of not-yet-melted snow. Karl stopped at a low brick building to read the plaque explaining 6,000 Russian soldiers had been shot there by Fascists. "I want to see what's in here," he said, stepping back to let me enter ahead of him.

"No," I planted my feet. "I'm not going in there." I felt loath to enter any enclosed buildings, imaging they were all fitted with gas nozzles. Was I being overly dramatic? I couldn't seem to make myself follow Karl.

If I hoped to avoid thinking about what happened there on that isolated hilltop, the silence itself was an indictment. As I stood there waiting for Karl to reappear, I imagined I could hear the voices of the victims, pleading for help, moaning above the sound of the wind. Off in the distance, I could see mountains and I wondered if the prisoners had stood here, looking out and despairing of ever escaping the living hell.

CHAPTER XXI

As we drove away from Buchenwald, Karl seemed grateful that I was doing the talking. I wasn't saying much other than how horrified and confused I was. Why had Gerhard been imprisoned?

When Karl remained silent, I said, "Where do you think we should go next? Should we go back and confront your father?"

"I think we need more information," he answered. "I wonder if we should talk to Tante Liska in Lobitzsch? She knew both my father and Gerhard. As children, they spent summers with her on the farm. Her husband Erich died some years ago. I remember them. I liked them."

That sounded reasonable. "We will have to drive pretty fast if we're going to get there before dark," I said, feeling a sense of urgency.

He glanced at me, acknowledging how unusual it was for me to encourage more speed. Despite our growing need to find answers, we decided to stop overnight in Zeitz, a town Karl remembered from childhood. He amazed me by driving unerringly to the street where he remembered the Three Swans hotel. Once a grand, stately and luxury accommodation, the Three Swans was now, by Western standards, decaying and unappealing. However, we learned from the hotel receptionist that a West German investor was putting $4 million into fixing it.

"It will be too expensive for us next time we come," said Karl.

In every town we drove through in the new lands—which is what the Germans were now calling the former East Germany— we found the same situation. People were busy trying to catch up on a half-century of missed progress. They were building car dealerships and furniture stores, apparently believing that driving a few kilometers to the next town wouldn't work nearly as well as having the consumer products available in their own villages. In every small town, where most of the roads were still made of cobblestones, there were massive traffic jams as new drivers tried to cope with the influx of visitors. Trucks streamed in carrying all manner of suddenly available goods, and cars seemed too big for the narrow, unplanned streets that wound through the towns and villages.

In Zeitz, there were four or five telephone stores in a few block area, side by side with nearly a dozen computer stores, some of them selling products that were incompatible with East German telephone systems or that were outdated by several years in other parts of the world.

"The national anthem of the new lands is the sound of a jack hammer," I laughed, remembering how nervous I had been about whether the East Germans and West Germans would have an orgy of militaristic celebration after the reunification. These people seemed too hell-bent on catching up to the materialistic twentieth century to give a damn about politics.

Although the hotel was primitive in some respects, with only one bathroom shared among forty rooms, the food in the restaurant was more than adequate and the room itself was pleasant. "This is really nice," I said as I undressed. "It has some really quaint touches. Almost antique-looking stuff."

Karl was already in bed, reclining on his pillow and watching me. "Come here," he said softly.

I walked slowly toward him, unbuttoning my skirt as I neared him. He reached out his hand and stroked my leg. Pulling me down on top of him, he began to kiss my neck, lips and, after pushing up my sweater, the tops of my breasts. "Too many distractions," he muttered, rolling me over and pushing my legs apart. "Not enough touching." He entered me and sighed.

"Mmm. This is nice."

I closed my eyes. The old man, the new lands, the mystery of Uncle Gerhard, all faded away. I began to rotate my hips and Karl grasped my shoulders. "You feel wonderful," he said, crying out his pleasure and grinning when he heard my response.

It wasn't until the next morning, when we were driving away from Zeitz, that I remembered how interested Der Alte had been in our itinerary and I wondered aloud why that was. Karl had no more answers than I did, but our musings were interrupted when we arrived in Nonnewitz, where Ingrid had walked those forty-some years before to deliver Karl and flee from the Russians.

Nonnewitz, hardly even big enough to be described as a town, stimulated my imagination. I pictured Ingrid, about to give birth to Karl and in fear of her life, trudging down the narrow country road toward her parents' house. The picture was so vivid I felt as though I had been there along with her, two women together, battling for survival.

Karl and I took pictures of the house where he was born. As several people pulled back their curtains to watch us, Karl said, "I think they are worried that we are from the West, former property owners maybe, intent on taking back our land."

Somehow, even though it wasn't on the map and he hadn't been there since childhood, Karl found his way from Nonnewitz to Lobitzsch, a village he remembered visiting, where relatives lived and farmed. "Here I remember driving a four-horse team when I was about ten," he said. "I remember we would come here to visit sometimes when I was a small boy and we were still hungry. The cousins would always give us fresh sausage to take home. Once, they mailed us a duck. It was rotten by the time it arrived. They always took care of my mother by giving her food in those days."

At the entrance to the small village, Karl slowed down. He had spotted an old man walking along the road. Karl pulled over and asked me to roll down the passenger window. In what Karl later told me was almost flawless Saxon dialect, he asked the man, "can you point out the house of Liska Schmidt?"

He hesitated a moment, then asked, "Why do you want to know where she lives?"

Karl explained, translating for me as he went along, that he was a relative, and he smiled, hoping to disarm the man. "I last saw her when I was fifteen. We want to visit her. She's my great aunt."

"Well," he said, "If you are related to Liska, then you are related to me. Whose are you?" Karl was puzzled about the meaning.

"I am Friedrich Schmidt's son," Karl said, hoping that was the right answer.

Apparently it was, because the man said, "Well, well, I see the resemblance in you. I am your Cousin Emil. Welcome back to Lobitzsch. Where have you been? The last time I saw you was when you were barely ten years old."

Karl said, "I now live in America. I've been there for the last thirty years."

Emil looked amazed. "That's a long way away, my boy, but at least you still know your way home." He pointed to Liska's house and shook hands with Karl. "Well, I imagine you won't want to visit everyone. I'll pass the word at the pub that you are home. Maybe I'll see you later, Karl." With that, he walked on.

Liska recognized Karl the moment she opened the door. "You look just like your father. You have our eyebrows." She was clearly delighted Karl remembered her. He introduced me and she nodded.

Karl said to me, almost in a whisper, that Liska had become very frail. Indeed, this very thin, bird-like woman, was bent over, holding onto furniture as she walked.

They reminisced about the old days, Karl telling her what he remembered about the farm. "Do you remember my Uncle Gerhard?" he asked her eventually.

"Oh yes, that one, what a rebel," she said, clasping her hands over her heart. "He never wanted to do what he was told. In the early years, in the thirties, once there was a parade through the city. Everyone was expected to lift their arms and say 'Sieg Heil', but Gerhard, he refused."

Karl asked, "So he was always rebellious. He didn't want to follow anyone's rules. What happened?"

Tante Liska's expression darkened. "The man who was leading the parade, a big shot, he stopped the parade in its tracks and ordered Gerhard to raise his arm, but he wouldn't, so the leader slapped him, just so." She waved her arm across her face.

"Some people later said that Gerhard resisted the Nazis and that it was all political. Yes, he was classified as a political prisoner, but Erich and I thought all along that Gerhard just wouldn't allow himself to be pushed or bullied. He was a person, by himself and for himself. The Nazis were exactly the opposite. Gerhard had strong principles. He just would not bend or compromise. He thought the Nazis were wrong and were ruining Germany."

Liska rose and stiffly walked over to the sink. She began to make coffee and to lay the table for an afternoon meal with bread and meats. Karl and I looked at each other with an implied agreement that even though she had little for herself, to refuse would have been rude.

"Now your father, he was different," said Liska. "I remember his neighborhood in Leipzig was built mostly by a Socialist savings organization, but not everyone who lived there was a Socialist, including your grandfather, the policeman. Many of his friends were Socialists. When their children grew up, they wanted to become officers in the Nazi Party, but someone had to vouch for them, because as the children of Socialists, they weren't acceptable."

Karl asked, "Who vouched for them?"

"Why, your father. He once told me, 'After all, I was a Nazi. I could do that'."

"But not just any Nazi, right? He had to be an Alter

Kaempfer?" Karl had gotten so engrossed that he had stopped translating and I had lost the thread of the conversation. Karl explained it to me and I said, "But what does that mean? An old camper?"

Karl twisted his mouth into a half-smile."Sort of. It means old fighter. The real McCoy, the inner circle. So I suppose if he could get the neighbor children into the party, he could have gotten Gerhard out of the camp."

"Or into it," I said.

Karl asked Liska if she knew why or how Gerhard had died.

"Well, yes, I remember your grandfather saying they had seen the body and it had no marks on it, so that was how it was. I remember going to a memorial service then after he died." Karl and I exchanged another look. Could this story of Liska's be yet another family myth to add to the growing collection?

After some hesitation, probably in deference to her age, Karl said, almost mumbling, "Did you know that Gerhard was imprisoned in Buchenwald?"

Tante Liska looked off into the distance and folded her arms across her chest. "You know. This all happened so long ago. Maybe you should talk to your father about this."

It was clear that was all Liska was going to say.

Before we left Lobitzsch and Tante Liska, Karl slipped her a 100 mark bill. "You were always so good to us," he said, looking around her small, cramped house, threadbare furniture, broken television and ancient appliances.

As she thanked him and hugged Karl good-bye and shook hands with me, she said, almost as an afterthought, "You know, your father and Gerhard came here every summer when they were children and then Gerhard stayed here for a while when he was a young man. Erich and I enjoyed him very much. Everyone who knew him in Leipzig always said he was a troublemaker— stubborn and contrary. But when he was here, he was entirely different. He was happy, friendly and helpful.

He talked freely to everyone. I think he felt we were all family and he knew he was safe and loved. At least for a while."

Her eyes misted over when she mentioned her long-dead husband—or maybe they were tears for the nephew she hadn't been able to protect. Before she turned away, bent and feeble, she handed Karl a paper bag with a homemade sausage and said, "Give this to your father. He always liked it. She was back inside the house with the door closed before Karl and I drove away."

CHAPTER XXII

Driving back to Heidelberg, Karl and I discussed how we were going to confront Der Alte. We didn't think we should tell him what we'd found at the Leipzig house or that we'd been to Buchenwald or that Tante Liska had told us to ask him what had happened to Gerhard.

"He's an old man. It would upset him to think we'd been there," I said, wondering why I was trying to protect him. Although we debated all the way to Heidelberg, by the time we got there, we still hadn't resolved how to talk to him. Instead, when we arrived, we presented Tante Liska's sausage to Ingrid with a flourish and regaled Der Alte with tales of the new lands.

He was obviously gratified by our observations and interested in discussing the politics of the Wiedervereinigung, but it was clear that even in the two weeks we'd been gone, his energy level had dropped. He looked more and more like a haggard and frail old man, and less and less like an imposing Nazi official.

When we awoke the next day–it was Karl's birthday—both of us were aware that it might be the last time we would celebrate the event with Der Alte. Perhaps Der Alte had the same thoughts, because in addition to Ingrid's predictable cake and coffee, he had gone to the store and bought German beer, meat and cheese.

"This is pretty ironic," Karl said in an aside to me. "In all of my growing up years, I don't recall him ever doing anything to acknowledge my birthday."

We told Karl's parents we had been to Nonnewitz. "I recalled your story about Karl's birth," I said to Ingrid. "I felt as if I had been there with you." Ingrid seemed touched, and placed a hand on my arm.

In the fading light, while Der Alte uncapped another bottle of beer, I turned to him and, driven by a sense of urgency because we were leaving the next day, said, "Didn't you get discouraged as the war went on and people disappeared—wasn't it difficult to cope with situations like the one with your brother?"

The old man seemed unperturbed, almost nonchalant about the question, as if we talked about it daily. I had to remind myself that Karl had never discussed the topic with his father and that no one in the family admitted to knowing what really happened to Gerhard.

"Well, I was away for a lot of the time. I was a soldier."

"But what really happened to him?" I asked.

Making a tent of his fingers, the old man said slowly, "He was involved in a Nazi youth group. The leader was someone who had been in England for years, then returned. He was, secretly, a Communist. He led the group astray, Gerhard among them."

Describing the years before and during the war, the old man outlined a confusing chronology that involved an arrest of Gerhard by the police, imprisonment in the Dresden city jail, release so Gerhard could find a place to live. Gerhard disappeared for a while, but when the Germans marched into Vienna, there was Gerhard again. He was arrested in Vienna, questioned, released and finally re-arrested in Dresden. Whatever the sequence of events and their causes, somehow, Gerhard seemed to have ended up finally in the Dresden jail, where he died.

"He died in the Dresden city jail?" I repeated.

"Yes. In the Gestapo jail," Der Alte paused. "I tried to find out why. But it would be folly to try to make inquiries now," he waved his hand in a dismissive way. "The commander of the jail was transferred to a combat battalion in the Balkans and finally hung himself. And of course, any records would be destroyed by the bombing and the firestorm in Dresden. It's too late. What would be the point?"

For the first time that night, his voice rose. He appeared fearful that my curiosity would lead me to delve further.

I decided to change the subject to assuage his suspicion. "Since this is Karl's birthday," I said. "I'd love to know where were you the day Karl was born."

Karl translated my question and when the old man rose with difficulty to his feet and shuffled across the room, I thought we had at last gone too far in our questioning, that he was leaving the room, and we would never find out more about Gerhard. But instead, Der Alte took a key out of a drawer in his desk, walked over to an armoire in the corner of the living room and pulled out a worn notebook.

"I'll read you from my diary about that day and the days following," he said. I could barely allow myself to look at Karl and see a reflection of my own amazement on his face. Never had a diary been mentioned. The old man had never once offered to describe any of his feelings or thoughts from that period.

While we waited with hushed expectancy for Der Alte to begin reading, Ingrid decided she had had enough. She pulled herself out of her chair, mumbling about old Nazis, sighed heavily and said goodnight. Amid the choruses of good-nights, thank-yous and see-you-in-the-mornings, the old man sat silently, opening the notebook to a page and peering at it.

"It was May 1 and I was leading my unit south into Bavaria, hoping we could elude the Allied troops and make it to safety in the mountains," he said as an introduction before starting to read aloud. "I was riding in the sidecar of a motorcycle with my aide. It was very foggy. We almost missed the old farmer in the gloom. 'You. Have you seen the enemy nearby?' I asked him in a low tone, squinting to see him. He was dressed in shabby clothes and carried a long staff."

165

" 'Ja. The enemy is all around us,' said the man, not bothering to stop." Where he was going, Der Alte said wasn't clear, but he surely had no intention of lingering to talk to a German officer.

Karl translated for me every few sentences. "Reaching the top of the rise, I motioned for the aide to turn off the motorcycle. We coasted down the hill silently and when we reached the bottom, the fog parted and there, before us, was an American tank. The soldier at the top lowered the machine gun with one motion, fired a burst in our direction, killing my motorcycle driver instantly. But because we were so close to the tank, the machine gunner could not lower his weapon enough to shoot me."

Swinging his legs over the edge of the sidecar, he threw down his gun, put up his hands and there, in the Bavarian countryside, with the mist dripping off his helmet, the war ended for Friedrich Schmidt.

"So, I was in a prisoner-of-war camp that day Karl was born, two weeks later. Eight days after we officially surrendered," Der Alte said. "I didn't know for several months about his birth, but on that day, I wrote this," he said, reading from his diary.

"'The war, as I expected, is lost and now it is left for me to decide what I will do with my life. The school, of course, is gone and it will not be possible for me to teach. I should like, above all things, to become an adventurer, try out different careers, travel the world, be carefree and footloose. It is true, I don't really want to find myself back in a family, with the responsibility of children and a wife. There is so much to see and do."

Der Alte seemed unaware that he was reading this excerpt to his son and that he was sharing his thoughts, not of the magnitude of the carnage the Nazis had wrought or the shame that Germany once again was to experience, but instead, his own personal distaste for resuming the life to which he had to return.

166

"How long did you stay in that prisoner-of war-camp and what was it like there?" I asked, thinking of Buchenwald, Bergen-Belsen, Auschwitz and the other camps, determined not to feel a scintilla of pity for whatever he said.

"It wasn't pleasant. We were all in a big field. It was damp and soon we all had bladder problems. There wasn't enough food. But I was able to read books shared with other prisoners and write in my diary and even sometimes get messages from the outside." He was silent for a short time, maybe remembering that field or perhaps trying to decide whether to continue his story.

"I probably would have remained there, or in another prison for a good long time," he said. "After all, when I was leading the school in Sonthofen, my superior was Baldur von Schirach. He was the Education and Youth Minister and was accused by the Allies of misleading the German youth. He was tried and convicted at Nuremberg. But an ignorant mistake by the Americans allowed me to go free."

"What happened?" Karl asked, apparently forgetting for a moment that he had vowed only to translate. Maybe because Der Alte seemed so comfortable telling the story, Karl was able to think just for a moment that perhaps there really were no terrible secrets to hide and that the old man, after all, had been nothing but a regular soldier in the German army.

"We were all asked to complete a form, describing what we had done during the war. I didn't think it was worth concealing what I had been doing, because I thought they would find out anyway, so I completed the form truthfully. I said I had been a Hauptbannfuehrer."

I stole a look at Karl to see if he was responding to that information with horror or surprise. He didn't look either shocked or amazed; I assumed he knew what that rank signified.

"I expected they would transfer me immediately to another, more secure prison or question me, because already we had heard about the Allies' plan for some kind of war trials," Der Alte continued. "But instead, to my surprise, they told me their major priority was getting the infrastructure of the country, including the trains, going again, and since I was a railroad official, I was free to leave."

The old man began laughing, a feeble laugh that made him clutch his chest. I was confused. Why had the Americans made such a ridiculous mistake?

Karl explained to me. "You see, the word for train is Bahn, not bann, but the Americans obviously misunderstood, so they let him go."

After that, the old man had made his way to Kiel, where he had agreed to meet his wife. Although all Germans were subsequently ordered to appear at de-Nazification hearings to describe what their roles in the war had been, Der Alte never kept his appointment.

Abruptly, he put the diary away and said good night. This had been our last night before we were to fly home. I wondered if there were any chance we would ever find out more.

"I remember," Karl told me when we were getting ready for bed and holding a whispered debriefing in one of our bedrooms before parting. "I remember him hiding out, I think. When we were living in the attic, I think some officials came and he didn't come home for days, waiting for them to give up and go away. They did."

He grasped my hand and said, "Maybe after he dies, we'll be able to read the journals and find out the entire truth at last." Karl paused. "It's amazing. After years and years of silence, mostly enforced by my mother, Der Alte talks. It is almost as if he knows that he does not have much time left and finally has a need to be understood, to be seen the way he sees himself. He almost challenges you to ask, and then answers every question you have. It is nearly half a century since he penciled his diary. Do you think I have even so much as heard of its existence before? No. And not only does he show it to me, he shows me where he has locked it away. He brings it out and reads from it. I am sure he has never done that before, or else I would have heard of the diary. I have the distinct feeling that he did this on purpose so that someday after his death I should go back and get it."

I had a more pressing question. "What exactly was a Hauptbannfuehrer?" I imagined Der Alte sporting medals and ribbons, marching and saluting.

Karl shrugged. "I have no idea. They gave everyone grand sounding titles that may or may not have had anything to do with what their actual job was. This is the first I've heard of that rank. I think it's made up. Bann is an ancient word. The whole thing translates as a superhigh area commander. It makes no sense. It's not really translatable from German to English. He told us he outranks a colonel in the Austrian army. That's all we know.

CHAPTER XXIII

I packed our bags after I dressed in the morning, leaving Karl free to linger over breakfast with his mother before we left for the airport. Karl told me she had complained he hadn't spent enough time with her.

"Karl," I called when I reached the living room where we had talked the night before. But today, the living room was empty. Sounds from the kitchen indicated that Ingrid was busy with food preparation. Karl and his father were in the study. When I approached, I saw that the old man was sitting at his huge, antique desk, with Karl standing behind him.

"Come look here," said Karl quietly, waving a document at me. As I reached his side, he handed it to me, and then another and another. They were letters and postcards, with the masthead of concentration camp Buchenwald printed across the top.

"Who are these from?" I asked the old man, but I already knew. These were copies of what we had found in the attic of Karl's grandfather's house. The old man didn't answer, saying instead, "And these, these are from the Gestapo." Karl was skimming the letters, translating quickly. "The Gestapo said they are detaining Gerhard for questioning. That he cannot be released."

Karl handed me a letter printed in the old style German font. "See this? This is from the Gestapo Directorate in Dresden, addressed to my grandfather. It's dated January 9, 1941. It states in three sentences that 'Your son died last night in our custody unexpectedly. With his death our investigation into his activities is now closed. Since this was a case of State

Security no inquiries will be responded to. Heil Hitler' and then a signature of someone I can't make out. And here is a death certificate. It says that he died of 'heart failure.' And this to top it all off: a postal receipt for human ashes. 'Gerhard Schmidt,' it says. 'Postage Due.' I think I am going to be sick," Karl groaned.

The old man seemed oblivious to our discussion. He did not look at us or comment as he silently handed Karl the papers. And then abruptly, almost as if he regretted sharing these documents, he gathered everything up, put them into a drawer of the desk, locked it and went toward the kitchen.

So was this finally the truth? There was no time to ask any more questions.

As we said good-bye after breakfast, I hugged Der Alte, reminding myself this was Karl's father, who would, likely, be dead soon. But that he might die with the secret of his brother and the real truth of what he did during the war made it more difficult to be sincere in my wishes for his good health.

On the way to the airport, I asked Karl how his Aunt Liska had been able to say there were no marks on Gerhard's body. "If there was a receipt for his ashes, how could she or anyone else have seen his body?"

Karl shrugged. "Yet another un-answered question. Quite obviously someone isn't telling the truth." Then he added, "If I were a German cop and had to investigate this I would treat Gerhard's death as a homicide. I would certainly consider my father to be a person of interest in the investigation, given his political influence."

"What do you mean? Surely you don't think he killed Gerhard?"

"Of course not, but considering his rank and his access to the inner circle, wouldn't you think he could have protected him, gotten him released, prevented his death? And since he didn't, isn't it possible that he actually implicated Gerhard to prove his loyalty to the Reich?"

171

CHAPTER XXIV

Karl waited until we were on the plane, headed back to California, to tell me about his last conversation with Der Alte. The old man had taken Karl aside after breakfast. Karl had emerged from the discussion looking shaken, but there had been no time for us to talk about what happened.

I assumed that the old man had either given Karl some money, as he sometimes did, or that he, ever a realist, was saying good-bye to his son, recognizing that as his health was failing fast, it might be the last time the two would be together.

Karl shook his head when I asked if that was what had been discussed. "Not hardly," he said.

"I talked to your friend pretty openly," Der Alte had told Karl. "But I know she is a Jewish journalist. I hope that none of what I said will ever show up in print in the American press. It could mean suicide."

"Suicide?" I cringed. "I wouldn't want to do anything to cause his death. Although at this point, I'm not really sure he said anything that really amounts to much."

I thought ruefully about how complicated the situation had become. Probably in years past, if I thought there were ex-Nazis like Der Alte on the loose, I would have been adamant about the need to bring them to justice. Now my conflict about relentlessly pursuing truth from a sick old man was prompting me to even give up on trying to find more information. And I had to admit that the old man's evasive and ambiguous answers had strained my reporting skills. I wasn't sure if I was even capable of ferreting out anything more and finding what might—or might not—be the truth.

Karl looked at me solemnly. "I think you might have missed his point. He specifically said, 'if this shows up in print, it would mean suicide.' Whose suicide was he talking about?"

I said slowly, "I assumed he meant it could be dangerous for him. Are you saying he implied I could be killed if I published any of this? Is that what he meant?"

"I don't know," I realized Karl was whispering. "I think he specifically left it open to interpretation. It's up to us to decide." I shook my head in amazement, but made an effort to be objective. "Maybe he just did not explain himself clearly, maybe he was just tired."

But Karl was adamant. "No. I know him and I know how he uses language. Nothing is an accident. He means everything he says and chooses his words carefully. He has always done that. If he was ambiguous, then he was ambiguous on purpose. He wanted us to think about the meaning and discuss all implications. I think this was a very indirect threat."

We looked at each other in consternation. What exactly had Der Alte said that was too dangerous to be published? Could he really carry out such an ominous warning? Karl didn't need me to tell him that he had followed his usual pattern with his father, a pattern established over a lifetime. He'd asked for no clarification about the old man's words, but let them settle over him in suffocating silence.

During the rest of our flight, we alternately debated what the old man had meant and whether I should write about him. We were so focused on the implied threat that we barely discussed how we should pursue finding out more about Gerhard.

When I noticed Karl glancing around and scrutinizing the other passengers, he confessed he was uneasy.

"I know it's ridiculous, but I keep wondering if he has spies watching us." I nodded in agreement. I had been feeling the same way and had, several times, surreptitiously moved the tiny audio tape we used to record our conversations with Der

Alte to more secure spots in my purse. We tried to make light of our fears by concocting fanciful stories about the motives of unlikely passengers, but our laughter only partially dissipated our unease.

Near the end of the flight, Karl said, "We have to get on with our lives too. We did have some nice times on this trip. It wasn't all gloom and doom, looking for Uncle Gerhard, trying to find out the truth about my old man and seeing Buchenwald."

He put his hand on my thigh. "I liked making love to my Sarah in exotic and strange places." He leaned over and breathed my scent. "Ah yes, this is still my Sarah."

I sighed, trying to relax. I knew Karl was trying to distract me. I thought it would be a long time before the images of Buchenwald faded from my mind. I turned his face toward me and kissed him, putting my tongue into his mouth, tasting his maleness. "I'm glad we're almost home," I said. But arriving home also meant that we would now have to go to our separate houses. That would feel strange after the intense togetherness we had just shared.

We decided to take a shower to celebrate our return to the convenience of American bathrooms, where crouching at the bottom of the bathtub and holding the spray attachment in one hand wasn't part of the routine of bathing.

"Boy, I'm glad to be back with you, in our country," Karl grinned.

He was clearly admiring me and I thought I didn't look at all bad for a woman of my age who had just flown across two continents, an ocean, a cultural barrier—and come face to face with the past.

CHAPTER XXV

In the end, the real meaning of the old man's warning was a moot point. When I wrote the story for the Jewish newspaper about the trip, explaining the old people's attitude toward me and the war, the paper cut out all reference to the old man.

"Visiting an old Nazi and not coming across in the article strongly about your feelings of revulsion for him meant that part had to be cut," said Bruce Kaplan.

It amazed me how sure Kaplan was that his attitude was right and how unmoved he was about the possibility that he might be censoring information his readers might want to hear.

I didn't tell Kaplan or anybody else about the old man's threat and as the trip began to fade a little in our memory, that piece seemed almost unreal. Had Karl misinterpreted what his father said? Had he mistaken humor for a serious conversation? There was no way of knowing, but the old man never mentioned the issue again, even as I encouraged Karl to call his parents more often.

"They're old, you should do it," I said, thinking not about Der Alte, the Nazi, but an old man in his twilight years. "And I confess, I keep hoping he'll bring up something, anything, about his brother."

Karl said, "The bottom line is, I don't think we'll know a thing until the old man dies and we get our hands on his diaries and other papers, including Uncle Gerhard's letters and postcards. And maybe even then we won't know."

We talked about why we hadn't just taken all the letters from the Leipzig house when we could. "They weren't mine," was Karl's explanation.

If we were unsuccessful in getting information about Der Alte and his past, telling my mother about Der Alte and the adventures we had in Germany seemed to fascinate her.

"I can hardly believe you went there, met the old man and sat and talked with him. I never imagined hearing the stories from the other perspective," my mother said, adding, "And to think, you were able to behave civilly."

Sensing some reproach, I said, "Well Mom, he's a sick old man and he's Karl's father. Besides, I'm a reporter. I'm used to hearing people say egregious things and not reacting. I can't say I loved everything he said, but he wasn't as outrageous as I expected. It almost seemed like he wanted me to understand what happened."

When I told my mother about Gerhard and Buchenwald and the Gestapo jail, she was as stunned as we had been. She asked why he was there and we told her we had read on the card that he was a political prisoner. "We think he died for his principles." I did not tell my mother some of the more disturbing aspects of the old man's comments. I wasn't sure why, but it was probably because I didn't want her to think badly of Karl. I didn't tell her about the warning or about the lies.

"Your family are now her *machetunim*," I explained to Karl, who didn't recognize the word, which almost defied translating. "It's a sort of extension of the in-law concept that makes the whole family on both sides somehow related. I can't totally bad-mouth the old man to her."

I didn't like to think about my mother's reaction to being related, if only by Jewish custom, to a Nazi.

It was several weeks after our trip, sitting in Brennan's, when Beth asked me about Karl's behavior in Germany. We had returned gratefully to our routine, he ordering his Irish coffee with a sigh of relief and commenting on how glad he was that he had emigrated. Sipping my beer, I turned to Karl and said, "You know, you were right, the German beer we drank on our trip makes this American beer seem like yellow water."

But although Beth smiled, she was more concerned with my trip than the quality of German beer. "Did he turn into a Nazi, more of a fascist pig than cops are just naturally?" Beth asked with a wicked grin at Karl. She herself was beginning to get comfortable with him and appreciate his finer points, but she didn't like to acknowledge her softening attitude.

I laughed. I understood my friend's vigilance and knew Beth's observations were sometimes ways to give voice to my own fears and anxieties.

"He was fine, basically the same as he always is," I said, telling Beth about the episode that resulted in me sleeping with the penknife in hand. Feeling foolish, I hadn't even told Karl about it.

"So his father was a monster?" Beth said.

"Actually not. I certainly wouldn't describe him as sweet, but he was very charming, very concerned about entertaining us, showing us the sights. He seemed very open about talking to me and answering my questions." I didn't tell Beth either about the old man's veiled threat. It all seemed so remote and unbelievable, sitting there in Brennan's and drinking beer. I wondered if he had really been that open, or whether it had all been a game, just a way for the old man to test whether his lies would be believed.

Strangely, that history now seemed to have very little to do with Karl. The trip had worked not to link him in my mind to his German past but to separate him finally in my thinking from his parents, the Third Reich and Germany. Despite his accent, he had become more of an American than a German. I saw that clearly for the first time.

Maybe that was what made it possible for us to finally look ahead to a future together.

CHAPTER XXVI

We began to live together some months after our return from Germany. Der Alte died not too long after that. Karl attended the funeral alone.

A former student from the Adolf Hitler Schule delivered the eulogy, which, besides describing Der Alte's rise to power in the NSDAP and his success after the war, included this surprisingly frank reflection, which Karl shared with me:

"There are memories of relatives who knew him as a child in Leipzig and Lobitzsch. We at the school knew that he played ragtime on his violin in the village pub to entertain himself and to confuse the farmers in Lobitzsch. We knew that he early on made a decision to join the NSDAP because, as he said, he wanted to do his part to erase the injustices of the Versailles Treaty and wanted to see the German people again as an equal member of the family of nations."

"At the same time, his younger brother Gerhard decided to work against the regime and he paid for that early in January 1941 with his life in the Gestapo prison in Dresden. Friedrich never spoke about his brother. However, in the last years of his life, he had a picture of himself and his brother on a shelf in his library."

When Karl got home from the funeral, he pulled out the photo he'd snapped of that picture during our visit and hung it on the wall of our house. He told me that when he asked his mother for Der Alte's papers, she'd made it pretty clear that, as far as she was concerned, there were no papers. Karl was angry but unwilling to upset her.

After our visit to Germany, Karl had tried to talk to his sisters about Der Alte's role in the Reich, and about Gerhard's fate. Both women discouraged Karl from pursuing more information and warned him not to even think about letting me write about it. They insisted that as a Jewish journalist, I could not be trusted to be impartial.

When Karl visited Germany several times more after his father's death, it was apparent that his mother was failing. She began to have difficulty breathing, walking and hearing. He was warned by his sister on each visit not to discuss anything that might worry her.

Karl and I bought a house after deciding that mine was too small for us, the dog and all of our books and other things we had collected over the years. As we set up our household, old photos of both of our families were hung in the hallway, the Jews facing the Germans.

We established our family rituals, including Christmas, Passover, Thanksgiving and birthdays.

When Karl's mother died just a few years after our first visit, Karl repeated his request to his sisters, who similarly denied any knowledge of diaries, letters, postcards or other documents— either Der Alte's or anything related to Gerhard.

We might have believed this, were it not for an unexpected visit from his older sister's now ex-husband. With no prompting, he told Karl as he was leaving after a pleasant dinner, "There's one thing I never forgot. Your sister had a shoebox of correspondence in her basement from your uncle, from the concentration camp. It's been there since your father died. I remember reading a postcard where Gerhard described his glasses being smashed and having lost his teeth. I will never forget that," he repeated.

After one of Karl's requests to his younger sister for information, and although she insisted that there were no documents, she suggested that if Karl were interested in preserving Gerhard's story, he should consider installing a Stolperstein—a bronze plaque—in front of the house in

Leipzig marking Gerhard's birth and death. "Maybe all three of us kids can do this together," she said.

When Karl told me about this conversation, I had no idea what a Stolperstein was. His sister had explained that recently a German artist had begun creating and dedicating little square bronze plaques to the memory of specific Holocaust victims. The Stolperstein was placed into the pavement of the sidewalk in the front of the person's last known address. Engraved on each one, besides a name, was the date of birth and date and place of death.

"Stolperstein literally means stumbling stone. It's an inconvenient reminder of the victims," Karl explained. "My sister says they are starting to appear not only all over Germany, but even in other countries."

After she made the suggestion, Karl and I debated where Gerhard's Stolperstein could be placed. One option, of course, was Leipzig, where Gerhard lived in his youth and where his rebellion had begun. Another choice might be Lobitzsch.

"I think he was happy there," Karl said. "Remember that my aunt commented that she and Erich enjoyed his stay very much."

We also discussed, somewhat sarcastically, what might be engraved on Gerhard's Stolperstein. "We could put his name and birth date—and since we don't know what happened to him—we could borrow the notation from his Buchenwald card," I suggested.

"Ueberfuehrt—transported in custody," Karl mumbled. "Right. Fitting."

The Red Cross Tracing service never contacted us again to provide any additional information.

We began to warm to the idea of dedicating the Stolperstein, yet whenever the subject came up, we couldn't seem to move ahead with the plan. Maybe it seemed too final, too much closure when we didn't have the information we had been looking for.

Ten years after the death of Der Alte, Karl's sisters, without comment, finally sent Karl a package containing some postcards, letters and records, some of which we had seen in Leipzig, and some of Der Alte's papers from the desk and cabinet. The diary, sadly, had vanished.

Going through the package contents, Karl read me from a letter his grandfather had written in September, 1945, to a government agency that apparently provided financial payments to Germans who lost family members to the Nazi regime.

Using his Police Inspector title, Karl's grandfather detailed the progression of Gerhard's troubles, beginning when he was eighteen years old and a student. It chronicled his arrest and incarceration in multiple places, including Buchenwald, Prague and Vienna. It referred to ten documents enclosed to corroborate his facts.

"Unbelievable. What nerve. He's making a case that his son was a victim of the Nazis—which he surely was—while simply ignoring that his other son was a high-ranking Nazi," Karl said.

To shore up his claim, Gustaf Schmidt had included testimony from a number of neighbors claiming he was an anti-Fascist, even though he remained a police official throughout the war and must have actively supported the Nazi regime.

Dated October 17, 1938 was a postcard from the State Police, headquartered in Vienna, to Karl's grandfather. "In response to your letter, I am informing you that your son was transferred from here on August 19, 1938 into the custody of the State Police in Dresden." The card was unsigned.

And there were a few letters and postcards from Gerhard in Buchenwald, one from 1939 telling his father that families of prisoners were now, despite the rules on the preprinted paper, permitted to send packages containing clothes.

Karl laughed sarcastically at that. "They must have needed warm sweaters for the camp personnel. I'm sure Gerhard never saw any of that stuff."

Also in the box was the death certificate, recording Gerhard's death on January 9, 1941, between 4:30-5:15 p.m., just days after he was transferred from Buchenwald to the Gestapo headquarters in Dresden. When Karl checked the address on the document of where the death occurred, it was the Gestapo headquarters.

Months later, after reading through all the material, Karl made a suggestion. "I've been thinking about my sister's proposal to place a Stolperstein in Leipzig. But I think I have a better idea. Instead of a small plaque just listing his name and some dates, why don't we take the papers and reconstruct Gerhard's story?"

The more we thought about that idea and the more we read and re-read the papers, the more that approach sounded compelling.

"We can also try getting information at the Holocaust Memorial Museum in Washington, D.C. and other places. They keep releasing new material," I said.

"Yes," Karl agreed. "Yes. Writing his story can be the memorial to him. The Nazis in the end were able to silence him. If we write his story, he will finally get what he truly deserves. His voice can still be heard."

PART III

Gerhard's Stumbling Stone

September 1932   Leipzig

Gerhard Schmidt was on the way home from school. He hated school, always had, perhaps with the exception of first grade. Gerhard did not like to be told what to do, when to do it, and what to enjoy.

He liked to pick his own pleasures. He could totally absorb himself in watching a flower, noting the way the petals subtly change color in different lights, and then drawing it with his pastel crayons. He liked to listen to music, especially Bach. He loved the brilliance of the trumpets, the festive chorales, the intricate continuo of cello and harpsichord.

Yes, music and art, those were the exceptions, but everything else in school he not only disliked but hated. That included the teachers—self-important pompous civil servants whose lives were divided into 45-minute lessons, forcing everyone to fake rapt attention when what they had to offer was unimportant and in no way connected to the reality of life.

Gerhard was angry. He was seventeen years old and therefore not yet entitled to freedom. He had to do what his parents wanted, what his teachers wanted. He comforted himself with the thought that soon—when he finished high school and went to the university—maybe then he would have more liberty to choose his own preferences, his own destiny.

It certainly did not help that his father was a police officer in Leipzig. A fiercely nationalistic man who had lost one leg in the World War in France, Gustaf Schmidt still rode his bicycle to work, refused to use a cane when walking, and only attended to his war injury in the practical matter of oiling his artificial leg when the knee-joint started squeaking. He detested the French and did not want to credit them even with the loss of his leg. It was probably hard enough to work under his supervision, but it was even harder to be his child.

Gerhard's life was regimented from the minute he got up in the morning until he finished his homework and went to bed. Well, maybe with the short exceptions of daydreaming or drawing something that he liked.

As he rounded the corner to Schillerstrasse on his way home, he heard it. Marching music, overpowering all other sounds. "Prussia's Glory." Actually, Gerhard thought, the band was decent. No sour notes, good instruments, and the piece itself well played. Quite a far cry from the marching bands of the Communist Party, which were usually a hodgepodge of well-meaning workers, trying to play as well as they could, but usually failing in the struggle against their instruments.

Gerhard stopped to watch. There were about 200 jackbooted Storm Troopers marching behind the band. Their uniforms were impeccable; they were in perfect step and arranged according to size. No tall marcher was next to a short one. At the head of the column was Schleicher, the Nazi leader in Leipzig, a ruthless commander.

Gerhard had seen photos and heard many stories about Schleicher from his brother Friedrich, who was five years older. Schleicher and Friedrich had joined the German National Socialist Workers Party—NSDAP, the Nazi Party— about the same time and had become friends. Gustaf Schmidt listened tolerantly to Friedrich's stories about the NSDAP and their antics. With a look of approval, he said, "Friedrich, I support your anti-communism and I also wish for a more disciplined Germany, but please, do not embarrass me by being arrested. It really does not look good if I have to let you go 'for insufficient evidence.' So watch yourself."

That day, Gerhard—an insignificant, skinny teenager standing and waiting for the parade to reach him— wondered as he often did why his father could be so forgiving of Friedrich's escapades and so judgmental and intolerant when it came to him.

Gerhard heard the trumpets and tubas echo from the

buildings on both sides of the street; he heard the "crack-crack-crack" of leather jackboots on the cobblestones. All street traffic had come to a halt. Everyone was watching; cars had pulled to the curb ahead of the marching column. Streetcars stopped. Gerhard watched along with the rest, fascinated yet disturbed by the show of force.

"Deeetaiiil, Halt!" Schleicher commanded. The music ended, while the jackboots cracked exactly three more times onto the pavement. Then the marching column stood still; the stormtroopers remained at attention with eyes straight ahead. The street was suddenly filled with eerie silence. Schleicher executed a smart right turn and marched directly towards Gerhard. His eyes were fixed on the eyes of the boy, like a snake will look at a bird just before striking.

Gerhard wanted to run but decided not to. Schleicher stopped within arm's length.

"Come to attention, damn it." Schleicher screamed and pointed at Gerhard. "I'm speaking to you. What is your problem? Why will you not salute the flag of Germany's future like everyone else?"

Suddenly Gerhard became aware of his own posture, leaning against a lamppost, both hands in his pants pockets. He looked around. Everyone else in the street had raised their outstretched right arms in the salute of the Nazis, toward the flags of the marchers.

Schleicher struck out with his flat hand, hitting Gerhard in the face. His teeth cut into his lip, his nose instantly trickled blood, his eyes filled with tears. "Greet the flag, damn it!" Schleicher commanded.

Gerhard tasted blood. His face stung and for a second he did not know what to do. He had been so surprised by the sudden attack that he had not moved. He still had both hands in his pockets; he was still was leaning against the lamppost. "Nun gerade nicht."[1] Gerhard said walking away, slowly at first and then at a trot.

---

[1] Now, certainly not!

As he gathered speed, he began to smirk. He liked saying "Nun gerade nicht" because it so clearly captured his anger and protest. He felt that it was a succinct way of saying, "Now that I know what your conditions are, I will deliberately disobey your orders." And it also conveyed his utter contempt for authority.

Gerhard heard Schleicher scream, "This is the scum we will eradicate! The future is ours. Deeetaiiiil! March!" "Prussia's Glory" again filled the street.

Spring 1934   Leipzig

Friedrich Schmidt was visiting his family home in Leipzig, on leave from his university. He had not joined one of the traditional student fraternities whose members drank a lot, were fiercely patriotic and still fenced with sabers, giving each other the scars of distinction. He looked down on these groups with disdain. They were symbols of Germany's past, whereas he wanted to work towards Germany's future.

At the dinner table, Friedrich confronted Gerhard, who could tell by the glances they exchanged that his father and brother had planned this ambush.

"So, have you joined one of the true German organizations yet? Have you decided to join the HJ, the Hitler Youth?" Friedrich asked, staring hard at Gerhard.

Gerhard did not know what to say. Whenever he heard his older brother talk about the great fellowship and the wonderful evenings among his Nazi party friends, Gerhard felt lonely. Friedrich would sometimes come home from some of the street battles and, encouraged by his father, boast about what had happened.

"We heard about a meeting of the Communist party in Gohlis. So we took about 100 of the biggest and strongest SA men and a lot of flares. Our marching column was to go right through the Commie area towards their head-quarters—a cheap workers' pub, of course. We naturally expected opposition. This is where the flares come in. It looks triumphant and festive when we march in a tight formation, every man on the outside of the formation with a lit flare in his right hand, but there is another reason for them."

Gustaf Schmidt nodded vigorously, and against his will Gerhard was drawn into the story.

"Well as you can imagine," Friedrich said, leaning forward toward his father with a big grin on his face, "when we entered their neighborhood, marching and singing, they did not like that. Some of their biggest bullies came from the apartment houses and back alleys. What we usually do is let them get real close and then, bang, we stuff the lit flares right into their faces," he chuckled. His father encouraged him to continue the tale.

"We got to the pub and crashed through the front and back doors at the same time. Schleicher, the devil, he was the first one in. 'Die, Commie pigs,' we screamed, broke tables and chairs before anyone could move and started cracking their heads. They ran like rabbits. The pub is a ruin."

"I know," Gustaf said approvingly. "I read the police report. The responding officers wrote that it most likely was an altercation between warring factions of Communist gangs."

Gerhard was troubled. He wanted to be part of something. But the Nazis? When he thought of the Nazis, he always recalled Schleicher with his marching band and his Storm Troopers. He remembered the public humiliation and the taste of blood in his mouth. To join them? Never! Nun gerade nicht.

But he had to tell Friedrich and his father something. "We have a teacher named Mr. Krause," said Gerhard. "He emigrated with his family to England before the World War. They have returned, and it's said that Mr. Krause speaks

191

English like a native. He asked me and some other students to join the Wandervogel. They hike a lot. They have meetings and they love Germany. I'm thinking of joining next week."

"Good," Friedrich nodded. "You'll like it."

And just as Gerhard was congratulating himself on finding a good answer, Friedrich said, "We are preparing for the "Gleichschaltung" —the incorporation of all youth organizations, all student associations into the great hierarchy of the Nazi party. So, if you join the Wandervogel, you'll eventually end up with the Hitler Youth anyway—and soon.

Friedrich knew about the incident with Schleicher and Gerhard. He had smoothed it over as a big misunderstanding by his immature kid brother. He also knew that Gerhard was reluctant to join the Nazis. Friedrich had kept up the pressure on his younger brother, albeit subtly. He knew it did no good to order Gerhard to do anything. That was only a sure way to get him to resist.

In fact, Gerhard had already been part of the Wandervogel under his teacher for almost two months and had come to like his teacher even more in that time, especially outside school. He felt like an older friend. When they talked, it became clear that although his teacher was a patriot, he was no friend of the Nazis. He called them "herd animals" who tolerated no independence, no opposition and who would eventually run Germany into the ground rather than make it great, as they promised. Gerhard finally had found someone whom he could trust, with whom he could talk and share opinions.

What Gerhard didn't tell Friedrich or his father was that Krause gave the Wandervogel group, and sometimes even his English class, assignments to write and design leaflets questioning the ways of the Nazis. Gerhard also didn't tell Friedrich that Krause, Gerhard and other club members often duplicated and distributed the leaflets throughout Leipzig.

When he arrived at school one morning and learned that Krause had been dismissed from his position the day before, Gerhard was devastated. The school secretary, who had a soft spot in her heart for Gerhard in spite of his rebelliousness, told him the school officials had wanted Krause to join the National Socialist Teacher's Organization and he had refused. The principal of the school was a Nazi, Gerhard knew. He had joined the party a long time ago and had demanded that Krause join the organization as a symbol of his loyalty to the Fatherland and its future, the youth.

"I proved my loyalty by returning from England. I don't have to prove anything further," the secretary reported Krause had shouted.

"Well, let me prove something to you," the principal had told Krause, bellowing so the secretary could hear clearly and imagine his icy smile. "We will no longer tolerate or humor opposition. You are part of Germany's future or you are part of its past. Will you join?"

"If you put it that way, then I am very happy not to be part of your particular future," Krause had said, opening the door and leaving so rapidly that only the secretary heard the principal roar, "You are fired!"

Krause had left the old gray building carrying some books and his lunch in his briefcase. The secretary noticed that as Krause walked away, he was followed by two men in long gray coats.

When they heard the news about Krause, some of Gerhard's classmates, the ones wearing the uniform of the Hitler Youth, were elated. Some of them weren't doing too well in English, but they said that was not the reason they were happy to see Krause gone. They criticized Krause's use of humor and provocative viewpoints to keep the students' attention. The Hitler Youth just wanted military discipline and toughness.

"He just doesn't have it. England made him soft. Too many Jews in London!" They broke into collective laughter.

Gerhard felt left out again. While he was mourning for the teacher—his youth leader—whom he had just lost, he was suddenly interrupted.

"Schmidt, Gerhard! Principal's office, now!" An older student from one of the upper classes, wearing the now-too-familiar uniform of the Hitler Youth, bellowed into the open classroom door.

Gerhard immediately felt guilty. What could he have done? You were only called to the principal if you had made a very big transgression. His first thought was to run. Where to?

Calm down, he thought to himself. I have done nothing. You can't punish someone when they haven't done anything wrong.

He strode quickly down the hall and then, slowly and fearfully, Gerhard opened the office door. The principal, Herr Fieseler, was sitting at his almost-black, oak desk. Behind him, on the wall, was a photograph of Adolf Hitler. Next to the principal stood two men. They did not say who they were. In fact, they did not say anything. Gerhard only noticed their long gray coats.

Gerhard moved to the only empty chair left in the room and began to sit.

"Have you completely lost your mind? Stand when I am addressing you!" Herr Fieseler yelled. "What the hell is this, and this, and this!? Explain!! Now!"

The principal punctuated his questions by waving the little triangular pennant of the Wandervogel. Gerhard and his friends had carried it with them on their Sunday hikes. Herr Fieseler was also holding up what looked like a list of members of the group. The third item Gerhard had never seen. When he reached out for the unfamiliar book. the Fieseler slapped his cheek hard. "You will not touch this trash again. You most certainly will not touch anything in my office without my permission! We know what you were up to. Your teacher, the self-professed patriot, is a Communist. You are all Communists! Hiding as the

Wandervogel! This, my friend—as if you didn't know—is the Communist *Das Kapital,* brought along from London. We found it in his house. We don't tolerate this Jewish trash here. We do not tolerate Communist groups in our midst. The Communist International may be your dream but we will destroy all of you vermin!"

With that, he again struck Gerhard in the face. The two men in the gray coats stood impassive, watching silently.

Gerhard could again taste blood in his mouth. He suddenly felt more alone than ever. He was thinking of Schleicher and his stormtroopers. "Nun gerade, nicht. Fuck you, asshole," Gerhard said quietly, remembering his own words.

Fieseler's face became red and his eyes widened. His voice rose even more. "You are out out out! Pigs of your ilk are no longer tolerated here. As of now you have been expelled from school. Get out of my sight!" Gerhard turned and ran. He was glad to be free of the choking oppression of the principal's office. But as he raced through the streets, he began to realize that a worse confrontation might be ahead of him when he reached home.

Hours later, after walking aimlessly, he found himself standing in front of his father's house. Still, he did not go in immediately. He no longer felt at home there either. His father seemed never to let up on him, never understanding him. The longer his brother Friedrich was a member of the Nazi party, the more Gerhard felt like an outsider in the family. He looked at the lone sunflower in the front yard and noticed the bold colors and the subtle play of light and shadow in the petals. He wished he could be suspended, forever, just he and the sunflower and time itself.

Later that night, when his father came home from work. Gerhard met him in the hallway. "My English teacher has been fired for being a Communist. All of our group of Wandervogel are suspected with him. They searched his house. I got expelled from school."

Gerhard's father hung up his coat and his hat. Next to the

wardrobe, in an umbrella stand, was a cane. Gerhard's father picked it up and said, "A hiking group? You got expelled for belonging to a hiking group?"

With that, he raised the cane and gave Gerhard a beating prolonged enough to cause welts. Gustaf Schmidt said nothing, except to grunt from time to time with the effort. Gerhard somehow managed to remain quiet despite the pain. He protected his head as best as he could with his arm and surrendered. He would not give his father the satisfaction of knowing that he was hurting his son. After a while Gerhard thought of nothing but the sunflower. And then eventually the beating was over.

"Tomorrow," said Gustaf, his face flushed, "I will find some apprenticeship for you. You will learn something. You will be out of my house and no longer my responsibility. You are a disgrace! You will not eat dinner tonight. Go to your room."

Slowly Gerhard got off the floor and went upstairs. His body ached but all he felt was an angry determination not to give in. "Fuck you, asshole. Nun gerade nicht," he whispered to himself as he closed the door to his bedroom. No one talked to him that night and his stepmother, whom he resented at best, remained tight-lipped at breakfast. His father wasn't anywhere to be seen. Gerhard returned to his room after the silent meal, picked up his pastels and his drawing pad, staying there all day.

When his father returned in the evening, he called Gerhard downstairs and told him to sit. "You will listen to me and you will listen carefully. I am a ranking Police Officer in this city and I will not tolerate dissension. You have brought shame on yourself and me. You not only have shown loyalty to this anti-German immigrant from England but you also have defied your principal. I should just throw you out of my house and let you fend for yourself."

Gustaf was pacing now, barely looking at Gerhard. "Against my better judgment and since I am still your father,

I have made a call on your former principal. Maybe it was what I said, maybe it was my uniform, maybe it was a combination of both, but here is what we decided. Your disciplinary dismissal from school has been changed into a voluntary withdrawal. Additionally I have enrolled you in an agricultural training school near Meissen. Your mother had farmers as forebears, so maybe you might like that sort of life in the long run. Tomorrow you will pack a cardboard box with your most urgent belongings and I will accompany you to the railroad station. There will be no need for clothing other than underwear and shoes."

Gerhard was stunned, his mouth was dry.

"This afternoon your Wandervogel was incorporated into the Hitler Youth. At your arrival at Meissen you will be issued one of their uniforms. Have I made myself clear?"

He felt so weak he simply nodded.

"Then go to your room. You may come into the kitchen later. There will be a sandwich for you. Go!"

Gerhard held onto the banister as he walked up the creaky wooden steps.

Two weeks later   Meissen

Gerhard had not gotten along well at the school in Meissen from the beginning. He was made to sweep the floors, clean the plows, tend to the draft horses and their harnesses. This went on for nine hours a day. Then, after attending meetings of the Hitler Youth he had barely enough time to sleep before the next day started at 5 a.m when the livestock had to be watered and fed and taken out to the fields. He was less than 100 kilometers from Leipzig, but Meissen felt like another world.

Nobody seemed to like the way Gerhard talked. One could tell from his choice of words that he did not belong to the working class but instead spoke the language of the middle class. His classmates ridiculed him, mimicked his

197

voice and talked in impossibly long words which meant nothing and which they made up. They laughed uproariously, slapped each other's shoulders and threw dirt clods at Gerhard.

He shared a room with two other students. While they were the same age as Gerhard, they were dramatically different from each other. Hans, who wore civilian clothes that were rough and often mended, was quiet but friendly with Gerhard. Siegfried, who did not pay attention in class, always wore his Hitler youth uniform—unlike Gerhard, who only wore it when he had to go to the mandatory meetings or when he washed the clothes he was wearing when he left home. Gerhard and Hans talked to each other often during breaks. Hans' father ran the family farm and wanted his son to learn all he could about modern agricultural techniques and machinery in order to increase the production of their land.

Siegfried, on the other hand, did not come from a farming family. He proudly proclaimed that his father was a prominent functionary of the Nazi Party in Weissenfels. Siegfried's father believed that Germany deserved "Lebensraum" —room to expand—in the east. When this happened, farms would be taken from the conquered peoples and they needed to be run by Germans. Siegfried saw himself as a future National Socialist land baron owning and overseeing a very large farm seized from the enemy. He bragged that his only interest in the agricultural school was to learn enough of techniques to know when his workers were cheating him.

During the Hitler Youth meetings Siegfried was even more animated than usual. He could clearly see his future, which he described in detail. He could not stop talking about ruling the "backward" Poles and Rumanians who would experience the iron fist of superior German rule in the near future. Gerhard sat through these meetings and was less and less able to contain his anger.

Damn, he thought to himself. I have no idea how I will make it through three years of this— or even one more night of meetings. You can't just leave the Hitler Youth, even though I never joined them. They're the ones who stole my organization and forced me into their uniform. While his thoughts strayed, he no longer listened to the other Hitler Youths who had similar idiotic ideas as Siegfried.

"So, what about you, Gerhard, what do you think?" A familiar voice interrupted his private thoughts.

"Think about what?"

"Well what we just talked about, naturally," said Siegfried with a smirk. "It is less important to really learn how to farm the dirt than it is how to rule over those lesser people. We are destined to do this because we are superior Germanic stock. You naturally agree, Gerhard, don't you?"

"Well, let's see," Gerhard slowly began, "All I see is that most of you—and I mean most of you—wearing the Hitler Youth uniform are here because you want something from other people. The only exception here is Hans, who wants to make his family's farm more productive. I am here because my father sent me by force. I have no interest in farming, and as far as this uniform I'm wearing, I should be wearing the Wandervogel uniform, if any. I am only wearing this outfit right now because I have no other choice." He paused and then blurted out what he felt was the truth. "I want to be an artist in my own clothes. I don't even like you guys. All of you seem to be a bunch of incompetent people who know nothing and can do nothing."

Gerhard was quaking with rage when he finished.

"You will take that back immediately," their leader shouted.

"Nun gerade nicht!" Gerhard shouted back and stood. He felt his knees shaking. "Raus! Get out of my sight," the leader yelled. As Gerhard left the meeting hall, running, he heard the leader say, "I will make a complete report of this."

September 1934   Lobitzsch

In flight once again, Gerhard had found his way to Lobitzsch, where his Aunt Liska took him in. In a few short sentences, he told her what had happened in Meissen.

"Gerhard, Gerhard. How could you?" said Liska, no rancor in her voice. "You are always such a contrary boy. Why do you always resist? Now you lost your place in this school too. I worry about you."

As she said this with a shake of her head, she cut him two slices of home-baked bread. "Here, Gerhard, first eat like a man. We'll see what we can do for you."

Gerhard was exhausted. He had walked 100 kilometers in four days and had slept in the barns of farmers. He was famished and it felt good to hear Liska's kind voice again. It reminded him of the happier times when he and Friedrich would come to the farm for the summer.

While making his way to Lobitzsch, Gerhard had thought long and hard about his lifelong problems with bullies. It appeared that they were deliberately seeking him out. All he really wanted to do was draw, paint, and be left alone. It seemed that the Nazis were obsessed with doing everything en masse. You not only had to join them, but also you had to be part of their mob. You had to wear their uniform, sing their songs, march in unison, and bash anyone who got in the way. Gerhard was not a sheep. He felt like doing things by himself or with one or two friends of his choosing, not with uniformed, shouting, marching groups.

Now Gerhard reflected on his father's warning that the Gestapo were watching him and the other Wandervogel "sympathizers." "Stay on the straight and narrow," his father had warned, but Gerhard had left the school in Meissen suddenly, wearing his uniform, leaving all his belongings behind. Taking the uniform was technically theft of government property. That crime, combined with his being ejected from high school, and being a member of a recalcitrant youth group, was certainly sufficient cause for the Gestapo to look for him.

Lobitzsch seemed to be the answer. Gerhard and his brother had spent most of their vacations in the village. You ate well, you worked on the farm and you visited with the other folks. It was small enough that almost everyone was a cousin of some sort and everyone treated you as a family member. Gerhard longed to be where he was welcome and could feel secure. When his Aunt Liska offered him homemade smoked sausage and bread, still warm from the oven, he felt safe for the first time since Schleicher had struck him in the face for failing to give the Nazis their salute.

Slowly Gerhard began to tell Liska in more detail what had happened. Not everything he told was in the order in which events had unfolded and not everything made immediate sense. Liska did not rush Gerhard and gave him time to tell his story. At the end, she rubbed her hands together in agitation.

"What can I say? You were always too smart for your own good. I am not saying that you were wrong to do and say what you did, but if you continually try to punch through everything like an angry bull with his horns, then you will end up doing harm to yourself. You are as strong-willed as a bull, my boy, but your head is not as hard. You should learn to be a bit more like your brother. He works for the Nazis and is one of them. And you see what has happened? He is rising faster in their ranks than anyone I have known. They took him right out of the University and now he is leading an important school in Bavaria. He is commanding a lot of people at that school, which is going to turn out Germany's finest. Your brother knows how to 'nod and smile.' Why do you always have to fight against the Nazis?"

Gerhard was surprised to hear about Friedrich's promotion. It had been fast, but his brother had been committed and was being rewarded. It made sense. He shrugged and said quietly, "I can't go along with things I think are wrong."

In spite of her strong words, Liska gave him a hug. "Well, my boy, whatever has happened, has happened. You can stay with us and help Uncle Erich to bring in the wheat. That should earn your keep."

Gerhard wanted to cry. Here in the village it did not matter what you thought, it only mattered what was in your heart.

Later in the afternoon, when Uncle Erich came in from the fields, he obviously had been told to expect Gerhard. He greeted his nephew with a strong handshake and his leathery, tanned face beamed.

"You still like to drive the four horse team?"

Gerhard nodded, remembering how his uncle had carefully taught him to drive the team of powerful horses. He remembered how proud he felt when he had managed to bring the very long team-and-wagon combination in one perfect circle around the village oak.

"Yes," Gerhard answered, not only relieved but overjoyed to be taken in. "I'll drive your team throughout the harvest and do whatever else you want."

"Be careful, Gerhard, I may want to use your hard head to drive some nails!" Erich laughed.

Several months later   Lobitzsch

Gerhard and Erich were sitting in the village pub having a beer or two and going over the schedule of chores for the next week. The harvest had gone well. Gerhard had proved to be an asset and had done more than his share. From a skinny kid, he was quickly developing into a well-muscled young man. Early that day, Liska had told Gerhard she had received a letter from his father saying he had been notified some months before by the school of Gerhard's disappearance and asking if Gerhard had come to Lobitzsch.

"What do you want me to tell him?" she had asked. He said he didn't know. "Let me think about it."

That night Franz Tollmann, who owned a medium-sized farm at the north end of the village, came over and sat down at their table. They had not invited him. Tollmann was not part of the extended family. His folks had come from Poland after the World War, when German farmers had to give their land to Polish people and leave. Tollmann was still considered a newcomer and was not well-liked. It was widely known that he had recently joined the Nazi party.

"Well, Sieg Heil, you two. Erich, I trust you will support my appointment as mayor of Lobitzsch by unanimous acclaim. I know we have not had a mayor here since the Kaiser's time. But I feel things are changing and a new wind is blowing, even here. We need a mayor to properly represent us locally and at the national level. We are proud members of the profession that feeds our great nation. I feel we need a strong mayor who is, without question, a National Socialist! What do you think?"

Before Erich answered, Gerhard took a deep breath. It was quite obvious that he wanted to say something. He was sitting straight up on the wooden bench against the small window. His knuckles were white and he had just broken the pencil with which he had been drawing on a piece of paper.

But before Gerhard could speak a word, Uncle Erich nudged him hard under the table and said, "Guten Tag, Franz, and yes, you may sit down. In answer to your question, I will support you. Mind you, as you just said, since the Kaiser's time we have not had a mayor. I personally don't see why we need to be represented. We are 256 people in this village. I am counting women, children and farm hands. We have always taken care of each other, helped each other with the harvest and even traded fields if one of us is caught with only poor fields. Franz—and

I don't know how it was in your old village in the East—if you feel you want to be mayor of Lobitzsch, then I will support you."

Franz looked grim, staring at Erich.

"Erich, you misunderstand me. I feel it is my duty to serve as a mayor in order to help in the struggle to erase the shame of the Versailles Treaty, which was designed to make us a second class nation condemned to poverty. When you say you will support me because I want the job, then you are belittling me. You really are in no position to do that. I know very well that your farm hand, even though he is your nephew, is an enemy of the National Socialist state. I know about his subversive group in Leipzig, I also know about his subversive anti-German attitude at the training school in Meissen, and there is also a report that he has stolen some government property."

Tollmann glanced at Gerhard with a sneer. "If you are not fully behind me, I will see to it that Gerhard here gets what he should have gotten a long time ago: an appointment with the Gestapo."

Erich said with a chill in his voice. "Franz, let me assure you, I'm on your side."

Locking eyes with Erich, Tollmann stood up and said, "I knew that I could count on you. Heil Hitler." He walked away without another word and joined a group at the next table.

There was a long pause in which neither Erich nor Gerhard said a word. Both were looking at the rough wood of the table. Gerhard began absentmindedly to draw with his index finger in some spilled beer. When he saw the beginning of a sunflower emerging, he wiped it off.

"Gerhard, somehow I don't feel like being here anymore," Erich announced. "Let's get a couple of bottles of beer and go home. Agreed?"

"Sure," Gerhard said quickly, pushing his bench back. "We can talk some more in the barn if you want. I meant to check the drive belt for the threshing machine anyway."

They got their beers at the bar and left for home.

As they were entering the big archway of the wagon gate at Erich's farm, Gerhard said, "I could have slugged that guy! What balls! He knows he needs your approval to be appointed mayor, but to threaten you?"

"Now, now, Gerhard, calm down. Don't get so excited. I don't exactly know if he really threatened me. You, maybe, but not me. Franz is really a coward. As a farmer, he doesn't amount to much. He has got the same acreage as I do, but year after year, he asks the county government for financial aid. He always insists that he is trying to make up for losses incurred as a result of his expulsion from the East. I think this is just blustery talk. You know how the Nazis are."

When they entered the barn, Erich lit a lantern and set it on the edge of the hay wagon while Gerhard busied himself with the threshing machine. "Here is your beer, Gerhard."

Gerhard laid aside the wrench and took his beer with a nod of thanks. "You know, I appreciate how you kept me from speaking up and telling Franz where to go with his Nazi ideas. I'm getting better, no? Maybe learning more when to keep my mouth shut? I know that I am too fast with my mouth. Perhaps if I speeded up my brain they would both perform at the same speed."

Erich laughed. "Gerhard, your brain is not your problem. You think mighty fast. Maybe even faster than your brother. You have the right ideas, all right. What you don't have is even a horse's sense. You think you have to tell everyone what you think. The less they want to hear your ideas, the more you want to tell them. My boy, it is necessary to have ideas. It is not necessary to talk about them."

Gerhard didn't want to get angry, especially with Uncle Erich. "We can't let them bully us like that, Uncle Erich. We have to do something about the Nazis!"

Erich sighed and took a swig of his beer. "What is there to be done? They have the government, the army, the police, the press, the courts."

"I don't know what to do, but I know that my old English teacher was right: We have to resist or we are in compliance with them! He taught us to go out and drop leaflets by the University, City Hall, the army barracks. We have to create doubt in the Nazis. Then we can organize and fight them! I am really grateful that you took me in when I had nowhere to go, Uncle Erich, but sometimes these days, I feel like a prisoner in Lobitzsch, and all I can do is preach to you and the horses!"

Summer 1935   *Lobitzsch*

Gerhard had come to hate Franz Tollmann. He hated Franz's silly mustache. It was clipped like Hitler's, with neither a right nor left side. Just the middle—laughable. He hated his uniform, which he wore whenever he was not working the fields, and he hated his insistence on bringing along copies of the *Voelkischer Beobachter*, the official Nazi newspaper. What he hated most were his constant attempts to involve everyone around him in discussions on Nazi politics and recent speeches by Dr. Goebbels, the Reich's Minister of Information. Gerhard knew what Franz intended to do. He would figure out who was opposing the Nazis and eradicate them from "his" village.

Recent legislation outlawed not only Communism but also any opposition to the NSDAP. The Gestapo was given authority to ferret out and apprehend anyone who was opposed to the Nazis.

"Gerhard," Aunt Liska said to him one night. "Do yourself a favor, come along. The meeting is only two hours. Everyone will be there. Don't say anything. Just think what you want to think. Look agreeable and nod from time to time. Take paper and pencil and draw something pretty." Gerhard knew he worried Liska. She watched him sometimes when she thought he wasn't paying attention, as if he were an unpredictable wild animal, loose in her parlor.

"All right, I'll go. I just don't know how much longer I can sit there while this idiot preaches and pretends that he is the "Fuehrer" of this village!" Gerhard told her, as they walked to the pub.

As usual, to the left of the bar was a small podium from which Franz would give his inspirational talk with all the imitated, fake-sounding pathos that his beloved Fuehrer used. To the left and right of the podium were two Nazi banners, with the swastika in its white circle on a red field.

For god's sake, this is a farmers' pub in a small village! Gerhard thought, knowing better than to say the words aloud. Sometimes I think I am stuck in a very bad dream and can't seem to get out of it.

When Gerhard, Liska and Erich had taken their seats and nodded uncomfortably to everyone, the room grew quiet. Franz Tollmann came into the bar, strutting, in full uniform. His left hand was clasping his belt buckle and his highly polished boots slammed their heels together. His right arm shot out and up in the Nazi salute. "Heil Hitler!!" he bellowed, as if he were trying to get the attention of thousands. "Hrrup, Hrruump, Ler!" The farmers responded, decidedly unenthusiastic.

"Today's topic, and indeed one of utmost importance for our nation, is that of identifying, isolating and finally exterminating inner rot. We as a Nation that is setting an example for every other state on this planet, must lead the way. The more singular the purpose of our Nation is, the more united we are in overcoming everything and everyone who is opposed to us, the more we will achieve as a Nation. We—as Germans who are thinking with a German mind—will therefore seek to stamp out and henceforth totally eliminate those maggots who are feeding on our successes but will not work for us, indeed who are secretly and openly opposed to us. We will not allow them to undermine our national will; we will squash them like the maggots and vermin that they are."

Try as he might, Gerhard could not ignore his own distress. The more he listened, the more he became cold inside. This was a new theme. Up to this point, Tollmann had given speeches centering about national pride and having one purpose—marching together. These were slogans one could ignore. Tonight's tirade, however, was something entirely different. It seemed this was the beginning of a witch hunt for everyone who thought differently. Secretly, the villagers were shooting each other nervous glances. They too had noticed the change in tone. As people were starting to shift uneasily in their seats and to look around, they noticed two men standing by the door. They were not from the village. They looked at no one. They were not even sitting down but rather standing by the door like sentries.

"...and that, in short, is our national determination as outlined in the Capitol only yesterday by Dr. Goebbels," Tollmann bellowed on. "For those of you, and I am sure most of you are interested, who want to read Dr. Goebbels' speech in its entirety, I have as usual brought several copies of the *Voelkischer Beobachter* for you to share. Are there any questions from the audience?"

"Yes," one of the villagers stood up. "Who are the two city folks back by the door?" There was a murmur of support for that question, which would prove to be the only one tonight.

"Those gentlemen," Franz Tollmann answered with an icy smile, "they are from the county commissariat of the Gestapo. As of yesterday, 12 noon, their job is protecting patriotic meetings like these from Communists, subversives, Jews, and other un-German elements. We can live secure in the knowledge that these elements will be actively sought out, isolated and apprehended. No longer will we feed, shelter and tolerate the saboteurs in our midst."

No one was willing to respond to Tollmann. People were getting up in haste to go home. As they were heading for the door, they noticed that the two Gestapo men had left.

Gerhard, Erich, and Liska took the short walk home in silence. The openly declared war on anyone who did not support the Nazis was a very real threat for Gerhard. It seemed just a matter of time before the Gestapo would come for him, even here in the little farm community.

"Liska, leave us alone, Gerhard and I have to have some man talk," Erich said as he steered Gerhard into the barn. "No beer tonight," he said. "We have to think what we must do. It is no longer safe for you to be here. Our little village has become like Leipzig. The Nazis run everything and everyone. Now the Gestapo is here. If they come for you, they will also come for us, if for no other reason than we have taken you in. They don't care that we are family."

Gerhard was using a stick to draw a pattern of some sort into the packed-clay floor as his uncle was speaking. He knew that Erich was right. He had to leave. Everything in him wanted to cry out and fight. He felt tired and sad when he finally spoke.

"I know. I have to leave. They say I am a subversive and stole my uniform. Tollmann told us that he knew that. Where else could he have found out, except from his friends in the Gestapo?" Gerhard laughed painfully. "Maybe that jerk is, in reality, not so bad, and maybe he was trying to warn me." He trailed off, still tracing the pattern on the floor, willing himself not to give into his grief.

"You know what," he continued, "right after he joined the Nazi party, my brother Friedrich tried to make me read Hitler's *Mein Kampf.* I could not get through it, but I remember Hitler describing how horrible he felt about all the different people—Jews, foreigners, Communists and others—in 'his' Vienna. When I read that chapter and saw how Hitler hated to be there, the more did I think that Vienna would be a great place to be. They speak German, but they are a foreign country. The Nazis don't rule there. I hear that they even have an art institute there. Maybe I should...."

Erich interrupted him. "Don't say any more. It is better for Liska and me that we not know your plans. It is better for you too, safer." Erich reached out and pulled Gerhard into his arms. "Go with God," said the older man. "Keep yourself safe."

A little after midnight Gerhard dressed in warm clothes and packed a small knapsack with food and a little money Aunt Liska had left on the kitchen table for him. He went into the tool shed, took a shovel, which he shouldered, and quietly slipped out of the village, heading south on foot. No one seemed to have noticed him in the dark. He walked quietly trying not to kick rocks on the unpaved road. When dawn broke, and people began walking to work in their fields, he hoped to blend in as just another worker carrying a shovel.

Ten days later   On the run

Gerhard's feet hurt and he was utterly exhausted. When he went to sleep for a few hours now and then in bushes and ditches by the side of the road, he did not dare take off his boots. His feet were so swollen that he was sure he would be unable to put them back on, and he knew that he could never reach the border walking in his socks.

The terrain rose and became hilly. As he trudged on, he noticed that the villages, which usually were spaced out every five kilometers or so, became more and more sparse. Between the fields more and larger forests appeared and in the distance he was able to see the Erzgebirge, the low mountain chain that marked the border to Czechoslovakia. The closer he got, the tenser he got. He had to overcome the urge to drop his bundle and the shovel, which had served him well, and run.

With each step he repeated to himself: *Walk, walk, walk, walk slowly. Walk.* He fought the rising panic. Finally, as he reached the crest of the hill, he saw a little round sign on a post by the side of the dirt road, which was a mere path here. "Halt! Reichsgrenze." "Stop! Border of the Reich." Only about 50 yards.

Where are they hiding? I don't see anyone guarding this crossing! Should I run for it? If they see me, will they follow me across the border and take me back?

He forced himself to walk casually, not change his pace and not make any noise. *Step, step, step.* He noticed that he was holding his breath.

He slowly passed the sign, walked on and took a shallow inhale, feeling that a thousand eyes were watching him from behind. He continued like this for about 100 yards and then at a bend in the road began to run. He considered just dropping the shovel but then thought better of it. He could swing it as a weapon if he had to. His knuckles were white as he clutched the handle. After about a quarter mile his knees shook so hard and his breath came so raggedly that he stumbled and fell into a depression by the side of the road. There he lay for about a half hour listening for any sound of border guards who may have followed. He heard only the wind in the trees, an occasional bird calling, and the buzzing of insects. There were no border guards.

Gerhard began to laugh—first silently, then a mere giggle, and finally a full-throated laugh. He suddenly stopped himself. Again he listened. Still quiet. Slowly he picked up his shovel and his small bundle and began walking again. But a few miles later, he dropped the shovel as though leaving an old friend from Lobitzsch. He thought he would have no need for it anymore.

After two more hours of walking, he chewed the last bite of hard smoked sausage Aunt Liska had slipped into his bundle. This was the first food he had allowed himself in the last twenty-four hours. He was ravenous. The salty mouthful was not enough but at least it stopped his empty stomach from hurting. Hearing the engine whine of a truck behind him, he stepped off the road, prepared to hide. It was an old truck, maybe surplus from the World War, leaden with what appeared to be sacks of potatoes. The lone driver in the open cab seemed to be a farmer. When the truck slowed, Gerhard overcame the instinct to run, instead stepping back onto the roadside. The truck stopped and the driver called something out to Gerhard in Czech, but Gerhard did not understand.

To Gerhard's relief, the driver repeated in German, "Well boy, where are you headed?" Gerhard panicked all over again. *Where am I headed?* He had not thought of it. All he knew was where he headed from: South, away from the Nazis, the bullies, the Gestapo. He was headed to freedom. "Prague. That's where I am going."

"That's a long walk. Want a ride? I'm headed for the farmer's market in Prague. I'm delivering my potatoes. In exchange for the ride you can help me unload the sacks."

Gratefully Gerhard climbed into the cab. He fell asleep immediately. He was only dimly aware of the change in engine sound as the farmer shifted gears. Now and then he felt the truck take turns but could not rouse himself. Only the sudden silence woke him with a start.

"Lunchtime, my boy. Would you like part of my sandwich?" the farmer asked. He had pulled over to the side of the road, which was paved, and had turned off the engine. Gerhard looked at the enormous sandwich which the farmer was unwrapping from a newspaper page and nodded weakly. He took the part that the farmer offered him and began biting, chewing and swallowing all at once.

"Slow down, slow down, boy. You seem to be inhaling the food. Pace yourself, enjoy what my wife made for me!"

Gerhard apologized. He realized that he had eaten like a starving animal. Come to think of it, that's who I am, he thought. He slowed down and smiled. "Food, at last. Wonderful."

In the late afternoon they pulled into the big warehouse of the farmers' market. Gerhard helped unload the dozens of heavy sacks of potatoes, working up a sweat. When they were done, he washed his face at a faucet and drank and drank. He was parched and hot and the cold water tasted delicious.

"So, where are you off to now?" the farmer asked him.

"The railroad station," Gerhard replied.

When the farmer asked where he wanted to go, Gerhard only said, "Actually I need to be somewhere." He did not want to tell the farmer that he had no real goal, but he thought that in the waiting hall of the railroad station he could sit down, blend in, and think of what to do next.

"Well, then good luck to you. If you walk about 15 minutes in that direction, you'll find the station. Can't really miss it, because it is a large building connected to a lot of railroad tracks."

Both of them grinned at the lame joke and Gerhard set off. He turned, waved and said, "Thanks for the ride—and tell your wife thanks for the sandwich."

Gerhard found the station and its cavernous waiting hall. He sat down and began to assess his situation. He only spoke German, some English and a little less French. German would work near the borders of Czechoslovakia because of the majority of ethnic Germans living there. But here in Prague, Czech was spoken exclusively. Gerhard could not understand the announcements coming over the loud-speaker. He also could not read the signs posted almost everywhere. He could not even find the bathroom. He began to watch people come and go. Then he saw men go into a door and after a while come back out. At the other end of the hall was a similar door where women and small children disappeared and reappeared. He looked at the signs on the door and tried to remember the one for the

213

men. Slowly he got up and strolled as casually as he could to that door and indeed, it was the men's room.

After waiting for an empty stall, he took time washing his hands and face. So far so good, he thought.

Back on the bench where he had been sitting, he pondered what he could do next.

He remembered that most larger German railroad stations had a room with tables and cots; this was a service for travelers who were stranded for a day or night. Usually they were run by non-denominational Christian organizations and provided a simple free hot meal and a cot at the end of the day. Gerhard hoped that this station had such a room, but how to find it?

Looking around, he studied the signs, but they were no help. He began to walk around, gazing into open doors, searching for the telltale signs of a travelers' rest area. He also used his nose to find the smell of food. It was too early in the day for stranded travelers, but he reasoned it could not hurt to plan ahead. After he had checked everywhere unsuccessfully he became disheartened. He went back to his bench but found his seat occupied. He strolled out of the station and began to explore the immediate area. Maybe he could find a restaurant, bakery or food store that had discarded old food in a back alley.

As he walked, from time to time he smelled a garbage can, but he also found a locked door in front of it. After about an hour he gave up his search and returned to the station. Again he took a seat in the waiting hall. He noticed that the announcements about train arrivals and departures did not come as often as earlier; the shafts of dusty light from the windows were at a shallow angle and the big clock at the far end of the hall showed that it was getting late.

Gerhard's stomach rumbled. He watched as one of the travelers finally got up from the bench, took his small suitcase and slowly went to one of the doors that had been closed all day. About 15 minutes later a woman with a small child on her arm also entered through this door. He waited another hour, watching a steady stream of travelers enter the doors and not come back out.

Gerhard thought he had found it, and decided to follow them. The smell of coffee and some sort of stew drew him into the room. He took a seat at one of the tables next to the man he saw first enter. The man looked friendly and immediately began to talk. Gerhard understood nothing, but he smiled hopefully.

The man continued to talk and Gerhard continued to smile. Then, with a very strong Bohemian-German accent, the man said," You are not from here. Are you from Sudetenland?" Gerhard nodded.

The two of them talked for a while about their missed connections because of delayed trains and being stranded for the night. Gerhard started to relax. A window near the back wall opened and he could now smell the aromas of meat and potatoes. A line of people began forming and both Gerhard and his tablemate joined those waiting for their free meal. As he had guessed, it was a stew. Thick and delicious. He sat down with his tin bowl and began to eat hungrily.

Noticing people who had finished were rejoining the line for a second helping, Gerhard was just about to get up when he saw the main door open and what appeared to be three policemen enter. They said something in Czech and his tablemate translated.

"Don't worry, they are only making a routine check of papers. They do that all the time."

Gerhard rapidly considered his options. Should he run? One of the policemen was still standing at the door and apparently guarding it. The other two were going from table to table and casually looking at ID cards. Both the people and the police were relaxed. This was not like the Gestapo in Nazi Germany. There was no intimidation or fear. Gerhard decided to wait things out. When the officers came to his table and the other man showed his papers, Gerhard just continued to scrape food from his bowl. One officer addressed him and the man translated.

"They want to see your ID card. Show it to them."

"I don't have any," Gerhard said. "I am a refugee from Germany. I am running from the Nazis."

One of the officers spoke German to him and said, " OK That may be possible, but you still need papers. You understand that you will have to come with us."

Gerhard was tired but not really afraid. He just said, "I understand."

He walked out of the dining hall accompanied by the three officers. They escorted him to another part of the station, which contained a small police office. He was placed in a tiny room containing only a chair and a table.

"Please wait," one of them said. They closed the door and locked it.

Later that night he was moved to a regular cell, which contained a bed and a toilet. He was also given another hot meal—for which he was grateful.

The next morning he was brought into a room, which looked almost like his classroom at school. One of the policemen from the previous night was there and nodded to him with a friendly expression. Then an official in dark civilian clothes entered and took a seat behind the table. He asked Gerhard to identify himself and state his reason for being in Czechoslovakia without a passport or a visa. Gerhard complied and told his story. The official took careful notes, and now and then interrupted Gerhard with questions. His German was excellent.

Finally the official said, "Here is what we will have to do. Even though you give very good reasons for why you are here without papers, the fact remains that you are here and you have no permission to be here. Not from the Germans and not from us. Usually we drive illegal entrants straight to the border where they came from. With you I am not so sure. I will sentence you to the minimum of three months in jail for illegally crossing the border into Czechoslovakia. In three months we will see what will have to be done next."

Gerhard only heard three months of food, shelter and safety and so he said, "Thank you, your honor." The policeman then took him to the jail in the city center.

Three months later   Prague

Gerhard had been thinking of little else during his short jail sentence than what would happen when he was released. Mainly, he hoped that somehow he would be granted political asylum, but as time passed he had more and more doubts. He had heard from other prisoners who were able to speak German that the Nazis were putting increasing pressure on the Czechs to give up their territories along the border. There was talk of disturbances between ethnic Germans and Czechs. There was also talk of political negotiations.

When the day of his release came, he was brought to the courtroom at the railroad station. There he met the same judge as before.

"Gerhard Schmidt," the judge began. "You have been detained for entering Czechoslovakia without benefit of a passport or visa. You have served your sentence of three months in city jail quietly and you have obeyed all regulations. You have even volunteered for work details whenever the need arose. I remember your story of persecution by the Nazis in Germany, but I have the unfortunate duty to inform you that your application for political asylum has been rejected. This is undoubtedly one of the consequences of recent high-level negotiations and is therefore out of my hands. The law states that you must be deported to your country of origin."

Gerhard's knees buckled. He sat back down onto the chair from which he had risen as he was addressed by the judge. His breath became ragged.

"I can see how you feel," the judge continued, still speaking his accented German. "I have therefore made some changes in your file. I will order you deported back to your native Austria and the city from which you came, Vienna. One of the officers here will transport you to the border."

Gerhard could not believe his incredible luck in having met this compassionate judge. All he could say again was "thank you, your Honor."

He was immediately led to a police van, and without another word, he was on his way to Austria.

December 1937   Vienna

During the three years that Gerhard had spent in Vienna, he slowly came to know the Austrian way of life and appreciate its capital city. Almost everything was different—much different—than in Leipzig. He was excited by the architecture, the history, the coffee houses and the tempo. There were people from many different cultures and countries. In contrast to the state-enforced drab conformity in Germany, Austria teemed with diversity. It appeared to Gerhard that almost any political viewpoint was accepted.

By day, Gerhard worked at menial jobs like loading and unloading trucks and cleaning up stores. Occasionally he saved up enough money to attend art classes at the Academy. He lacked the means to attend full-time, but someday, he told himself, he would do it.

By night Gerhard often sat in one of the city's many pubs, at first just watching the scene, then entertaining himself by having casual chats with acquaintances, eavesdropping on nearby conversations and keeping his pulse on what was happening politically.

He learned that black clouds hung over even Vienna. Just the year before Gerhard had arrived, the Austrian SS occupied the government building and murdered the Chancellor.

More and more, there were rumors that the Germans would arrive any day and take control, but Gerhard tried not to hear the worst and kept his opinions to himself. While he had not taken an active role in denouncing the Nazis, he carefully listened to news reports, read leaflets when he could find them, and attended debates about the future of Europe.

Lately, the discussions he heard disturbed him.

One night, Gerhard sat in the corner of Sattler's Bierstube, slowly nursing a half-liter glass of light beer and watching people come and go. Five young men sat down at the round table next to Gerhard, and it was not very difficult to catch bits and pieces of their conversation. All appeared very committed and made no attempt to keep their voices down.

"I think it is an open secret. Germany is getting ready to swallow us up," one said. "All you have to do is read the *Voelkischer Beobachter* and compare it to what the middle class out in the street is saying. They are talking the same line! I tell you, when—and I purposefully don't say 'if'—the Nazis march into Austria, the Gestapo will come after us, after any group that is not in conformity with their goals. We will most likely face arrest!"

"Arrest for what?" his friend argued. "Arrest for having a political opinion? Don't be ridiculous. If this were true, then they would have to arrest all members of the political opposition, the independent and leftist labor unions, newspaper writers etc., etc. I don't believe it could happen. For one, where would they put all these arrestees? There aren't enough courts to try everyone. No, I think there will be a hell of a lot of pressure to conform but outright arrest, that I don't see." Most of the group nodded in agreement.

Gerhard desperately wanted to participate in the discussion, but forced himself to listen instead. It was so tempting to tell them about his own experience, and to warn them.

"What we really need to do is the following," said one of the students. "We have to post leaflets at the various buildings of the University, at the Art Academy and near the military training grounds as well at police barracks. We have to alert those who can think and organize and those who are trained to act—before the Nazis take over. I do not think that we can prevent Austria from losing its independence, but I think that we are a small enough country to establish a strong opposition so that Hitler will have to tread very lightly in Austria." There were more nods of agreement.

As the students began dividing up the tasks of printing the leaflets, delivering them, hanging them up as well as handing them out, Gerhard became more and more agitated. Finally he could hold back no longer, and turned around in his chair.

"You know," he said slowly. "In Germany I belonged to a group just like yours. Well, not quite. We were younger than you and still in school. Mostly, we were a hiking group." He paused, looking around to see whether anyone else in the pub was listening to him and lowered his voice before continuing. "We made leaflets and distributed them to see if people could be organized. Our leader was arrested by the Gestapo, and I don't know what happened to him. I assume that at least several of my friends from the group were also arrested. Well, let me tell you, we were mere boys with a teacher as our leader. And still, they went after us."

The students were listening intently. A few of them began glancing nervously over their shoulders.

Gerhard felt as if he could not stop talking even if he wanted to. Words that had been bottled up for years came pouring out. "I had to leave school. I lost my home. Eventually, I even had to flee my hometown. I worked hard on a farm in a tiny village. The Nazis came there too. Let me tell you, once they take over, they will come after everyone opposed to them."

Gerhard saw that the students were listening avidly as he went on. "I don't get it! It seems that all of you are convinced that the Nazis will take over Austria. Well if they do, and I for one hope and believe they will not, but suppose they do. Why are you guys talking so openly about opposing the coming regime? If you are right, and the Nazis are coming, then you certainly will be identified and arrested as opposition!" By that time, Gerhard had turned his chair around, but he took care to keep his voice down.

"So what are you? Students who are out on a dare? Or are you really opposed to the Nazis and want to do something? If you are serious, then you have to stop advertising in public who you are!" Gerhard suddenly banged his fist on the table in anger. He was convinced that for these students, all of this was an intellectual exercise. They looked like they had never worked with their hands and were being supported by their parents. Certainly they did not anticipate appearing on an enemy list of the Gestapo one day.

"Who are you?" asked the blond student, the one who thought that the Nazis would have to tread lightly in Austria. "Come join us, I am sure you know what you are talking about."

Gerhard hesitated. If he had just shut up! He had come here to Vienna to escape the Nazis, to avoid almost certain arrest by the Gestapo. He had given up his job, his home and his country. He had run, but at least here, he was free. Why was he now endangering everything again by talking to this fledgling and probably doomed opposition group?

"No thank you," he said, forcing himself to breathe and calm himself down. "Thanks for the invitation. I have just come here to quietly enjoy my beer. Sorry, I intruded into your conversation."

"Oh no, not at all," the student said. "My name is Dieter. Come join us, I insist." Gerhard remained reluctant. He had been in Vienna for three years but had not made any close friends. The truth was, he felt lonely and really wanted someone to talk to.

"OK" Gerhard said, shaking hands with each member of the group. "My name is Gerhard. I am from Leipzig in the Empire of our new leader Adolf Hitler. I guess he is from around here."

The students laughed. "Sit down. Let us buy you another beer. You sound like a kindred spirit." Dieter introduced the rest of the group—Max, Hans, little Joseph and his older brother Xavier. "We are members of the Socialist Students organization at the University here," Dieter said, not lowering his voice.

"Well," Gerhard said. "Nice to meet you all. Sorry again about telling you when and where to be open. But I have unfortunately already experienced what it's like to live under the Nazis and the Gestapo."

"Ah, forget it," said Dieter. "Actually we feel somewhat honored to have you in our midst. We really only know from newspapers and radio what it is like in Germany. And then of course, you have to keep in mind that everyone who writes or works at the radio stations is committed to one position or another. In these times, hardly anyone is neutral or objective any longer. You, Gerhard, can tell us what it really is like."

So that night and in the weeks to come, Gerhard began sharing his experiences about the Nazis. He told the students about Schleicher and his marching column in Leipzig, his group and the English teacher, how he was forced into the Hitler Youth, and about his ejection from the agriculture school. He told of Lobitzsch and Franz Tollmann. He also described the Gestapo in the village, whose job it was to arrest dissenters. It felt good to have someone listen to him at last.

Mostly, when Gerhard talked, there was respectful silence. Then the students, especially Dieter, would begin asking questions. "What exactly were the contents of the leaflets your group had handed out in Leipzig?" "What did the farmers in Lobitzsch think about Tollmann?" "Did your uncle take you in as a farmhand because you were running from the Gestapo or did he take you in just because you are his nephew?" And on and on. Gerhard answered them all, wishing to help the students avoid the mistakes he had made. In particular, he was drawn to Dieter as he had not been to anyone since the Wandervogel group.

January 1938   *Vienna*

After some weeks, Dieter said, "Gerhard, you feel like a long lost brother to me. You are a refugee, you have little income. I invite you to stay with me as long as you want. My parents are paying my expenses, and they will never have to know whether they are supporting one or two sons."

Gerhard was touched. He had found new friends and also a better place to stay. From now on, he was sure, his future was safe in Austria. Still, he waited several weeks before deciding to give up his cheap room and move in with Dieter. But their continued nightly sessions at the pub gave Gerhard a warm sense of belonging and acceptance.

As they arrived at Dieter's student quarters in the Maierstrasse that first night, Dieter showed Gerhard where he could sleep, where he could put his few clothes and where he would find something to eat. Gerhard was grateful as he prepared his bed.

Dieter began searching for something in the room, then began patting down his pants and jacket pockets. "Damn, did you see them?" He asked Gerhard.

"See what?" Gerhard answered, confused.

"My cigarettes. I must have forgotten my cigarettes at the pub. Damn. I had hoped to talk for a while longer and smoke a couple more cigarettes before turning in." Dieter said, visibly annoyed with himself. "Ah well. I can always buy more tomorrow at the tobacco store."

"Don't be silly," Gerhard said to him. "I saw one of those new cigarette machines at the corner. Why don't we go, grab some fresh air and buy you some?"

"Now, why didn't I think of that?" Dieter said and the two of them left.

By this time, the streets were almost deserted. The gaslights that dimly illuminated the sidewalks were hissing, but otherwise it was quiet. They arrived at the cigarette machine and when one of the coins jammed, Dieter pounded the machine with his fist.

Whether it was the noise of the banging or just bad luck, a policeman, walking nearby noticed them, crossed the street and called out, "What are you doing?"

Dieter explained and it all seemed like just a routine discussion until the policeman said, "OK I believe you, but let me see your papers in any case." He stretched out his hand to Gerhard, who hadn't uttered a word.

Dieter handed his I.D. card to the officer and Gerhard stood still. He and the policeman looked at each other and Gerhard said, 'I have no I.D."

"How far away do you live? We can walk there and get it," said the official.

Gerhard started to sweat but at the same time felt ice cold. His mouth was dry as he said, "I do not have any papers. Going to my home is no use. I am a political refugee from Germany."

Although they had by now shared almost all of their stories, Gerhard had never told Dieter that he had no papers and had been arrested in Prague for that offense. Gerhard tried to calm himself down, remembering his good fortune with the Czech judge. He smiled at Dieter, hoping to reassure him.

The officer handed Dieter his I.D. and, looking at Gerhard

said, "You'll have to come with me." He pulled a pair of handcuffs from his pocket and quickly cuffed Gerhard.

After three days in a jail cell, similar to the one in Prague, Gerhard was brought before a judge and sentenced to three months, an outcome that made him oddly optimistic. He held out hope that he could somehow resume his life in Vienna soon. And maybe this time he would be given political asylum.

March 13, 1938 Vienna

Just before he was due to be released and while his request for political asylum was being considered, Gerhard was told that Germany had annexed Austria.

"Your request for political asylum is no longer active. Instead of being released, you are being sent to Weimar," said the jailer.

Gerhard was stunned but utterly helpless. On the long ride to Weimar, he had more time to think than he wanted. He remembered that, feeling secure, he had told Dieter and the other students what had motivated his uncle Erich to hide him from the Gestapo, why he had fled Germany, what the Wandervogel had done and what had been the contents of the leaflets—everything that he had kept a secret in Germany. He had opened up to Dieter, believing their friendship would keep him safe. And now, he was sure that the Gestapo would find all of this out from Dieter eventually.

December 24, 1940 Buchenwald

It was early in the morning on what was, ironically Gerhard's 23rd birthday—maybe because it was his birthday—that Metzger, the sadistic prison guard, came for him, pulling him out of the mustering of prisoners lined up for the interminable body count.

"Good news, kid, and Merry Christmas to you." Metzger smirked, his ruddy fat face always glistened when he tried to look pleasant. He looked that way when he was with his "children" and when something very bad was about to happen.

"My child, there is someone here to see you on your birthday, for Christmas, so to speak. Follow me," Metzger drawled out the words as if he were savoring them. Gerhard wasn't sure whether it was worse to be treated like a nameless, faceless prisoner—vermin—or to have Metzger single you out for special attention and call you "child."

Gerhard nodded. He did not change the expression on his face because usually Metzger would kick you in the groin if you frowned, shrugged or if you said anything. He did not want you to look at him, or respond in any way except with silent compliance.

Most of the SS were not this predictable. You never knew when they decided to punish you for something. With Metzger you always knew.

Metzger swaggered towards the iron front gate, Gerhard trailing behind. "Jedem das Seine." These words were meticulously wrought in iron and placed into the gate about face-high so that you couldn't miss them when you entered— or left—the Concentration Camp Buchenwald. "Everyone gets what he deserves."

Gerhard suppressed any emotion while he thought, *Funny, this is all wrong. We are getting it, but they deserve it.* Gerhard knew he would soon be "getting" something unpleasant. It was rare to be taken out through the front gates. He didn't believe for a minute that Metzger was planning to release him. The two SS sentries shut the gate after guard and prisoner had made their way through it.

The second building to the left, up the hill, was where the Gestapo had their office. *They are taking me to the Gestapo.* Gerhard became cold with fear, but he willed himself not to show any outward reaction.

Gerhard was pushed through a doorway by Metzger. The door slammed shut and Gerhard heard the key being turned twice. When Gerhard turned and saw two Gestapo men, he felt they looked familiar. *Maybe it is just the long grey coats*, Gerhard thought.

"Prisoner 632," the younger one said. That was all that was left of Gerhard's identity. The almost-shaved haircut was alike for all prisoners; so were the threadbare pants and jackets. Shoes were whatever covering prisoners could find for their feet, but it was the hollow cheeks and the vacant eyes that made the prisoners all look alike.

"632, Schmidt, Gerhard, 12-24-17, Leipzig, unemployed farmhand, no permanent residence. Arrested: Vienna, 04-07-38. Political prisoner. Protective custody." The younger one had finished reading from his papers.

Funny, Gerhard thought. I've almost forgotten now after more than two years that I was someone with a name and a life outside of this camp.

"My, my, it is your birthday today, my boy," the Gestapo official laughed, and Gerhard became even more convinced that they had chosen his birthday to stage this event deliberately.

"Well, how would you like to go home to your mother today? You can sit in her warm living room, look at the wonderful Christmas tree and eat some of her roasted Christmas goose. Would you like that, boy?"

Gerhard thought of his stepmother. He had not heard from her since his arrest. He had heard from his father, though. Gerhard wrote his father postcards twice a month, as the camp rules allowed. Not all of the prisoners could write or receive mail. Gerhard did not want his father or brother to forget that there was an entirely different side to all the so-called "nice" things that the Nazis had brought to Germany. Gerhard tried to tell his father what it was like in Buchenwald, though this was difficult. The prisoners could only write on small, pre-printed postcards and letters.

"Konzentrationslager Buchenwald," it announced across the top in red print. "Write clearly! Illegible writing will be discarded by the censor!" And then there were a few pre-printed blank lines on which you could compose your message. Gerhard certainly gave it his best shot to get the meaning across. His father had to know what it was like here.

Surely the German public, if only they knew the truth, would not tolerate what was being done here. They did not know and had to be told! Gerhard wondered how much was left of his postcards after the censor got through with them. That was a strange concept to fully comprehend—a censor—a faceless person who had the power to obliterate all of Gerhard's communication.

But although Gerhard received postcards in return, he really did not know how to interpret them. His father wrote back as if he had not read Gerhard's cards. All Gerhard ever got was some sort of acknowledgment that he was in Buchenwald. He might have been in a summer camp for kids. Maybe his father didn't want to know, refused to understand Gerhard's coded words.

He was also directed nearly every month to initial some sort of ledger sheet showing a deposit to his "account." This page showed withdrawals from the account as well, but Gerhard never saw any money. He assumed his father was sending it to him, expecting he'd buy something at the non-existent store. Maybe his father believed the pre-printed instructions on the card that said, "In the Camp, everything can be purchased."

Instead, he seemed to be serving as a bank for the SS.

Maybe that explained his work assignment too. Instead of being sent out to do forced labor with most of the other prisoners from sunup to sundown, he worked as a janitor at the SS barracks each day, on the edge of the camp. There he was subjected to constant verbal abuse and taunting from the sadistic SS personnel.

"Do you understand what I have just told you?" the Gestapo official shouted. "You can leave here, today, now. We are not at all happy about the way you have shown your gratitude to the Fuehrer. Gratitude for the rapid rise of your older brother, who has become a rather big animal on the food-chain, and gratitude for being placed into such a nice camp. Well as I said, you can leave. You are free."

Gerhard wondered, briefly, what it meant that they would mention his brother. *Was this, perhaps, a good sign? Maybe,* he allowed himself to hope, *he really was free to go.*

The older one, a Bavarian by his accent, continued, "All you have to do is tell us where your original group members from Leipzig are now. You, my boy, can trade places with them, so to speak, of course. You understand that this is a birthday and Christmas present rolled all in one. What do you say?"

There was a long silence. Gerhard pictured the roasted goose—even cooked badly by his stepmother; the decorated Christmas tree; the faces of his father and his brother. He could almost smell the food being prepared. His stomach started to hurt, the way it does when you are very hungry for a long time and have nothing to eat and no hope of eating. Gerhard thought of the wrought-iron gate: "Jedem das Seine."

For the first time since he had entered the room, he made eye contact with the two Gestapo men. Gerhard stood upright, looked into their faces, and said, "Nun gerade nicht. Fuck you, assholes, both of you!"

He said it calmly, clearly and with pride. The fact was that he had no idea where the Leipzig group was. He had been imprisoned now for more than two years, and he hadn't known since the day the Wandervogel leader left school where any of the members or Krause had gone.

The smile froze on the older one's face. "What did you

say?" The younger one slammed Gerhard against the wall and kicked him in the stomach.

This hurts a lot less on an empty stomach, Gerhard thought. *At least you don't vomit.*

Gerhard felt his legs being kicked out from under him, causing him to fall to the ground. He felt splinters from the wooden floor bite into his face. A blinding star exploded in front of his eyes. He heard his eyeglasses being shattered. Then another kick. Gerhard could not breathe for a minute. He vomited bile and tasted blood, coppery blood. When he felt in his mouth with his tongue, he noticed that most of his teeth were gone.

Gerhard tried to sit up and wipe his chin with the back of his hand. There was more warm blood coming from the holes where his teeth had been. When he tried to swallow, he gagged and threw up again—a slimy mix of bile and blood. He groaned and lay back down on the floor.

"Get up, you miserable piece of shit!" the Bavarian yelled, "Get up!" Gerhard pulled himself to stand, using the wall for support. His hands left bloody smears on the whitewash. He turned around to face his tormentors again.

"Well my boy, happy birthday again," The younger Gestapo man smirked, "Now you know what it is like when we ask you nicely. The next time we ask you, you will answer us. I guarantee it. And to think, you could have had roast goose." The Bavarian unlocked the door and called to Metzger. "Take this piece of shit back to his playpen!"

Back outside, Gerhard staggered along beside Metzger. He wondered whether, if he had given the Gestapo information, or even said he had no idea, if they would really have released him. Was it all some elaborate game? Why had they mentioned his brother?

"My, my, kid, you must have really given them shit. Look at you! Boy, do you look colorful with all that festive red around your face. Look happy!" Metzger was at his sadistic best.

Gerhard forced a grimace through his bleeding mouth.

"Yessir," Metzger resumed in a hearty voice, "looks a hell of a lot better now. Look at the bright side. You can now forget about brushing your teeth." Metzger laughed his loathesome laugh that always ended in a cough.

Gerhard struggled to walk upright. His midsection was cramping and he wanted to double over. His mouth hung open, trickling blood and thin saliva. When they reached the iron gate he again saw "Jedem das Seine" —everyone gets what he deserves.

He believed in it still. *JEDEM! Sooner or later, they will have it coming too, only they don't think so yet*. His thoughts trailed off. The pain was too excruciating.

At his barracks Metzger stopped, "Almost forgot, my child, here is what your parents sent you for Christmas. Don't forget to thank them properly." With that he handed Gerhard a piece of paper. It was a list of contents of his Christmas package. Gerhard could make out the neat and methodical handwriting of his father.

1) Smoked homemade pork sausage
2) Cookies
3) Knitted sweater (brown)

The piece of paper was the closest Gerhard would get to his Christmas package. Did his parents realize they were mailing gifts to the SS?

"The less fortunate members of our society thank you for your contribution, my boy," Metzger chuckled as he walked away.

Gerhard leaned against the door frame of the barracks until Metzger had rounded the corner. He did not want him to see that his knees were giving out as he slowly sank onto the frozen dirty snow. Merry Christmas indeed.

The next day, Gerhard felt only marginally better. He staggered through the day in a haze of pain, unable to eat even the liquidy slop served up at day's end. Now, since the sun had gone down behind the trees, the cold was numbing. Gerhard moaned to himself as he stood waiting for the roll call to finish. He looked north across the barbed wire fence, past the stand of wind-blown oaks over the valley. There in the distance were mountaintops. Gerhard imagined those far-off peaks. They had no barbed wire, no SS, no dog patrols and no stench of people packed together without the possibility to ever take a bath.

When Gerhard squinted his eyes even without his shattered glasses, he was able to make out the distant mountains, without seeing the fence or the watchtower or the barracks. He could almost convince himself that he was not on the inside but that he was just there, looking across the valley while on a hike with his long-lost friends.

All around him on the ground, there was dirty snow. It had been blown there by the constant wind, into a thin drift, extending out from the building onto the walkway. The black speckles of soot melted into it seemed to Gerhard to be the only contact to Weimar, which lay on the other side of the hill, in the direction of the railroad station, where new prisoners were unloaded. Now, on a winter day, if the wind was right, you could smell the coal smoke from Weimar's chimneys.

Gerhard bent down to take a closer look at the snow but could not see anymore. He had forgotten. His glasses were smashed. Gerhard took a full hand of dirty snow and slowly put it into his mouth. The throbbing, violent pain became bearable.

This is not so bad, Gerhard thought. *The pain won't get any worse. I can make it bearable with snow. At least they can't ever do this again.* His broken, cut lips started to bleed again, but Gerhard did not notice.

January 1941   Buchenwald

Three weeks had passed since the Gestapo kicked Gerhard's teeth out. The pain had lasted for ten days or so and the infection seemed to be getting better. Only from time to time did Gerhard have the sweet taste in his mouth that came from the draining sockets in his gums.

Five days after Christmas, when the twice-monthly mailing privilege was granted, Gerhard had written his father a thank-you note for the package he had never received. The SS demanded a separate list of contents in every package or "It will be destroyed"—or so the instructions read. In reality, it was a neat trick. No prisoner ever seemed to get the packages; the list of contents was given to the prisoners so that they could send thank-you post cards.

Gerhard was unwavering in his determination to let his father know what had happened to him. "Konzentrazionslager Buchenwald"—Write clearly! Illegible writing will be destroyed by Censor! Underneath the red standard printing, Gerhard wrote:

"Dear Father and Mother. Thank you very much for the package which arrived on time for Christmas and my birthday. I like the brown sweater very much. We don't have many clothes and in the winter the warmth of the sweater is very good under my prison uniform. My fellow prisoners liked the sausage very much. They have not had a treat like that in a very long time. I had to give the sausage away since I don't have teeth anymore and was not able to eat it. I enjoyed the cookies very much. I was able to dissolve them in my mouth and so had a nice treat from home.

P.S. Father, could you perhaps check if my prescription for my glasses is still in my bed stand? I need a new pair. My present pair is all smashed up. I am sure that the prescription has not changed much. Thank you again. Your son Gerhard."

The short reply that Gerhard got from his father several weeks later at first amazed and then angered him: "I have found the prescription for your glasses. The optician says he can make a new pair. He said the price for the glasses is the same as when you purchased the original pair. You can write to him directly and order them. He says that you will have to send him money up front. Your father."

Gerhard had tried to tell his father what had been done to him, in the only way he could without arousing too much suspicion from the censor. Not only did his father not seem to understand what he was saying, he also appeared not to want to help.

Now, standing there in the early morning chill at the endless roll call, Gerhard wondered with little hope whether there could have been a hidden message in his father's letter. If not, his father, in fact, had told him: "What is happening to you is none of my concern. If you need help, help yourself."

Gerhard felt lonelier than he ever had before. His instinct, for the first time since he had arrived at Buchenwald more than two years before, was to cry. He felt his vision blur with tears welling up, but immediately caught himself. He blinked hard and looked into the distance, to the north. He saw the valley and the mountain top. There was a lead-gray sky with dark snow clouds above it.

Snow, Gerhard thought. He looked down and saw the soot from the coal stoves of Weimar in the melting ice at his feet. Until now, he liked the soot. It came from warm homes on the outside. He liked to imagine those homes. He thought about being in one of them with a family.

Now he wished for fresh snow to cover up the soot. There was no hope on the outside either. Again Gerhard looked towards the mountain.

"That is how they do it. They want us to be weak. But

when we are weak, we will die. I may die anyway," Gerhard whispered to himself, "but I will not die weak."

"Starting to talk to yourself, are you now, my boy?" Metzger walked up behind Gerhard. "Seems like you are one of the popular ones around here. You can leave this roll call and skip work today. You've got visitors. Follow me."

Gerhard had been standing outside his barracks for quite a while, trying to escape the stench. He was cold from the wind blowing through the camp. His lips and fingertips had turned blue. Now, the word "visitors" made him feel chilled to the bone. The Gestapo was back. Gerhard wondered what new lies they would utter, what questions they had come to ask, what horrible price they would make him pay and why, particularly, they had singled him out.

Gerhard followed Metzger out of the wrought-iron gate, past the SS men with their dogs, and trudged to the "interview room." Once inside he recognized the two long-coated Gestapo men who had kicked in his teeth and mangled his glasses on Christmas. He tried to breathe easy but fear gripped him.

"Time to take a little trip. Move!" said one of them. They grasped him, twisted his arms behind his back and shoved him out of the room. There was a windowless van outside. They threw him into the darkness and slammed the door shut. There was nothing to hold on to and nothing to sit on. He heard an SS dog bark as the motor coughed to life and the van got underway.

Gerhard knew perfectly well that the trip away from Buchenwald didn't mean freedom. In the Gestapo's scheme of things, he had done nothing to earn it. But where were they going? Could anything be worse than where he had been?

The trip took hours. From time to time the van sped up, turned corners and slowed down again. Though completely sealed, it was drafty inside. Gerhard examined the back door with his fingers and could feel that there was no interior door lock to be opened. Occasionally, when the van was traveling over cobblestone pavement, he pounded on the doors to hear how thick they were. He found that they had been reinforced. He felt dazed, too sodden to think. Somehow, he propped himself up in a corner and began to doze.

January 9, 1941 Dresden

After an eternity, he felt the van turn a sharp corner and slow down. He heard two dogs barking and a large iron gate clank shut. The van stopped and the doors were opened. Gerhard was blinded by the sudden light. He squinted. Someone yelled, "Out!"

He hurried out of the van and found his footing on the wet pavement. The same voice yelled, "Inside, hurry up." As Gerhard opened his eyes to see where he was supposed to hurry to, he was struck from behind with a heavy truncheon.

He saw that he was in a courtyard outside of what appeared to be large gray building. One of the Gestapo men pointed to an open door and Gerhard went quickly towards it. He was not fast enough. On the short run, the truncheon hit him twice more. Once he was inside, the door was slammed shut from the outside. Gerhard could hear that it was a metal door and that it was heavy.

He waited. That was all he could do. *Why did they bring me here? If they wanted to torture me, they could have done that in Buchenwald. If they wanted to interrogate me, they also could have done that at the camp. They had done so before. If they wanted to kill me, they could have done that also in Buchenwald. God knows, they killed prisoners there every day for various reasons. Sometimes for no reason at all. And they could.* He thought bitterly of what he had seen in Buchenwald. It seemed as if almost everyone in the camp died eventually from overwork, diseases, lack of food or beatings.

What was different now? Something had changed. Most prisoners left the camp only when they died, when they cooperated or when they were to be interrogated. Gerhard had never cooperated and he had been tortured and interrogated. What was happening now that was different?

Something must have happened on the outside that made a difference. He tried to remember if there was anything in the postcards from his father that he might have missed. Was there any sign? Was this somehow related to his brother? And why couldn't his brother, seemingly rising higher and higher as Gerhard rotted away in Buchenwald, why couldn't Friedrich save him?

Finally, after what seemed like hours, he heard footsteps approaching the door to the room where he was being held. He could hear a key in the lock and the door opened.

Gerhard saw two men in grey suits. Gerhard was puzzled. It had been a long time since he had seen civilian clothes. In the camp the prisoners wore grayish jackets and pants with black stripes. The SS wore their black uniforms. The Gestapo that he had seen all wore long grey coats. The last time he had seen civilian clothes was when he had been arrested. How long had that been? He had lost track of time.

One of the men said, "Get up. Come with us." It was an order. It was curt, but it was not shouted. What was happening? Could there be any chance that they would actually release him?

Gerhard left his narrow cell and walked ahead of them as they indicated. At the end of the long hallway, which had iron doors on either side, he saw a staircase leading up. Gerhard was not sure what to do, but walked towards the staircase. When he reached the first landing he was told to turn left, which he did.

Walking down a long corridor, they passed close enough to the signs on office doors so even without his glasses he could read: Criminal Commissariat, Robbery, Forgery, Sex

Crimes. Gerhard knew that he was in Gestapo headquarters. He stopped reading and began squinting at the light reflected off the meticulously waxed brown linoleum floor. At the end of the long hallway to the right there was an open door. Gerhard was ordered to enter. Neither of the men entered with him.

Behind a large desk, and with his back to the window, sat a smallish man.

"Sit down, Schmidt." Gerhard hesitated, then sat. He had not expected a chair and if there was a chair, he had not expected to be allowed to sit down. As Gerhard sat, he began to study the man on the other side of the desk, who was only a few feet away.

The man had a head that seemed too large for his body. He wore a wrinkled gray suit. The cheap cloth was slightly worn. His hair was longer than that worn by the SS. He reminded Gerhard of a typical civil servant who might sell postage stamps. He was wearing nickel-frame glasses with small circular lenses. Behind the thick lenses were piercing blue eyes.

He was reading a file. Gerhard saw the cover. "Schmidt, Gerhard, 12-24-17, Leipzig. POLITICAL." It was his file the man was studying. Gerhard waited. The room was quiet. From time to time Gerhard heard a faint tick-tick from the steam radiator under the window. After what seemed an eternity, the man looked up from the file.

"I have a problem. The problem is you." He focused on Gerhard and paused. "You have the solution to my problem. We will find out what it is." Gerhard noticed the nasal twang of the man's northern German accent. "Your brother has risen quite successfully in our hierarchy. He is a god-damn Hauptbannfuehrer! You know what that means? Do you? It means that you, my boy, are an embarrassment. You are an embarrassment to your brother, to the Reich, and to me."

Gerhard wondered suddenly if Friedrich had requested that this man meet with Gerhard and explain to him what a problem he posed to Friedrich's career.

"That you are an embarrassment," the man said, "is in itself no tragedy. You see, since the Fuehrer assumed power in Germany, things have changed a lot. We have systematically eliminated institutions, laws and conditions which were designed by the enemies of Germany to weaken us. We took a look at what it was that sapped the German spirit. We overturned the Versailles stab-in-the-back; we eliminated the joke that called itself the Reichstag—the so-called parliament. We were able to put Germany back to work and we eliminated the power bases of the obstructionists who say 'no' to any positive change."

The diatribe sounded all too familiar to Gerhard. He willed himself to listen. There was usually a point eventually. He stifled the urge to tell the little man to save his breath.

He continued, "Gone are the Communists, the Jewish money-bags, criminals and other social and biological deviants. We have improved vastly our physical and biological infrastructure. And here are you. You are the brother of one of the founders of the National Socialist Workers' state! You carry the same heritage, bloodlines which are pure and have been free of Jewish influence for as far as we can trace back. You and your brother have had the same biological, Nordic and ethnic heritage as well as upbringing."

"Yet he is one of our leaders and you are in custody as a political enemy of the Reich."

The little man stood up suddenly and came around the desk to stand closer to Gerhard. "There is a possibility that you are either stupid, terminally stupid, criminally stupid, or perhaps that you were misled at one time and, for circumstances beyond anyone's control, were not able to see the light."

By now, the man was pacing. "It has been requested that I a) examine your case as a black mark reflecting on your brother b) that I speak to you to find out what motivates you, and c) see what you think you owe to your brother's commitment to the Reich so maybe we can eliminate this black mark once and for all. And this, my boy, I will do today. I owe that to your brother, so to speak."

He thumped the file and said, "I have read and studied your file. Quite impressive. It appears that you are just as determined as your brother. But, while reading your file there is one open question. I need your cooperation in order to find a satisfying answer. I have that, don't I?"

Gerhard had been lulled into a near-trance by the little man's ranting and nearly missed the question, but without waiting for an answer from Gerhard, he continued to talk, a continuous slight smile on his thin lips. Gerhard noticed though, that there was no smile in his eyes.

"What puzzles me is the following: you joined a Hitler Youth group. It says here on your application that you followed the example and advice of your brother. Very good, my boy. The leader of this group was employed by the Reich as a teacher of English and geography. This teacher was born and raised by German emigrants in Birmingham, England. They had emigrated after the collapse of the Emperor's Reich at the end of the World War. Well, understandable, the situation seemed hopeless."

Gerhard was surprised to hear that the Wandervogel was now being called a Hitler Youth group. When had it stopped being considered a subversive club?

"When Germany arose again, the Krauses returned, as countless other families have done from all parts of the world. The assumption, of course, was that they felt obligated as loyal Germans to participate in the rebuilding of our nation. The problem was, as we now know, that your English-teaching leader was a swine. He had been indoctrinated by mongrel politics and was subverting us from within, eating the German substance like a maggot.

Now, my boy, it is quite likely that you were misled by him, led astray, so to speak. That you were confused as a young impressionable youth and turned away from your heritage, your destiny as a German."

"It is my job to answer that question. While reading your file, I see that curiously enough, this question was never answered. Maybe it was never asked. Maybe it was never really thought to be important because your brother—although he is a proud bearer of the golden Party pin reserved for those only who joined the NSDAP prior to our Fuehrer's Assumption of Power—your brother was just a teacher in Sonthofen, and a second Lieutenant in the 1st Mountaineering Division. Now that he has risen in the ranks, the contrast becomes an embarrassment to all of us as well as your family, and the question becomes essential."

Gerhard had lost track of the meanderings of the little man's mind. He seemed to be saying that if Friedrich Schmidt had remained an insignificant nobody in the party, Gerhard's transgressions could have been ignored. But as Friedrich grew more important, the need to redeem Gerhard became paramount.

It seemed that the man behind the desk was talking more to himself than to Gerhard. He was preparing himself for something. He had stated his intention. *There is embarrassment. The embarrassment must end.*

Gerhard became calmer and calmer. The man wanted something Gerhard knew he could not give.

"So, my boy, is it that you joined the Hitler youth group because you wanted to be part of the rise of Germany, or did you join this supposedly loyal group because you knew that the leader, although pretending to be a loyal German, was in fact, loyal to the Communists and was using your services to distribute anti-German propaganda in schools and city offices, all the while wearing and besmirching the uniform dedicated to Germany's youth?"

As Gerhard wondered, almost hysterically, whether he could ask to have the question rephrased to be more succinct, the little man screamed suddenly. "Which is it?" Throwing down the file that he had held so carefully earlier and pounding with his flat hand on the oak of the desk top, he still smiled. And his eyes behind the thick lenses still looked cold and small.

Gerhard quickly considered his choices. He could simply admit he had been misled and wanted only what the Nazis wanted for the Fatherland. He wouldn't be lying. Thinking back, he knew he had joined Wandervogel originally because he had admired the English teacher and was looking for friends.

Gerhard thought of the arrest by the Gestapo in Vienna, the brutal beatings by the SS thugs in Buchenwald. He thought of his glasses, his teeth and his unanswered post cards. It was hopeless. No one wanted to listen. He was alone, and filled with grief.

Looking up and focusing on the little grey man's face, he felt drained and empty. With a clear voice he said, "Nun gerade nicht. Fuck you, asshole." Instead of defiance in his voice, there was finality.

"Very well then. Plan B." The little man placed both hands on the desk and shouted, "Get him out of here!!" Instantly, the door flew open and the two men in gray suits were in the office. They had been waiting just outside the door. They grabbed Gerhard roughly by the arms and shoved and pushed him back down the hallway and the stairs, the way they had come earlier. Gerhard was being returned to his cell. While he was allowed to walk at his own pace earlier, he was being pushed and shoved now. He nearly lost his balance on the stairs. Pushed inside his cell, as he stumbled against the opposite wall, he heard the iron door behind him shut and the key being turned. The lights went out.

Gerhard had just sat down in the far corner of his cell when the lights came on again.

Two burly men in rumpled grey uniforms burst in. One of them yelled, "You swine! Get up!"

Gerhard tried to scramble up but was hit by a tremendous blow in his left leg. The second man, the one with the fat sweaty face, hit him in the left knee with an iron bar. There was an ugly crunching sound and Gerhard saw his leg bend at an awkward angle. It buckled and he fell.

"You maggot!" the ruddy face yelled and hit him again. "You will learn respect!" the other uniform shouted and jumped on him.

While one of the men held him down, the other tied his feet together. Gerhard wanted to cry out in pain but was not able to because of the weight of the man sitting on his chest. They lifted him from the ground, feet first. Gerhard saw a hook in the ceiling. They hung the cord, tying his feet to the hook. Then they let go of Gerhard. The full and sudden weight of his body hanging upside down pulled the ends of his broken legs apart and tore the muscles. Gerhard heard himself screaming.

As his leg muscles gave way, his body did a slow half turn. He saw the one with the iron bar swing another blow which hit him squarely in the back. To Gerhard, it sounded like a rope snapping and he felt something like a tremendous electrical shock between his shoulder blades. He noticed that he could not feel the pain in his legs anymore, bringing an odd relief.

The man with the iron bar lifted it again. He swung back sideways and Gerhard saw the iron bar come towards his head. Then he saw and heard nothing more.

Afterword

While we are calling this a work of fiction, it is inspired by the actual events that took place during the period described in the book. The patterns of distrust and the prejudices that Sarah and Karl experienced as their relationship grew mirrors our own true life experience as a couple.

The trip to Germany, Sarah's talks with Ingrid and Der Alte, the visits to Buchenwald and Weimar were also real; so is most of the narrative about Der Alte and his brother Gerhard.

The reason that *Stumbling Stone* is a work of fiction is because in trying to recreate Gerhard's story, we want to acknowledge that not everything could be known, as is true of many Holocaust victims. We filled in the gaps using information that we gathered from family documents, interviews, the United States Holocaust Memorial Museum in Washington, D.C., the Berlin documents of the National Archives in Virginia, the Weimar state records in Germany, the archives at the Buchenwald concentration camp and with our imagination based on a variety of stories we had heard.

Rudi Raab and Julie Freestone

This book is dedicated to Gerhard Raab, Buchenwald prisoner 632. He was murdered January 9, 1941 at the Gestapo headquarters in Dresden, Germany.

Acknowledgements

Since we've worked on this book for more than two decades, we have so many people to thank it would take another whole book.

For starters, Armand Volkas introduced us to his lifetime commitment to reconciliation, which led to the first version of *Stumbling Stone*.

Julie's book group and the Adventure Pals read the book and offered suggestions. Beverly Chilton did a masterful job of reading every line and making not only helpful edits but encouraging remarks that gave us confidence. Sally St.Lawrence suggested a radical and very valuable revision. Jane Zastrow edited the final proofs.

Liz Rosner, an old friend, brilliant poet and wonderful writer, became our inspirational editor who changed the focus of the book and offered kindly and professional improvements.

Kate Fowlie, Vicki Balladares and Nick Despota made it possible for us to launch a website to promote the book and share memories, photos and videos. And our wonderful crew of website reviewers helped refine stumbling-stone.com

Marsha Hebden and her El Cerrito High School World War II class made us realize that people were interested in our story and might buy our book.

Cousin A.D. Puchalski was able to cull from our vague suggestions a wonderful design for the book's cover.

Staff at the Buchenwald Concentration Camp, the United States Holocaust Memorial Museum in Washington, D.C. and others provided us with invaluable information about Gerhard Raab.

There are so many more of you who read the book, gave us encouragement, made suggestions and provided valuable insight. We thank you for being on this journey with us.

The Authors.

Rudi Raab and Julie Freestone
Julie Freestone was born in the Bronx, N.Y., to immigrant Jewish parents in 1944. Rudi Raab was born in Germany eight days after World War II ended in Europe. His father was a high-ranking Nazi. They met when Julie, a reporter, was doing a story and interviewed Rudi, a cop. They live in Richmond, California. In 1950, they both lived in Hamburg, Germany eight miles apart, where they each acquired the bears they are holding as toys.

Made in the USA
San Bernardino, CA
24 February 2019